Upon BUTTERFLY Wings

J. H. NELSON

This new adult contemporary romance is recom-
mended for readers 18+ due to mature content.

Cover design by 1231 Publishing
First Edition: September 2024

ISBN: 978-0-6451315-2-9

Published by J H Nelson

NOTE FROM THE AUTHOR

There is a saying throughout the autistic community that goes, 'if you've known/know one person with autism, you've known/know one person with autism.'

That is 100% accurate. Autism can't be defined or pigeon-holed into a certain or specific set of rules/traits. The challenges, deficits, strengths, and superpowers that one person with autism has can be the exact opposite of another. They might share a few traits or have completely different ones all together.

I wrote this story because autism is a subject close to my heart and because it is a story, I think needs to be told. Yet, after writing it… I was too scared to share it with the world. Why? Because I was afraid it wasn't 'politically correct' enough. I was (and still am) afraid that the autistic community would criticise me for my 'mild' character challenges/struggles and for my 'incorrect language'.

Labels are everywhere. Whether we like them or not. Society has labelled me things like loser, loner, weirdo, dumbass, social retard, etc. Bullies at school, bullies in the workplace, unsympathetic boyfriends. Then there are the professionals... I've had just about every label slapped on me by the medical world; depression, anxiety, bipolar, unipolar disorder (is that even a thing? I have no idea), borderline personality disorder, split personality disorder, PTSD. These labels all fit individual areas of my struggles, but each new diagnosis never quite covered/explained ALL of the elements that haunted (and continue to haunt) me. It wasn't until my son turned 4 and we were told to start looking into having him assessed that all my own puzzle pieces started falling into place.

That's right... I'm autistic. As are my 2 children and several other members of our extended family tree. Unlike my children, I wasn't diagnosed as a child. I spent the first 29 years of my life (along with my poor parents, who, at times, had no idea what to do with me) trying to make sense of 'me'. I sit somewhere between 'not autistic enough to be clever/genius like Rain Man but too autistic to cope in the neuro-typical world comfortably and without serious detriment to my mental health.

Dani is a fictional character with traits and challenges I have experienced, seen, read, or heard about in others. She is not me or any one person I know. Some of her quirks, however, resonate with me (especially when I was younger).

In the same way that one person cannot represent the entire autism spectrum in real life, Dani also is only the face of one person living with autism. She does not possess all the different complexities of every person living under the ASD umbrella. Autism is a multi-faceted diagnostic label and, as such, can't be defined or portrayed by any single character.

Between the crippling anxiety of needing to make 'that' appointment and trying to figure out how I'm going to tell hubby that I've forgotten to organise dinner *again*. I don't have enough spoons left in my day to make sure I'm using the 'correct' language/terminology.

If you don't like a word I've used, change it in your mind to whatever you want it to be as you read the story. You, as the reader, have the power to change the words you don't like. Use that power.

Trigger warning

This story contains an attempted rape scene. While writing this story, a few people told me I needed to remove this scene because it was too controversial for this otherwise low angst novel. I took this seriously and almost pulled the scene from the story, but the idea of chucking it niggled at my conscience, something I'd heard at an ASD seminar.

Did you know that people on the spectrum are at an increased risk of being sexually assaulted than those without ASD? Possibly because they can have trouble reading/interpreting social cues. Perhaps predators can sense this social vulnerability and take advantage of it. Regardless of the reasons why. I knew I couldn't scrap the scene. It's too important.

I want to raise awareness. For autism. For understanding and acceptance. For consent! If people take nothing else away from my novel, I hope they take with them how important consent is. You need to **have consent,** and you need to **give consent** before you move forward. Everyone needs to feel safe before you cross into each other's space.

If you find yourself in an impossible situation like Dani does... please seek help, confide in someone you trust and report sexual assault. If not for yourself... For the next victim that your assailant preys on.

1

—————

Danielle

I made it! I've finally finished my shift and head towards my little white hatchback. It's no race car but it's zippy enough for me and it has a great sound system and that's what is important to me.

Chucking my backpack on the passenger seat, I climb in and start her up. The stereo comes to life. *Hmm, MJ. Yep, I am in the mood for his awesome beat.* Leaving work behind, I turn up the stereo for 'Billie Jean' to vibrate through the steering wheel. I only work fifteen minutes from home.

Pulling into the driveway, I see Mum in the garage unloading grocery bags from her car. I park in the carport that my dad built for my sister and I when we got our own cars. Jumping out, I give her a hand carrying them inside.

"Hi sweetie. You're going to damage your hearing if you keep listening to your music so loud in that car of yours."

"Yes, Mum. So you've said."

We get to the kitchen and start putting the shopping away. I like to work in companionable silence, but Mum makes small talk, asking about my day.

"Yeah, it was good. Nothing exciting, just put stock away mostly." I am busy reorganising the pantry as I say this, so I doubt she's even heard me. As I turn around, I discover her standing right behind me, watching me intently. I have the good sense to be a little embarrassed, if not ashamed of my necessity to have everything in its correct place.

"Sorry." It probably doesn't cut it, but it is all I can think to say. I'm not going to lie and tell her I didn't mean it or something like that. She already knows I did mean it—kind of.

"It's fine. I was going to sort them out *after* I got all the cold items in the fridge. You just beat me to it."

She thinks she was about to fix it, but in truth, my poor mum wouldn't get everything in the right order. She tries, but it doesn't matter as much to her as it does to me.

"So, stock again, huh? You know that's because I'd bet no one in that whole shop does it as efficiently as you." Mum has her teasing smile on, so I know she is being nice to me, rather than trying to wind me up.

"Yeah," I chuckle. "Oh, and guess what Sean told me today? He reckons he is officially getting me to update *all* of the sale tags from now on, because he says I do them the best of anyone there. And he likes that I fix up any of the ones that aren't taped on straight n' stuff."

"Well, there you go! At this rate, it sounds like you'll be off registers in no time."

The shopping is all put away so I'm keen to escape work talk. "How long until tea? Have I got time to listen to some music?"

"Yeah, that's fine. Not too loud, though. And have a shower first so you don't dirty your quilt!" she yells after me.

Because I do that so often… not! I roll my eyes.

I shower quickly and drag a brush through my thick shoulder-length hair. I don't have much interest in primping or fashion. As long as I'm comfortable, I'm good.

Back in my room, I scroll through my CD's—there is something comforting about the repetition of good old CD's. The way you know the song order because it never changes. I'm chasing something soothing after my long day. The lights are always so insanely bright at work, making it hard for me to concentrate. Ah, Michael Bublé. Hitting play, I load up the pillows behind my head and lay down, listening. I clear my mind and focus on the instruments behind the words.

A movement on the bed startles me. Two pale blue eyes stare at me. Rebel, my Ragdoll cat, nudges my cheek, purring. He curls up beside me and we enjoy the soft music together.

By the time Mum knocks on my door, it is almost dark and my room is defined by shadows. She cracks open the door and a painfully bright shaft of light streams in from behind her.

"Dinner is ready. You gonna come out and have some?"

"Sure, Mum. Just gimme a minute and I'll be there."

She leaves, pulling the door closed behind her and I reach over, tapping my lamp once. It is a touch lamp that has three different levels of light. My dad bought it for me not long after I was diagnosed. He said he thought it might help since it started off soft. I was skeptical, but it's turned out well. Once my eyes adjust to the light, I tap it brighter. Brighter still. The smell of dinner wafts in, making my tummy rumble. I turn off my stereo before leaving the sanctuary that is my room.

Driving to work, I am surprised to hear my phone beep. I don't really have friends because most people can't relate to me and even if they try; I end up saying or doing something that scares them away. I have finally learnt not to chase after them. People get weird when I do that.

I wonder who's texting me? Probably Mum. I wait until I pull up in the carpark before grabbing it out of my bag. A memory flashes to mind of my driving instructor, giving me bonus points on my test because my phone had rung, and she thought I would answer it. Instead, I'd reminded her that using a mobile phone whilst operating a motor vehicle was against the law and I always followed the rules. The expression she'd given me at the time made me question if I had offended her, but I'd apparently just shocked her 'in a good way'. Whatever that means.

Agh, it is my sister, Michelle. She's getting married soon and I swear she thinks that every girl needs a man to be happy. *If only she knew the truth!* I love her, I do. And I'm glad she is happy and has found her fiancé, Luke. He seems nice enough and must make her happy, since they're getting married… but not all of us want to. Some of us are better off on our own. I wish now that I hadn't told her about the guy from despatch liking me. She is texting me to ask if anything has happened! *Ah no, not unless you count him asking to borrow my ID badge because he left his in his locker and couldn't get into the staffroom yesterday.* I decide against telling her that. She will undoubtedly spin it around into some ridiculous show of affection or a random declaration of love. Honestly, I don't want to lose my morning's toast! Silence is the best way to deal with her. Tucking the phone away, I head in to start work. Last day of four in a row, can't wait for it to be over.

2

Danielle

I am feeling much calmer now that I've been to the library. With another bundle of books, I can make it through the week.

~ Because you have ZERO friends! ~

Agh, meet She-Devil. She's my loud and obnoxious negativity who likes to pop in uninvited and make herself known! My first psychologist suggested I should give her a name. Something about taking the power back. I don't know that it changed anything. *Yes, thank you… Compliments of my non-existent social life!*

I am enjoying my drive home with Katy Perry pumping loudly as I turn into my street. Before I reach the driveway, I see Michelle's car in our carport. She has parked across the space, so I am forced to park on the nature strip out front. Happy feeling gone!

I grab my books and head inside, agitated about having to leave my car in the sun. *I live here!*

Multiple voices shout excitedly over each other within the house. It sounds like it's coming from the kitchen. I can hear Mum, Michelle and another voice talking and laughing. I wander in.

"Hi!" My sister beams at me. The unfamiliar voice I heard was Michelle's best friend and soon-to-be-bridesmaid, Susie. They are huddled around the breakfast bar looking through magazines. Bridesmaids' dresses, I'd guess, by the cover of one staring up at me.

"Have you forgotten how to park correctly since moving out?" I challenge. Her attitude annoys me, like most sisters, I'm sure.

"Sorry, love, I was excited to show mum the dresses we've picked. You wanna see? Have you changed your mind about being a bridesmaid?"

"Nope. I'm pretty sure you don't want me freaking out and having a meltdown in front of all your friends and making a scene. I know I'd rather not." My books are getting heavy and I'm not really needed in this conversation, so I decide to leave them to it and go put my books in my room.

"Hey, sweetheart." It's mum. "Why don't you put those down and then come pick out a dress that you might like to wear? Not a bridesmaid dress... just... something nice. As sister of the bride."

"Sure, Mum. Can you please put the jug on? I'll just put these away." In my room, I swing the door closed with my foot and drop the books on my bed. I immediately begin gnawing on my finger before stopping and taking a deep breath. *We've talked about this already.* Mum wants me to consider wearing a dress. The thought sends panic creeping in to smother me. I keep taking deep breaths the way my therapist has taught me to do. It helps, but the second I stop, the panic rises again. *Dresses make me crazy!* I visualise a wall of orange and black Monarch butterflies at the end of their long migration south. Visualisation is another strategy I use. It works enough that I can walk out of my bedroom, back to my mum. I decide to make myself a cup of tea before I take on the 'looking at dresses' challenge. The three women standing around the bench watch me in silence. It's as though I can actually feel their eyes on my skin. The phrase 'caged animal' springs to mind.

"Would anyone else like a cup while I'm making one?"

The girls snap their heads back towards their magazines and mutter no thank you's. I rinse my spoon and put it in the drainer. With no more distractions, I go to them and let them show me the dreaded magazines. Fortunately, I have missed most of the hype while I was out at the library, so the women don't inflict the 'magazine dresses' torture on me for very long. They head outside to gossip and whatever else girls do. I chase escape in my usual spot, fiction.

When my dad gets home in the late afternoon, my mum, sister and Susie have been out on the back deck most of the day talking and laughing. I've poked my head out a few times to pinch the odd carrot stick off the table. They keep asking me to join them, but I would rather read with my trusty little man, Rebel, beside me. The sun is setting in the sky and I can hear my dad tidying up out the front. I decide to go out and say hello. The girls are getting more rowdy as the afternoon wears on.

"Hi, Dad. How did you go today? Catch anything?"

"Hey, honey. The other guys caught a couple but nothing worth keeping, so we just threw 'em back in the end. Sounds like your mum and sister are into the wine."

"Mmm, I think so. I haven't been out there in a while now. Michelle has Susie over too. I thought I heard one of them say they'll get Luke to bring tea over and we can all eat together, but that might be wrong."

Luke arrives while I'm having a shower. He has brought with him enough Indian cuisine to feed an army. Turns out to be a good thing though, because my mum and sister have worked up an appetite. We all sit out on the back deck together around the big eight-seater table.

The girls are indeed 'into the wine' and getting louder by the minute. My dad and Luke have gone all out and made themselves creaming-soda spiders. He offered me one too, but I declined in favour of my usual diluted apple juice.

Sitting at the table, I find myself—surprisingly—enjoying the meal. I haven't had much to do with Luke. Michelle was already living out of home before she met him. He is—again, to my surprise—a quiet and sensible guy. My dad and he are having an in-depth chat about the economy and politics. I don't know too much about it but I am interested in their discussion. I wish I did though... it is much more interesting than my sister's bitch session about some girl who is supposed to be her friend.

I listen intently to Dad's opinion on what needs to happen to save the country's financial woes when I hear my name across the table.

"Sorry. What?"

"I said... How'd your date go with Despatch Dude? What's his name again? I was just telling Mum. I can't believe you haven't told her about him."

"That's because there isn't anything to tell. His name's Tom and we didn't go on any date. He asked me to the movies, but I said I was busy."

I'm such an idiot! Why did I open my mouth?

"Wait... what?" Michelle sputters and yells across at me. "Why'd you say no? I told you he likes you. Why don't you go out with him and see? He might be 'the one'." Michelle raises her eyebrow at me. She looks ridiculous!

"No, we work together! When it all goes sour, I will have to see him, and that would be horrible. I'm finally getting some shifts off the front counter, which means we're together more and I don't want to stuff that up." I raise my glass to my lips and turn back towards Dad and Luke as a sign of 'discussion closed.'

~ Freaks don't get soulmates, they end up living with a bunch of cats. ~

Oh fantastic! She-Devil *always knows when to jump on the 'thrash me' party!*

"Oh phooey! How do you know it will go bad, Miss Cynical? You're always looking for reasons why you shouldn't date ANY-ONE! Are you gay? Is that it?"

"Michelle!" Mum frowns at her and shakes her head.

"What? I'm not saying it's a bad thing, merely asking the question. It would explain her aversion to dating a man."

Great, now even Dad and Luke have abandoned their conversation to listen to Michelle's ranting accusations.

"Not that it's any of *your* business, Michelle… no, I'm not gay. My *aversion,* as you say, is not gender specific. I don't want to date anyone! I'm going to bed." Picking up my dirty plate and glass, I take them to the kitchen. With a quick rinse, I stack them in the dishwasher. I grab my special teacup from the cupboard and pour my nightly glass of milk before bed. I can still hear Michelle talking outside.

"What? I just think it would be nice for her to have someone other than us to talk to. Don't you? She finally has a boy who likes her, and she is alienating him before he even has a chance."

Somebody mutters something else and I hear her reply again. "Yes, I know that… But I swear sometimes she just uses her autism to cut herself off from the world!" Luke mutters something about 'time to take her home' and then there is rustling and shuffling. *Finally!* I'm still drinking my milk in the kitchen when they make their way through to the front door.

I leave my poor dad and Luke to get a very drunk Michelle and Susie into Michelle's car. Luke has parked his work ute on the front lawn behind my car—where it remains from this morning—I hear someone say they'll come back tomorrow for it. When Mum and Dad return from saying goodbye, I watch my dad 'dance' my mum towards their bedroom and close the door. Pretty sure that they're done for the night, I bring in all the dirty dishes from the deck. Setting them in the dishwasher, I pop a tablet in the dispenser and turn it on. The kitchen is tidy and the counters are wiped clean before I turn out the lights.

I can do this. I can get through this day. Clothes shopping is one of my worst nightmares and it's happening today! Worse than clothes, *dress* shopping! *Agh! Just kill me now!* Mum is taking me *dress* shopping for one I can wear to the wedding. No matter how many times I say the word 'dress' my mind still rejects the idea of wearing one.

I have stalled as long as I can, but with the wedding in just three short weeks, the time is now. I get up and turn on soft, soothing music while I get ready. Keeping my mind on the lyrics often helps me control my anxiety. Choosing what to wear stresses me out. A sure sign of imminent trouble. In the end I go with my denim three-quarter pants—even though the seams are itching my legs. I opt for two singlet tops, white over black. It will probably make trying on clothes harder, but it is what I feel comfortable in. My hair gets its usual ponytail and then I leave the safety of my bedroom to get breakfast before we go.

My mum and I have talked lots about today in the past couple of weeks. I feel fractionally better better since mum explained she only wants to find me a nice dress that I like and feel comfortable in. She understands my trouble with scratchy fabrics. We decided together that Michelle didn't need to come today. She can be too much for me to handle, even on a good day! Today will go smoother if she isn't there. Hopefully.

"So, I've found this little dress shop. It's a bit of a hike, but I think it'll be worth it and I'm really hoping we can find something you like there. I rang the lady, and she said she has lots of different styles and fabrics in stock."

"Sounds good, Mum." I give her a weak smile. My bravado is dropping now that we are in the car.

I am pleasantly surprised when we arrive. The place is silent apart from soft instrumental music coming from hidden speakers. Every wall of the building is lined with protruding racks that display the different styles. A range of different colours in each design hang behind the front one. I notice they are all in the same colour sequence, rack after rack. Looking around, I become overwhelmed. The task is too great and I don't know where to start. Trying to stay calm, I focus on the soft music.

"Good morning. Can I help you ladies? Or are you just happy browsing?" The sales lady is smartly dressed in a matching skirt and top set. It has a sequins type look of bronzy-gold. I would think it looked over the top if I'd seen it on a rack, but she looks pretty in it.

"Hi. I'm Beth. We spoke on the phone yesterday."

"Oh yes, lovely to meet you. And you must be Danielle? Well, why don't you have a look around and see if there is anything you like and we can organise for you to try on some styles? We can order any dress in any colour, so don't worry if you can't find your size or style in the colour you want. I'll just be over here if you need any help." She has a friendly smile and, considering I'm pretty sure my mum would have told her about me, she doesn't stare or have that 'pity look' that most people get when they know. I like her.

"Do you see anything that grabs your attention straight off?" Mum asks me quietly.

"There's so many I don't even know where to start." I scan around the room, looking for exactly that, a place to start. My middle finger and thumb connect. I rub the pads of each tip together in rhythmic circles.

"Well, should we feel a few of the different materials? Maybe we can rule out what you *don't* like. Did you have anything in mind about what type of dress you might feel better in? Long, short?" she pauses and waits for me to think about it.

"Um, I think maybe long? I don't want my feet showing." *Can't I just leave my feet—and the rest of me—at home and you can give them my present?* "Nothing strapless. I'll be worried about it falling off." *I'd literally die if my boobs fell out and I was forever known as 'the girl with the boobs issue!'* I cringe. My mum's smiling at me. I think it is one of those times that she wants to laugh at me. "What?"

"Nothing. I'm just impressed and proud that you're giving this a go. I love you." She kisses me quickly on my hair and walks off towards a pale pink dress hanging up. *I am* definitely *not wearing pink!*

By noon, we've finally finished, and I have my dress in hand. It took longer than I thought it would, but I am actually pleased with the one I chose. *Didn't think that was possible.* It has a high neckline with an oval cutout across my chest, giving the top a crisscross looking pattern. That part is satin—so it's soft—but then the rest of the dress falls into a slim-fit style, made of something called chiffon. It is a little scratchy, but it's lined so feels ok once it's on. It's a dark blue colour called Midnight. The best part is—because of my height—Mum said it was ok for me to wear my black ballet flats underneath because they won't even be seen. *Thank goodness I don't have to endure shoe shopping as well!*

3

———

Kevin

Pulling into the familiar driveway, Patch stands on the passenger seat beside me, tail wagging in excitement. Engaging the hand-brake, I turn off the car and release Patch from her harness. With better manners than some people I know, she waits for my say-so before leaping over me and out the door.

Before even making it to the front door of my childhood home, I hear the clanging of metal and a hose running out back. I follow the sound around to the side, Patch on my heels.

"Hi, Mum. Can Patch and I come through?" My mum cares for sick and injured wildlife. It isn't unusual for the yard to be hosting multiple creatures at any given time.

"Sure, hun, come on through. I'm just washing out food bowls."

With a flick of the latch, Patch and I are through the side gate. I'm careful to keep a sharp eye out for any such animals.

"Hi." Mum looks up from her scrubbing brush. "What brings you over this arvy?"

"Nothing much. Finished up early and didn't feel like hanging around home. Thought I'd drop in and see if you needed any help."

"Uh oh. Sounds like trouble. I'm just about to cut up some fruit for Minty and the crew. Why don't you come give me a hand and you can tell me all about it?"

"Sure, Mum. Patch, here." At the sound of her name, Patch leaves her perimeter check and returns to my side. She is my best friend.

Inside, the house is abnormally quiet. Dad must have gone to get the plumbing supplies for tomorrow's job after all, despite my offer to run the errand for him.

"When's the big day?" I pick up a spare knife and start cutting the apples she dumps in front of me, on a cutting board alongside mum who's doing the same with some peaches.

"Next Tuesday. I'll be sad. Always am, but he's more than ready. Showing great foraging skills! He'll get a tracker, so we might cross paths again. Only time will tell."

Back at home, where I live with one of my many cousins. I chuck my keys into the timber bowl by the front door, kick off my work boots and Patch takes off for the kitchen, no doubt in search of food.

"Kev! Hey, bud. I wasn't sure if you were home tonight or not. I cooked up that green curry for dinner. There's some leftover, if you wan' it?"

"Nuh, I'm good thanks, Mick. I was out at Mum and Dad's, so had a bite there. You know how Mum is." We chuckle together. Understanding how parents are, especially mums, always feeding their boys.

"Uh, where's mine then? Think I'll 'ave to message her and remind her, I still live here too, she's *obviously* forgotten!" Mick laughs.

"Huh, one word… Dad! He can eat, man! He polished off every last scrap. Mum even looked half pissed that she was clearly not going to have leftovers for his lunch tomorrow." We both break into a belly laugh.

"Sounds like maybe you should take the curry for lunch and give ya poor ol' mum a break." Mick breaks into more laughter.

"Thanks, I think I might just do that. Your curries are good and Mum doesn't make hot food like that, so I'm sure he'd appreciate it."

"Sure thing. Oh hey, by the way… A letter came for ya in the mail today. I got one too. Invite to Lukey's wedding. You takin' a date?" One look at the smirk on Mick's face and I know he's fishing.

"Nuh. You?"

"Hell no! Who would I take? What about that little blondie you been seein' a bit of lately… she seems nice."

"Yeah, I thought so too. Turns out she's exactly like the rest of them. Thinks men are a handbag; you don't match the outfit, they leave you at home and take the other one."

"Oh Kev. Sorry, man. I didn't know."

"All good, bud. Who needs 'em? You're probably easier to live with than any woman would be anyway. And the fact that you're an awesome cook is just a bonus!" I wink at him, and we laugh easily. Mick goes in for a mock punch to my shoulder.

4

Kevin

Ah, the bittersweet arrival of the weekend. Don't have to go to work, but what to do? *Hmm, that is the question.* Rolling out of bed, Patch rises from her mat and shakes away the night's stillness. I chuck on some shorts and a long past used T-shirt that sports holes and tears, showing spots of bare skin. I should throw it out, but somehow it keeps getting washed and worn.

In the kitchen, I meet Mick, dressed only in shorts, eating cereal from a bowl whilst leaning over the sink.

"Morning," he says through a mouthful of milky slop.

"Hey." I open the refrigerator door in search of something cold to drink. "Finished with the milk?" I ask.

"Mm, yep. Sorry. What's on the go for today… anything?" he asks through another spoonful.

"Not much, I don't think. You?" I retrieve a glass from the cabinet and pour myself an orange juice.

"Few of the boys from work and I are heading up the coast. Maybe check out the surf, grab a bite to eat. Wanna come?"

"Still a bit chilly for surfing, isn't it? Nuh thanks, bud. I need to do some washing and I think I'll take Patch for a run."

"Sure thing. Just remember though… beers tonight for Lukey. He's insisted on not wanting a buck's party, which I'll concede to. But we're definitely getting together for beers at least. I told him you'd be there."

"Yep. Haven't forgotten. I'll be there. Six, wasn't it?"

"Five! Don't be late Mister Sensible. And be sure to bring your drinking arm!" He points his spoon at the end of my nose.

"Yes, sir!"

Waking up like this isn't something I do very often anymore. *Why, oh why, do I let that bonehead talk me into these situations?* With my head pounding and my mouth feeling like it's full of sand, I stagger out to the fridge. *Water, I need water!*

I hear shuffling and grunting coming from down the hallway and pour a second glass for Mick. Not knowing what state he will be in; I send Patch out the back and lock the pet door for a minute while she goes to do her business.

"Oh my god! What time did we get in last night? Where'd we end up? Agh, I need grease. Bacon and eggs?"

"Here." I hand him the glass. "I think that's the least you can do for me. I have a headache that'd kill a horse and I'm holding you responsible. Every time I wake up with a horrendous hangover, I think back to the night before, and you're always there. Mum was right… I would've been better off moving in with Luke!"

"Ouch! I'm wounded by that. You don't wanna' live with Luke. Can you imagine all the smooching you'd have had to put up with this past year with him and Michelle all over each other? Probably right there on the couch and everythin'. Eewww! Besides, you need me to keep you from dying from the boredom that is your life. How long do ya think we should wait before calling to see if Luke's alive?" Mick laughs but winces and stops short. *Yep, his head's as sore as mine. Good!*

"Just start cooking, chef boy. My life isn't boring, it's simple and predictable. The way I like it." My phone sends up a terribly loud trill. *Thank god I didn't take that to bed with me last night!* With a glance at the screen, "Huh, the man lives!"

"Hey! Why didn't he message me?" Mick digs around in the fridge, pulling out ingredients for breakfast.

"Probably because he's asking me to help him plot your murder. I take it he doesn't feel any better than we do. You have once again outdone yourself, Mick. I hope you're happy."

"I am actually!" He gives me a cheesy smirk and I rough up his hair with a strong arm. I hope it aggravates his headache.

"It was a rhetorical question, you jack-ass!" We wrestle playfully. Both giving as good as the other and getting the same in return. The tussle is short-lived with both of us tiring easily and with heads screaming.

5

Danielle

My Tuesday is off to a terrible start. Signing on for the day at work, I see that I am allocated to registers. A heavy sigh escapes me. My least favourite area. Water bottle in hand, I walk to the front service counter for my instructions.

"Oh, Dani, thank god you're finally here!" *Rebecca.* Glancing at my watch, I confirm I'm fifteen minutes early, as always. *Why is she talking at me like I'm late?*

"I'm not rostered to start until nine."

"Oh yeah, I know. Look… I need you to cover number one today. Once you've started, of course."

"One? But that's the busiest till?"

"Yeah, I know. You're the best with cash accuracy."

"But. But… I'm the worst with the customers." My mind is reeling in a feeble attempt to avoid the high volume of people. Before I get the chance to hyperventilate, my boss arrives. *I won't cope on a register all day!*

"Dani, hi," Sean says. "Change of plans, I'm afraid. I'm gonna need you out back. We're completely jammed with stock out there and you're the best man for the job. Figuratively speaking."

"Sean! You can't be serious? I need Danielle today. I'm a member down already!" Rebecca pouts at him in a way only cool girls can. *Do they go to some secret school of cool?*

"Don't worry, Beccy. I've sorted Jaz to come in for front-end to help you guys out instead."

"Oh, well in that case…" Beccy smiles and dances back towards her station. Jasmin and Rebecca are good friends, both 'cool kids'. It isn't a surprise she is happy to hear of the swap.

"Yeah, yeah, you can make it up to me later." Sean winks at her. *Agh, people make me nauseous!* Grabbing my water bottle from the counter, for what I hope is the last time. I follow Sean out the back to learn what the

29

priorities are. The loading bay is overflowing with stock.

"All the usual stuff, Dani. I need as much of this—as much as we can anyway—moved out onto the floor or stacked neatly. We need to get the door down tonight. We shouldn't be getting anything in today, but tomorrow'll be heavy again, so the more room we can make, the better."

"Okay, I'll do my best. Hey, um… thanks for getting me out of reg's."

"No sweat. Well, I'll leave you to it. Tom should be here soon to give you a hand."

Tom arrives within minutes of Sean's departure. Despite him having a crush on me and my turning him down, we work well together. Side by side we sort, shift and despatch stock to most areas of the store. The morning moves quickly while we clear a channel through the head-high sea of boxes and pallets.

By lunchtime, it is looking as though we will get most of the bay emptied out before home time. We take our lunch breaks in turn. Myself first, then Tom straight after.

Working over a box of assorted undergarments, I hear footsteps approach and, without turning, I smile. "You aren't due back yet. I told you to take your time." Tom always cuts his breaks short when he is working with me. I don't know if he does it with everyone or if it's because he likes me.

"Actually… I came to see how you were getting on. I knew I'd picked the right girl for the job." Sean's voice surprises me as he casually strides past me to the far end of the bay. "What's this lot down here?" He points to something behind a towering pallet. I'm forced to leave my work and step beyond him to see around the pallet he is pointing to.

As I manoeuvre around the far side, I don't have time to see or do anything before I feel Sean come up behind me. His hand brushes my forearm, surprising me. I flinch away from his touch and images of Jack's enraged face flash through my mind. I gasp. I don't get time to exorcise the troubling memories before I feel Sean all around me. He is in my bubble. Too close. His hands are on me. His tongue violates my mouth and I shove against him. "Stop. What are you—"

My words are cut off when my back slams into something hard. The sudden stop sends my head careening back and I hear a crack. *What was that? Was it my head? What's happening?* While trying to process, I feel a sharp pain tear through my left hip. Something rips. *Was that my shirt or my imagination?* I feel his full body weight leaning against me, holding me captive. Suddenly, it isn't Jack's face that is glaring down at me in anger. It's Sean's. My hands are pinned between the wall and my backside. *Not again! Please no!*

My brain goes into protection mode. It cares little of my physical self but instead focuses on shielding my mind from the offensive invasion I am about to endure. *Limp, go limp!* Fighting against him is a pointless exercise and I will only cause *myself* more injury by struggling.

Forcing my thoughts to drift far away from this reality. From this man I thought I knew. I wander into a beautiful, lush forest. I'm surrounded by gentle animals that come close to me for comfort. Taking grains from a pocket, I kneel and open my hand. Critters large and small eat from it, taking turns. A kangaroo joey nudges me, requesting a scratch behind the ears and I comply. A rabbit eats from my other food-laden hand. Birds sing their melodies from high in the trees above.

Breaking through my mental escape, I hear his—suddenly repulsive—voice close to my ear. "Good girl, don't fight me." He brushes the hair from my face and I flinch away from his touch. Purely a reaction despite my earlier decision not to fight. My already pounding head hits the wall again.

"Don't." My rainforest fades to black.

"You owe me. I got you outta front-end... I know you hate it there. I did you a favour."

"Please don't." Frustrated with my lack of words and ability, I plead again.

Cool air reaches my skin as he lifts my shirt aside. My blood freezes in my veins, fear raises goosebumps along my skin. I squeeze my eyes shut to block him out. His hand comes between us and he grasps my pants button, yanking them open. My torso twists with the momentum and a spasm of pain shoots through me, above the hip. Wincing, air whistles through my clenched teeth.

"Ow! I'm hurt." I say with fractured comprehension. Knowing what is to follow, my fists ball up behind me. *It will be worse to fight him.* I remind myself, but the instinct to do so is strong. Silent tears roll down my cheeks. How pitiful I must look.

"What the hell?" The weight against me vanishes and my legs buckle, sending me sliding to the floor. Clutching my injured side, I roll into the foetal position. Two men argue, but I pay them and their words no attention.

Unaware if one minute or one hour has passed. If I've slipped out of consciousness or not. I notice the world around me is quiet. My muscles are locked, not even my eyes will open on command. Feeling safe amongst the darkness of my closed lids, I stay a while longer. My capacity for thoughts, stunted.

"Danielle?" His voice is familiar. He sounds far away. *Who is it? Danger? Where am I?*

"It's me, Tom. Are you alright? He's gone. I don't know what to do. What can I do to help you, Dani?" Okay, he definitely sounds closer now. I manage to make my muscles work and unwind slowly from my tightly woven ball. My eyes open by degrees. The light's bright. I squint. Pulling myself up into a sitting position, I clutch my side and feel the frayed material of my ripped work shirt. *Mum's going to be so pissed!*

"Dani? Dani, you're bleeding! Shit!" Immediately I lift my shirt above the wound,

I don't want blood on it. I try to cover the cut—and bare belly—with a hand.

"Don't." Tom gently pulls my arm away. "Your hand's all dirty. I'll get some tissues. I saw them here just before," he mutters, looking around frantically. Sure enough, my hand is covered in dust and dirt when I turn it over to see. He returns with the box and I sit up properly, leaning against the wall.

"We need to go and report this." Tom squats down in front of me, staring. Looking grey. I shake my head at him.

"Who would we report it to? Sean's the manager. I just need to sit a minute while the bleeding stops, then I'll be right to get back into it." I smile bleakly.

"Fuck the boxes! You can't stay here. You need to go home, where your family can take care of you after... everything."

Just as I am about to argue the point, a wave of nausea hits me and I agree silently. *Don't let me vomit at work! Please let me get to my car before I puke everywhere!*

"Okay, slowly does it. I've got you on this side, but if it hurts too much, we'll stop. On three. One, two..." Rising slowly with Tom on my good side, I get to my feet.

He continues supporting me while I hobble my way through the store to the staff exit as customers and work colleagues look on. Self-consciously, I clutch a handful of the ripped and bloodied shirt in my free hand. Silently, we leave the building and questioning glances behind us.

At my car, he deposits me into the passenger seat. *I need to be in the other seat to drive. What is he doing?* He takes my keys, leaving me with firm instructions.

"Wait here! I'll be one minute." He walks a short distance away and pulls out his mobile, making a call. I hear him mumbling into the speaker, but I can't hear what he is saying or who he's talking to. His eyes never leave my slumped form as he makes the call.

"Sorry. Dave from Tech is going to follow us. I'll drive you home, then he can bring me back. Is your mum or someone at home?"

"Huh? I can drive myself home and that way neither of you are interrupted. Besides, I don't need the entire shop gossiping about me, so the less people involved, the better."

"I didn't tell Dave anything specific and even if I did, he isn't into gossip. Is there someone at home? Here comes Dave now.

Do you want to call your mum, or maybe it would be better if I called her and explained for you?"

"NO!" I shout too quickly. "No, I'll tell her. She is at work today though, so I'll tell her tonight when she gets home."

"Nuh uh, I am not leaving you home alone. Either you find someone to stay with you or I'm going to until I know you are safe and with family." He signals to Dave. "Put your belt on. Do you need help or are you right to do it?" Tom has become quite authoritative throughout the day's events. *I don't know if I like this Tom.*

"I can manage. I will have to call my sister. Just know... this is strictly under protest!" I sulk.

As Tom charters me away, I dial Michelle's number and secretly hope she won't answer. She answers on the third ring. *Terrific!*

"Hi, Michelle, it's me... Dani. Oh yeah, right. Sorry. Hey, do you think you could come over home? No, I got injured at work and they don't want me to be on my own." I scowl over my shoulder at Tom. "No, I'm okay. Yeah, Okay. Thanks. Bye." Tom returns a stern glance my way.

"You *are* going to tell her what actually happened, right? It's not my business, but I'm worried about you, Dani. That was… I'm shaken up, and it didn't happen to ME! Jesus! How can you be so calm? Maybe it's shock? I don't know what to do for shock. Is it shock that you shouldn't go to sleep…" Tom mutters to himself while driving. I don't contain the energy to explain to him that I've done all this before and worse. However, I do have the strength to correct his 'no sleep' confusion.

"I'm not in shock, but if I were… you would need to keep me warm. sleep is fine. You're getting shock and a concussion mixed up." He looks at me with his eyebrows knitted together. *Maybe I do have a concussion. How hard did I hit that wall with my head? It's throbbing fiercely. If I tell him that, I'll never get rid of him!* "You shouldn't sleep if you have a concussion. You know… when you've hit your head really hard." I resume staring out the windscreen and directing him through the maze of my estate.

Michelle's car is parked neatly on her side of the carport we once shared. *It's a miracle, she can park correctly when she knows I'm injured.* Tom parks my hatch in the driveway and Dave pulls in behind us. I grab my bag and tenderly get out of the car being careful not to reopen the wound and start it bleeding again. There is no way I'm going to give Tom any reason to insist on taking me to the Emergency Department. He holds my door open for me.

Michelle comes barreling out of the house, flinging the screen door back with a bang.

"Dani, are you all right? What happened? Shit, Dani, look at your shirt. Have you been to the doctors? Hi... I'm Michelle." She turns her attention to Tom.

"I'm fine. No need to fuss. I fell and caught my hip on a metal shelf. I just need to get cleaned up and lie down. Thanks, Tom. I appreciate your help and for bringing me home. Please thank Dave for me, too." I pray he doesn't say anything more to Michelle. Gossip queen doesn't need to know.

"Dani?" Tom questions. I raise my hand in a halting manner with my eyes trained on my shoes. With a deep breath and a prayer that he will understand, I look up into his eyes, begging him silently to stop talking. He does and I make my way inside. I just want to get washed up.

"Michelle, I'm fine." Shrugging her off sends more pain through my hip. She takes my bag from me but lets me go. Grabbing clean clothes and a fresh washer from a laundry basket on the dining table, I head to the bathroom, closing the door behind me. With the wet cloth, I wash the cut slowly and carefully. Inspecting it properly for the first time. It is larger than I realised. I wonder if it should be stitched. *If I can get rid of Michelle and convince her I just want to sleep, maybe I could take myself up to the doctor to do it.*

A soft knock interrupts my thoughts. Michelle's voice travels through the closed door.

"Can I come in for a minute? Please." *Agh, why is she always so attentive when I least want it?!* I'd love a nice hot shower but I'm scared the cut will start bleeding badly again. I pull on clean clothes before answering.

"It's open." I rinse out the washer and wipe away the stray water spots on the vanity with my dry towel. Cautious not to twist or reopen the cut. Michelle's and my eyes meet in the mirror before mine fall away. She looks sad or maybe scared, I can't tell.

"Tom told me. We need to get you looked at." My cheeks flush bright red but I refuse to budge.

"He shouldn't have told you. It isn't his business. Nothing happened, I'm fine. It's just the cut that hurts." I fiddle with the cloth in my hands.

"Dani, this is serious. I think you should see a doctor and then we need to take this to the police. I think we should call Mum, hey?"

"NO! Please don't call Mum, Michelle. She'll hover over me waiting for some kind of mental breakdown! Please, I'm absolutely fine! I only wonder if this needs stitches. I don't want an ugly scar that will remind me. Do you think it needs some or it'll be okay?" Lifting my baggy T-shirt for her to see, she kneels to have a closer look. The idea of having someone sew me up with needle and thread has my anxious fingernails pinching my arm, leaving half-moons etched in the skin.

"I think we should have it looked at. Besides, it looks like there could be some dirt in there and that should be cleaned out properly."

"Would you take me?" I ask quietly.

"You don't want Mum?" She swallows. I shake my head no.

"Okay, but we need to tell them the whole story. Yeah?"

"There's nothing to tell! Tom got there before Sean even got my pants fully undone. Nothing like last time. I promise, I'm fine." I hope I sound as convincing to her ears as I do to my own.

"Wait… WHAT?! Has this prick done this before?" her face turns into something resembling a wrinkled old tomato, with lips puckered, she explodes. Her outburst makes me jump, echoing in the small bathroom. *Damn it! Did I say that?* I retrace my words… *Oh.*

"No, no! He didn't do it. I didn't say that." I reach towards her, but she is backing out of the room. I can't comprehend why she's so upset or where she is going, so I follow her.

"Bullshit, Dani, don't protect that animal! I'm ringing Mum! She needs to come home and sort this out. Now!" She picks up the telephone in the kitchen.

"No! WAIT!" *Agh… I need to make my tongue work!* "Wait… WAIT!" With closed eyes, I breathe so deep I think my lungs will burst. Slowly, I release it, trying desperately not to think about the mess I'm in. "Please don't call mum! I'll explain. Please. Sean's never tried until today, I swear. And he didn't do anything physically to me… well, sexually anyway. Tom came and stopped him before he could.

"A few years back, I dated a guy. Anyway, he thought we should've been having sex before I wanted to. I broke up with him. I knew I wasn't making him happy. I tried to explain. He… He called me names and said I 'owed him for hanging out with a retard like me and getting nothing in return.' Then he took what he came for.

"I drove home. Had a shower. Prayed I wouldn't get pregnant and never saw him again."

Tears hang on Michelle's lower lids, the telephone receiver forgotten in her hand. She stares at me—for what feels like—a long time. I look around the kitchen, uncomfortable. She reaches towards me—maybe to hug me?—but I withdraw, like a turtle vanishing into its shell. From the corner of my eye, I see her retract her outstretched arm.

"Oh my god," she whispers. "I had no idea. And all this time, I've been pushing you. Who was it? Do I know him? I'm gonna chop off his dick and ram it down his own throat until he chokes on it!"

"It's irrelevant. I don't want to get into the details. It was so long ago. Can we please just go to the doctors?" I watch Michelle trying to decide.

"Yep… but this isn't over. We're gonna talk about this further. I'll phone ahead and let them know we're coming. You right to get in the car or do you need me to help you?"

"No, I should be fine. Promise me you won't tell the doctor what happened. I cut myself on a shelf. That's it. Yeah?" Michelle holds her breath.

"Reluctant, but yes, I promise." She hugs me carefully. She wants to comfort me, so I let her, but the whole thing feels weird to me. Breaking the awkwardness, she continues, "BUT… we're gonna keep talking about reporting this and the other time, okay? But for right now… yes, I promise not to say anything to the doctor until we can sort it out." I nod in agreement. *Hopefully, she'll forget.* The blip-blip of the phone keypad is loud in the otherwise quiet house.

Forty minutes later, Michelle and I are walking back out to the car. After deliberating, the doc thought it wiser to stitch my cut rather than glue, based on its location. He claimed that because it would be subject to strain every time I bent over and that my pants might rub, the stitches would hold it together more securely and with the water-proof dressing he gave me, it would be safe from germs and soft-waisted pants.

The trip home is non-eventful except for the persistent natter of Michelle's voice explaining the importance of reporting both incidents and something about telling mum. I have no clue what about; I stopped listening ten minutes ago. Pulling back into the driveway, the front door is open. *Shit... Mum's home.*

"We have to tell her. If you don't, I will. She needs to know... About today, at least."

"Mum's going to flip out. You know how she is. *And* I ripped my work shirt as well, which she won't be happy about."

"No... You were attacked! Your shirt was ripped in the assault. There is a HUGE difference!" Michelle brakes harder than necessary and we lurch to a stop. Thankfully, I am hanging on or we'd be turning right back around to have my sutures repaired.

"Injured, Michelle!" My fuse is short after the harrowing day.

"Sorry. I didn't actually mean to do that. I just wish you weren't so black and white all the time." She sighs. "Are you okay? Here comes Mum. You ready?" Michelle's out and around the car to help me before I have unclipped my seatbelt. I move carefully.

"What's happened? Dani?"

"I'm fine, Mum. Honest. Just a few stitches." I feel Michelle's eyes on me. *Okay… Seven, to be more precise.*

"Mum, go inside and put the jug on while I help Dani. We need to talk, all of us." Michelle waves Mum off. *I knew she'd fuss!* I am—for once—very grateful to have Michelle here with me.

6

Danielle

Darkness has fallen and we are all on our third cup of tea before the decision is made—hesitantly on my part. We are going to the police first thing in the morning to report Sean. Both Mum and Michelle are taking the day off to come and support me. Part of me thinks it's all a ruse to make sure I go. Regardless, their company on this occasion is welcome. Dad arrives home just as we are rising out of our chairs.

"Hi! What a surprise, Shell. How're you, honey?"

"I'm good, Dad," Michelle says. "But it's been a big day, so I'm heading off. I might see you in the morning if you haven't left before I get here."

"Oh? Everything okay? I thought you were back at work tomorrow?"

"Change of plans, but I'll let Mum and Dani fill you in. Night, Dad." She kisses him on the cheek before leaving.

"I'll walk you out, Michelle." I follow her out.

"You gonna be alright tonight?"

"Yeah, think so. Hey, um… Thanks for everything today."

"Of course. I'll be here first thing in the morning, okay? No doubt you're going to be worried by the time I arrive, but Mum and I'll be right there with you, so just remember that, hey?" I nod, unable to speak.

As I wave her off from the verandah, a soft breeze rustles the trees. I stay a moment, contemplating Michelle. *She was totally there for me today. She listened and took me seriously. She helped me with Mum when words stuck in my throat. She was caring. What if we could be close? What if this could bring us together? Like the strong sisterly bonds I've read about in my books and seen on telly. Wouldn't that be something?*

Dreams can be dangerous, though.

Inside, Dad looks at me with an odd expression that I don't understand. Mum gives me a small smile and I realise that she's told him. I sigh. *Nothing even happened! If only they knew about the other time, they'd realise how much better off I was this time.* But I managed to convince Michelle against telling them *that* story. And I'm certainly not changing my mind now!

Sitting across from Mum and Dad, the usual dinner time chatter is missing. I'd be happy staring into my pasta—like it held all the answers—if only they'd stop staring at me under the pretence of 'having a drink.' Every clink of silverware against bowls ricochets like smashing glass in the silence. I'm at my limit and in no way hungry. *I need to move.*

Excusing myself, I see the reluctance in my parent's faces as they would rather I stay where they can hover. They mean well, and everyone today has had the same reaction, so I have to assume it's only me who doesn't understand their need to watch over me, but I'll go nuts if I don't escape them. Soon! Without a valid reason why I should stay and eat, they watch me retreat to my room.

With all the drama, this is the first time since this morning that I've been back in here. Finally, being alone brings a fresh round of questions to mind. *Did Sean send me out back on purpose? Was this set up, or did he just take advantage of an opportunity? Would this still've happened if I'd stayed on reg's? What choice did I have? He told me I was working out the back. What if Tom'd taken first lunch… instead of me?…* Agh, useless questions that have no answers! I dig out an old stress ball from my drawer and flex it repeatedly in my hand.

Tonight is going to be one of those nights. My brain is on a loop. Round and round. Tomorrow is going to be hard enough. *I really need to sleep.*

~ They'll never believe you! He is the manager and you're just a socially crippled employee that read all the signs wrong! Don't know why you're even wasting everyone's time. ~

Oh, that's just perfect! Go away, She-Devil! We both know I agree, but it's irrelevant! I've already promised that I'll go, so just buzz off! I slam a CD into the stereo. *Music!*

Sliding in under my doona, I invite Rebel to join me with a pat on the mattress. He comes willingly and is content beneath the covers with me, purring comfortably. The soothing hum sends me to sleep surprisingly quickly.

Waking up, I hear birds outside. My room is brighter than usual. I check my watch. *Seven o'clock! I never sleep this late!* Rebel must have snuck out from under the covers at some point because he is now curled up on top of the doona at my feet. *Wow, I must've been tired.* As I become more coherent, I hear Mum and Dad shuffling around the kitchen together. *I'd better get up.* Leaving the security of my room proves as intense as I'd imagined. They both stop their breakfast preparations to stare at me as if horns are emerging from my skull.

Sitting alongside them at the breakfast bar, the crunch of my toast is loud in my ears. There is no conversation today. I am relieved to hear Michelle pull in the drive. *Thank you! Whoa. Since when am I glad to see Michelle? That's different!* Michelle lets herself in and reaches us in the kitchen just as Dad's rising out of his chair with dirty dishes.

"Morning, Shell." He pauses to kiss her on the forehead. She hugs him lightly while he holds the dishes aloft before she pinches his seat at the breakfast bar.

"Hey, Dad. Late start today?"

"Yeah. Thought I'd hang around here for a bit, for... well, you know how it is."

"Yeah." Michelle looks down the length of the bench at me.

"How you feeling, Dan?"

"Still don't want to go," I challenge.

"We know you don't, Dani, but you need to. Remember what we spoke about... It's the law." Mum interjects.

"Yes, Mum, I know." I say, defeated. *It's going to be a* long *day.*

The next four hours pass in a blur. I have a headache and I'm so exhausted that I just want quiet. I would take out my phone to play a mindless game, but in the angst of the morning, I forgot to grab it.

My annoying, analytical brain is stuck on a loop and keeps dragging me back through every word I spoke. Thanks to that one parting line from the police officer.

"If you remember or think of anything else, let us know." That right there was the permission that my brain needed to torture me with more questions and replays!

Mum offers to take us to lunch, but I decline. I just want to go home and escape to my bedroom. I feel fidgety and uncomfortable in my own skin. Given my susceptibility to anxiety and outbursts, I'd rather be at home, where I can run off any excess energy or cower in the corner if the need arises. Mum and Michelle settle for takeaway, but I can't stomach the idea of food.

"You should eat something, Dani. You hardly touched your breakfast."

"No thanks, Mum. I'm just not hungry. If I change my mind, I'll make myself a sandwich at home." I stare out through the rear window of the car, seeing nothing.

At home, Mum lets us out on the driveway before putting the car away. A sharp twinge reminds me to move carefully. With one hand on the car frame, I pull myself out. Gently, my other hand holds my pants aloft so they don't press on the stitches. Michelle gets out too, carrying the food and drinks.

"You did so well today. I'm really proud of you. You handled the whole thing like a star. I know Mum is proud too." She smiles at me.

"Yeah? Thanks, Michelle. I was pretty scared."

"Well, you didn't look it. You were so brave. You've done the right thing. I can see you're still turning it over in that mind of yours, but you *have* done the right thing." She ducks her head to see into my down-turned eyes. I nod in agreement, unable to speak.

Inside, Mum and Michelle set themselves up at the dining table with their lunch. Despite their invitations, I take myself off to my room where I can organise my thoughts and fall apart in private. One step inside, my phone is flashing on the bedside table. My fingers tremble as I reach to open the screen. I give them a flick to stop it and press the button. One new message. Tom wants to know how I am. He wants to visit me.

I flop down onto my bed. Rebel jolts awake with the movement and scrambles off, sneaking out through my all-but-closed bedroom door.

Great. Even Rebel doesn't want to be around me. The brain drain of the past two days leaves me in a sort of mental paralysis. Void of any further ability for comprehension and yet, still able to plague me with relentless, noisy chaos.

I stare blankly at the phone screen until it blackens again. Somewhere far back in my mind, I register its shift to sleep mode. Tom's message goes unanswered. My mind is stuck on replay, trying to make sense of everything.

What happened? Nothing happened! Will he say I provoked him? The police woman thinks I did. I never thought he was like that. Then again, I didn't think Jack was either, and I was definitely wrong about him! I thought Sean liked my work.

How could he try to do that to me? How could I have got it so... so ass-about? Why did it have to be me? I'm not strong enough to be different. I'm just... broken. This shouldn't keep happening, should it? No! I hate my stupid brain. HATE IT! Why can't I just be normal? Like Michelle. Like everyone else!

Tears line my cheeks, each one chasing the track of its predecessor. Faster they fall and I hear a sob through my own ears, as my vision blurs with each new salty tear. Falling to my bed, I roll away to face the wall and cry. Silently I release the hurt, anger and frustration that is my everyday struggle.

I know I'm not the easiest person to live with, but most of the time I manage by myself pretty well. I have my coping strategies and I work hard to keep myself in a positive mindset. Sometimes though, on days like today, the negative thoughts are loud and very easy to believe.

Eventually, my eyes run dry and I feel fractionally lighter despite the exhaustion that always follows an emotional meltdown. My breath is shaky from trying to cry soundlessly. With Mum and Michelle just outside, I don't want to draw their attention and have them crowding me; I just need this release. Privately.

Swollen and sore to the touch, my eyes hurt. I'm pretty sure my entire face is a mess if I cared enough to get up and check in the mirror. I don't. Rolling back onto my pillow, facing the ceiling, I close my eyes and imagine. I'm standing in the middle of a vast field that is skirted by dense forest and carpeted in colourful flowers that look like petunias.

There are butterflies fluttering everywhere amongst the blooms. I imagine them working together to lift me up above the blossom rainbow. I am flying and no one can touch me here. My body feels like a balloon, an exterior casing that is light and airy on the inside. They steer me along, sharing their incredible view of the flowers.

A soft knock on the door throws my vision into blackness.

With a sigh and a sniffle, I call. "Come in."

Michelle appears in the doorway. She frowns and I'm reminded that I must look horrible.

"Sorry," I say, feeling self-conscious. She comes and sits on the edge of my bed.

"Hey, why didn't you call us? What are you thinking about?" She brushes my hair back from my face.

"Just trying to work out where I got the signals wrong. And... and worried. No one is going to want anything to do with me after this."

"Why won't they? I don't understand." She frowns again.

"Because they'll think I asked for it or deserved it somehow, but I promise you, Michelle... I didn't do anything to give him the wrong idea!" I throw my arms around her, needing pressure. I nearly send us both flying off the bed as she hugs me and I begin weeping again.

"Hey, I know that! Gosh, do you honestly think that's what people think? What we're thinking? We know you'd never do anything like that!"

"B... But I... I'm al...ways mess...ing everything up!" I blubber.

"No, you aren't!" I look at her, knowing she's lying. "Okay, sometimes you get things a little muddled up. But if there is one thing that I *do* know—and *sometimes* it's a bad thing—it's that you tend to close yourself off from people! You're very hard to get to know, Dani. And like I said... usually I would call that a bad thing, but in this case... it's kinda good because it means everyone absolutely knows that you were not flirting or causing trouble with that pecker-head. You don't even engage in conversation with people unless they ask you something first." Calming down now, I can see her logic.

"Do you really think so? Even if I told you I let a boy kiss me on a first date? Only once, though."

"Seriously? It wasn't the other guy, was it? The one who assaulted you?" Michelle's smile fades. I shake my head and she continues. "I'm learning a lot about you this week, but yes, even knowing that. Letting a boy kiss you… even on a first date, doesn't make you a tease or easy, Dani. Hell, not even you kissing *them* on a first date would classify you a tease.

"Listen to me, at NO point is it okay for anyone to take or do anything to you that you don't want. No matter what's happened before that point. Understand me?" She dips her head to look at me, but I keep my eyes averted. It feels nice to have Michelle here, helping me. I don't know what's changed, but I hope it stays like this. Trying to think of something to say next, she hugs me tightly again.

7

Kevin

Mick balances a large pot on his lap in the passenger seat of my ute. We pull up out the front of Luke and Michelle's two-bedder cottage. We're so late that I struggle to find a vacant piece of curb as cars litter their lawn and driveway.

"Agh, man… Told ya we'd be late!" Mick curses, throwing his door open.

"The game doesn't start for another seventeen minutes. Stop your whinging! Besides, you're the one who insisted on making the damn curry!"

"Just get the beers."

Luke opens the door with a smile. "About time you guys got here. Thought we were gonna need to order pizzas. Come on in. Michelle's just finishing up the rice. Cold beers are in the fridge and hopefully there's still some space in the bottom for yours. Everyone's excited to try the new recipe."

Mick and Luke head for the kitchen while I hang back to greet my cousins loitering in the front lounge room.

"Kev, m' man! I thought you were bailing on us again."

"Hey, Josh." I squeeze past him, beers still in hand. The little place is crawling with my relatives and their partners. In the kitchen, filling couches and some are already deposited on the lounge room floor.

With mismatched china and cutlery, dinner is a self-serve affair. We fill our bowls with rice and fish curry, grab a beer and squish into the dinky little lounge room just in time for kickoff.

Dessert consists of mixed lollies and a block of chocolate that barely offers enough for a square each. Mock fights break out over the last few pieces.

Another goal and we erupt into roars of cheer. My phone blips, interrupting my concentration on the TV screen.

Angela: I miss you baby. Can we catch up for a drink?

I roll my eyes and return the phone to my pocket. As if I'd buy into that shit. I return my gaze to the TV, but my attention wanders and I'm done for the night. Having offered to drive Mick, so he could drink, I'm stuck here for the duration. *I knew there was a reason I stopped driving him!* With the lounge room so cramped and me no longer interested in the game, I rise from my piece of carpet and head for the kitchen. A little surprised, I find Lizzie, Josh's girlfriend, doing the dishes.

"Hey, why aren't you out watching the game with the rest of them?" I ask.

"Are you kidding? Way too crowded in there for me. Besides, footy isn't my thing, and I'd rather know the kitchen is clean." She smiles at me.

"Here, I'll dry for you." I grab the tea towel hanging from the oven handle.

"Thanks. How come you aren't watching the game?"

"Nuh, I've had enough. But I'm driving and Mick wants to keep watching."

"Hm." She nods. "You know, I'd almost buy your story if I didn't know the end score was the primary aim of watching footy. What's up?"

I consider what she's said. She is an observant girl. *Where do my cousins find these 'real' women? I sure as hell can't find any!* Lizzie stares at me, waiting for an answer.

"Can I ask you something, Liz?" I pause, searching for the right words to use and she nods, misinterpreting my sudden silence.

"How did you and Josh meet?" I ask. She turns a pretty shade of pink and I immediately regret my question. I stammer uncomfortably.

"What... what I mean is... you don't have to... what I meant was—"*Agh, just stop talking, Kevin!* I button my lips and my own cheeks warm with embarrassment. Lizzie chuckles.

"Nuh, it's fine. Josh was one of my clients at the shop." She averts her eyes to the dishwater. I'm confused.

"Really?" I ask. *What would Josh want with a beauty shop?!* My brain derails and I blurt out my initial thought. "What for?"

"He's my boyfriend... but I still have a code of confidentiality to keep where my work and clients are concerned." She smiles politely.

"Oh right! Sorry, course you do." I'm back to square one and my thoughts stray back to Ange. "Do all the *real* girls have a secret hideout that I should know about?"

She looks at me with a puzzled expression on her face.

"Huh?"

"Nothing. Ignore me. Just feeling sorry for myself. Feels like I'm the only one in this lot," I thumb over my shoulder, "that can't meet a nice girl." I polish the plate in my hands with extra force, thinking about Angela.

"Mick hasn't found anyone yet, has he?"

"Ha! Mick doesn't want to find one. He isn't looking! He likes the ones that scamper out with their handbag and high heels in their arms before he wakes... if you catch my drift?"

"Oh," she says, eyebrows raised.

"Yeah. And that's fine if he and his *friends* are happy, but I don't want to be the bachelor cousins who live together forever because I can't get a real relationship happening, you know?"

"For sure I do. It'll happen. I wasn't sure where I was ever going to meet someone. I mean, ninety percent of my clients are women! And building up the salon meant I never had time for socialising or partying. But then... Josh rang up, and I nearly said no because... well, I had my reasons. But I realised there was a market for males too, so I agreed. And it was the best thing I ever did. Josh and I hit it off straight away."

"Yeah? That's awesome, Liz. I'm happy for you guys. I know Josh's smitten." I say with a genuine smile, despite my own sore heart.

8

Danielle

Despite a good night's sleep, I wake early with a horrendous migraine. The kind that makes you want to vomit. Physically pushing 'send' on my resignation email last night was harder than I'd imagined it would be. That, combined with the stress of Michelle's impending wedding, has caught up with me. Reaching for the bucket from under my bed—the one I keep for this exact purpose—I sit up and retch. My head pounding with vicious ferocity brings another round of nausea to the forefront. Last night's dinner must be passed my stomach because nothing comes up. Mum barges through my door, a frown creasing her face.

"Dani, what's wrong?" It takes me a minute to catch my breath.

"Nothing, Mum, just a migraine." I'm surprised she hasn't been expecting it honestly. It's usually her who reminds me to 'slow down' before I crash in a heap.

"Damp cloth and tablets?" she asks knowingly.

"Please," I whisper with closed lids.

Block-out curtains keep my room surprisingly dark against the sun beyond my window. With summer still on its way, the temperature is cool enough to crave my doona. Pills in hand, Mum returns. After taking them, I sit the glass on my bedside table and drape the cloth over my eyes and forehead. It isn't long before I fall back asleep.

By the time I stir again, it is well past noon. Gingerly, I sit up, cautious not to jostle or induce a fresh round of pain and retching. Thankfully, the worst appears to have passed. All that is left now is a dull ache and fogginess. Both of which I actually welcome after the pain of this morning.

The house is bright beyond my door and I squint, but it isn't as bad as I expected.

"How's the head?" Mum has the telly on softly. Sounds like some midday soap opera.

"Better than this morning. How come you're home? Hope you didn't stay home just for me?" I move slowly and talk softly; I don't want to wake the monster again.

"Of course I did. With everything that's been going on around here, I wanted to make sure you were truly okay."

"You're silly. It's just a migraine. And now you have wasted almost a whole day because I was only sleeping, anyway." I fill my glass from the refrigerated water container.

"Nothing's wasted. I'm catching up on my daytime telly." She smiles at me. "How about I fix you a sandwich? Vegemite, or are you going to trust me with your order of a salad one?" She's trying to be cheeky.

"Just Vegemite, please. You'll never get the salad right." I take a seat at the breakfast bar opposite her. "No offence."

"What are you thinking about?" Mum quizzes me.

"Huh? Oh… I'm just trying to work out what I'll do for a job now. We both know I'm not the easiest person to interview, much less employ. Oh, but don't worry, I have some money saved so I will still be able to pay board."

"Sweetie, your dad and I aren't worried about you paying board right now. You've got a lot going on and your anxiety is up. We don't want you worrying about getting a job at the moment. For now, you just need to rest and reset." She hands me the sandwich.

"Thanks."

"Do you think it might be worth going back and talking to the psych about everything? We're worried and thought it might be a good idea." Mum is twisting the dish cloth around her finger. I watch the motion. Thinking.

"No, I'm fine, Mum. She'll just want me to go back on the meds again. But I promise, if I feel like it's getting on top of me… I'll organise a new referral. Okay?" I give her a faint smile to hopefully help reassure her; I mean what I say.

She stares at me for a few seconds, frowns and eventually nods softly, releasing her facial muscles. Either she has decided to trust me, or she has realised she can't actually force me into doing anything, since I'm legally an adult. Regardless, I know that I am okay, for the moment at least.

With my headache still threatening quietly at the back of my skull, reading is too risky. It could bring it all back on in a rush. I start sketching in my book instead. Rebel is curled up beside me, purring softly in a rhythmic beat. The vibration of it through the mattress calms me.

After dinner, Mum, Dad and I all watch some TV together. Although it isn't my favourite thing to do, it does have a kind of mind-numbing effect, which is good tonight, given that reading is still out of the question.

We sit watching an animal documentary. My parents are in their recliners and I'm stretched out along the matching three-seater. A leopard is dragging a full grown impala up a tree on the screen. Mum is gagging even though she has a cushion covering her face. When the house phone in the kitchen rings, she jumps up, keen to answer it. Dad and I share a chuckle at her weak stomach.

By the time she is finished the call, it is eight thirty and I am just about to get my milk and call it a night.

"Dani. That was my friend, Barb. Her son owns a DVD shop and when we got talking about you looking for work. She mentioned that he is looking for a new person to help them out with stocking shelves and covering lunch breaks and so on. Isn't that great? She said for you to give her your resume soon, so she can give it to him for you." Mum looks kind of breathless.

"Yeah. That's great, Mum, thanks." *What happened to 'don't worry about a job right now'? And a DVD shop? My retail career is going from bad to worse in the 'opportunity' department. On the upside though, my organisational skills could be great if they'll let me loose.* "I'll update my resume tomorrow for you. Do you mind giving it to your friend?"

"Of course, hun. That will work well actually. Barb and I are catching up tomorrow night after work for end of week drinks. Oh… unless you need me to be here, of course?"

"Huh? No, Mum. Go out, have fun. I'll email it to you, yeah?"

"Yeah, sounds great."

"Okay. Well, I'm going to bed, I think. See you guys in the morning. Night, Mum. Night, Dad."

"G'night, sweetie."

9

Danielle

By Saturday, things are looking brighter. Although I haven't heard back yet, I altered my resume, and Mum has forwarded it to the DVD guy. So now all I can do is wait and hope that he likes what he reads and calls me. Even if the thought of an interview makes me want to vomit.

In the meantime, there is plenty to keep my anxiety running strong. My work wants me to reconsider and come back, assuring me that Sean is no longer with them. I was so excited when I heard, but Mum and Dad don't think it's a good idea.

Michelle and Mum are in 'wedding' mode. It's become a familiar sight seeing them working at the dining table together most afternoons after Michelle finishes work. So far, they haven't asked me to help them. *Thank goodness!* Some nights I stay and talk with them, but most of it is over my head. Last night, they were working on table placements and seating. I'll never understand why people can't just pick their own seats. How can anyone be bothered with all that?

"Hiya, Dan," Michelle says, waltzing through the open front door.

"Hi," I reply without looking up from my novel. I'm at a good bit and just want to keep reading undisturbed.

Instead of heading down to the kitchen like usual, she comes and sits beside me on the couch. I try to ignore her, but I can feel her eyes on me. I look her way but drop my gaze almost immediately after.

"Why are you looking at me?" I ask.

"Because I want to ask you something, but I'm not sure how you'll take it."

"Probably wrong," I reply sarcastically. "What is it?" I close my book, jamming my finger between the pages to keep my place.

"I was wondering if you would maybe do a small piece of artwork for the ceremony booklets. I would love to have a little piece of you to remember of our special day."

"You know I'm coming, don't you? I'll actually be there." I ask, confused by her question. Michelle chuckles.

"No, silly. I know you'll be there on the day, but we'll keep one of the ceremony booklets and several other reminders of our day. It'd really mean a lot to me if you did the artwork. You don't want to be a bridesmaid and that's fine, I get it. But I'd love to have your stamp of approval, I guess you'd call it. Will you do it?"

"Um, I guess so. What do you want me to draw?" I ask her. Hesitant to open myself up for ridicule but wanting to please Michelle at the same time.

"I don't mind. Whatever you feel like doing. The bridal party are wearing mint green so if it could have this colour in it somewhere, that'd be wonderful, but not essential." She hands me a cut-out of a woman in a pale green dress on glossy paper, from a magazine, I presume. I take it from her, staring blankly. Along with the glossy clipping, she also gives me a folded piece of A4 paper with cursive writing scrawled in fancy font across it. All I can do is nod. I'm a fair bit confused and have no idea what she would like. *How do I say no, though?* With that, Michelle jumps up from the couch.

"What—" I try to ask.

"Whatever you feel like drawing. Surprise me!" She turns to look at me, still walking backwards out of the room. "Oh, and when I said 'it'd be good to get some mint green in there'… I didn't mean that's the only colour you can use. Get creative. You're always excellent with colour choices and combinations. I trust you." And then she's gone.

I sit staring, glancing between the glossy clipping and the cursive writing blankly, my book forgotten. *What am I supposed to draw? What do ceremony booklets normally have on them? I'd have to be the least experienced person for this. Drawing, yes. Knowing what to draw for a wedding, definitely not!*

My heart rate quickens the longer I think about it. I pull my phone from my jeans pocket and type into the internet search bar 'ceremony booklet artwork.' Jumping straight to images, I scroll through the hundreds of pictures on display. Most of the booklets don't have any art, so that's not helpful. The ones that do, mostly consist of flowers, wedding rings and one has doves on it. *Hm, fat lot of help that is! Maybe I can find something at the library.*

Finding nothing inspirational at the library, my options dwindle and I leave empty-handed. Waiting for a green traffic light, I fidget. Spying an imaginary imperfection in my pinky nail, it goes into my mouth without a thought. The sole survivor after another stressful week.

The nail slips between my teeth, and with a chomp and tear; the pinky matches its mates. The taste of blood dances on the tip of my tongue. Sliding the offending nail from my mouth, I flick it out of the window. I assess the damage with a frown. The corner has torn into the nail bed, explaining the blood.

At home, Mum and Dad are sitting out on the deck, having a cuppa together.

"Hi, Mum, Dad." I say.

"Hi, sweetie. Kettle's hot if you want a cuppa," Dad states.

"No thanks, Dad. Hey, Mum, can I get your help?"

"Sure, sweetie, what's up?" Mum asks.

"Did Michelle tell you she's asked me to draw something for the ceremony books for her wedding?" She nods at me with a smile. "Well, I've had a look online and at

the library but I don't know what to draw."
I stare again at my man-hand fingers. They
itch to be chewed.

"Well, what do you think of when you
think of a wedding?" She sips at her coffee
while I think.

*Loud music, wearing a dress, lots of drunk
strangers, family members hugging, Mum crying and
telling me it's 'cause she's happy.*

"Love?" I ask, uncertain of the right
answer. "But how do I draw that?" I sigh.

Mum chuckles.

"Hm, well, what do you *love* to draw?"

"That's easy, butterflies," I answer.

"Well, some people release butterflies
at their wedding, so I would say butterflies
are appropriate for weddings. Perhaps you
could have some flying from a cage or something. Or doves. People release doves sometimes, too. Or something around a love
heart. I'm sure whatever you decide will be
beautiful."

Mum's idea of releasing butterflies
gives me inspiration for an idea and I jump
up, keen to get started. "That's it!" I say.
"Thanks, Mum!" I bolt to my room to pull
out my sketch pad.

Now that I have an idea, my hand
glides over the page with a will of its own.

Colour choices and design happen as if by magic. The end result is intricate but clear. Individual butterflies trail and fly up into a myriad of them, forming the shape of a love heart. Colours varying from magenta through to mint green and black patterned wings. I check that the sizing fits against the sample booklet Michelle gave me. Perfect.

Jumping up, I grab my phone and take a photo of my creation and another of it next to the booklet for size reference. In a new message window to Michelle, I attach the pictures. Doubt strikes before I press send and my excitement fizzles. *What if she doesn't like it? What if it looks dumb? Is she going to laugh at me? At my work?* I stand frozen, processing. Without any way of knowing or figuring out these answers, I carefully pick up the drawing and the sample book.

"Mum?" I call out, searching the house.

"In here, sweetie," she replies, and I follow the sound.

"Mum, I've finished my drawing. But… I'm worried it might be silly. Would you take a look at it for me, please?" I ask, handing her the pieces of paper.

"Of course." She holds her hands out. "Oh, it's beautiful, Dani. I think Michelle is going to love it. You've done a wonderful job." She smiles at me.

"You don't think it's... dumb?" I ask in a whisper.

"What? No! It's stunning! Why would you think it was dumb? Have you shown Michelle yet?"

I shake my head. "I was about to, but I got worried. Do you honestly think she'll like it? I don't want her to be embarrassed by me in front of her friends."

"Oh, sweetie... Michelle loves you. You're not an embarrassment. And she wouldn't have asked you if she didn't want your help. I'm sure she's going to love your drawing. I certainly do. It's gorgeous. Send it to her, or better still... why don't you drive over there and show her in person? That way, you'll be able to see her reaction for yourself. I know she is at home. I just messaged her, and she said she was there. She'd probably love to see you, and I know she's excited to get the booklets printed so that she can check them off her list."

"Hm. Thanks mum. I think she's probably pretty busy. Think I'll just message her." I lean in and give her a—mostly awkward—hug before returning to my phone. My message still waits to be sent. Pictures still attached. Sucking in a deep breath, I push send. *I hope she likes it.*

10

Kevin

Ignoring Angela's messages proves fruitless. She is persistent and her messages are getting worse in her desperate ploy to get my attention. After switching off my lamp, I lay in bed thinking of tomorrow. I cringe momentarily at the idea of going to another wedding alone.

Maybe I should have invited Angela? At least I could pretend for a few hours that I'm successfully adulting. I shake the idea from my head. *Forget 'er, dude! She dropped you last week for that pimple-faced college douche in the convertible. She ain't what you're looking for.*

I roll over and clutch the spare pillow to my chest, blinking into the darkness and ignoring the buzz of my phone receiving more messages on the bedside table beside me. It is sometime after midnight that I fall asleep.

Dreading what she sent after I said good-night and put the phone down, I snag it up and have a look. Three unopened messages. *I'm gonna regret this for sure.* She was getting pushy before I cut her off. *Gee-zus! Does she honestly think that makes me want to date her? Flashing her bits at me in some cheap attempt to lure me back? Didn't take her long to get bored of douchebag. That or he figured out her game and dumped her arse!* I delete the images and block her number from my phone.

Patch scratches on the closed bedroom door, pulling me from my thoughts. "Yep, let's go, beautiful. Come on." Chucking on some shorts, I let her out. She races me to the back door and I crack it open enough for us both to slip out quietly. I scrub the sleep out of my eyes while she does her business.

With an all-over shake, Patch is a bundle of energy and she tears around the yard like a kid on whizz fizz. She sniffs madly, darting all over the lawn. I laugh affectionately. Snagging up her rope toy, she runs back to me and drops it at my feet before backing up, waiting.

After several runs for the rope toy, we have a brief game of tug. She is strong and pulls at it with fierce determination. Grunting around the rope, she gets the angle on me and I fall forward onto my knees. Bursting into laughter, Patch licks my face, still excited. With a loving cuddle, I rise and wipe away the dewy grass from my knees. "Come on, gorgeous, back inside. I gotta get some brekky and get ready." She barrels in behind me, tail wagging.

It's a last-minute dash to the finish line as Mick and I race around each other in the little, old, fifties style government house with only one bathroom. Between us, there are hair-care products all over the vanity and colognes thick in the air. With shoes and ties in hand, we jump into my ute—it's cleaner than Mick's—and race towards the church.

11

<hr>

Danielle

Watching from the first row, Michelle walks towards us in a powder-puff of white. Her hair hangs in soft curls to her shoulder blades. She is beautiful. Luke looks equally as handsome in his black on black suit with white and silver tie. He has two groomsmen by him. They too, are dressed in black on black suits but with ties of mint green to match the bridesmaids' dresses. Susie and a lady I don't know stand beside Michelle in their knee length dresses.

The church is modern and elegant. The ceremony seems long and I fidget, but I doubt anyone else thinks this, just me. Mum and Michelle argued last week over the length of the ceremony. I tried to tell my mum at the time that my issues aren't Michelle's worry. She doesn't always need to control everything, but I guess Mum will always be Mum. She forgets I'm not a child anymore.

Other than a few family photos at the church, I'm lucky to escape the worst, which is reserved for the bridal party only. My parents and I are put in charge of collecting all the altar flowers and transporting them to the reception. People gather outside the church in groups, most of my relatives among them. Michelle is having the 'big wedding'.

My parents are chatting with a group I don't recognise when I round the church corner with the last of the flowers. I'm not very good at small talk, so I slow my steps, wondering if mum has locked the car or not. *I'll just go and see for myself.* Before I move however, they all start walking towards the cars as well. I hesitate, unsure if I should hurry ahead of them—though long strides in this dress aren't likely to be successful— or hang back and let them get to the cars first? Almost everyone else has left for the reception already.

Standing amongst the unfamiliar group is a young man. I can't see from here if he looks my age, but he certainly looks younger than his current company.

Michelle and Luke's reception is held in a giant marquee at a fancy manicured garden centre especially designed for weddings. Most of the guests stay inside except the odd person who strays out to the gardens. One of these 'odd' people is me. The band in the tent is loud. Combined with the one hundred plus guests, cramped around tables, it is utterly overwhelming. I disappear regularly for much needed sanity breaks.

It is on my fifth escape, I decide to wander further away from the noise. Given that the grounds are designed for weddings, there are little alcoves and picturesque garden statues, waterfalls and bird-feeders hidden all over. During our arrival, we came down a few broad steps made of stone that were flanked on both sides by lush green hedges. If I can find my way back to it, it would be a nice place to sit for a minute. Maybe do some breathing exercises.

Away from the marquee windows, it is much harder to see with only very dim lights illuminating the path. *Staggering around in the dark, in a long dress, around a place you don't know... not your smartest move, Dani! Oh, hang on… Yay, you've found it.* Deciding whether the steps are dirty enough to mark my dress doesn't take long, I don't actually care. I sit. Now that night has fallen, the air is crisp. Deep breath in… one, two, three. Out… one, two, three.

Breathing and sitting, sitting and breathing. The cool air on my face is a welcome feeling, but my legs disagree and I tuck them up under the long fabric of my dress to keep warm. I sit for what feels like several minutes before I feel someone's eyes watching me. Looking up, I see the shadow of someone standing over me, goosebumps rise along my arms.

"Hey… are you okay?" The voice is male and not one I recognise, but I can't tell any more than that.

"I'm fine. Just getting some air." I keep it brief having no idea who the stranger is. I'm uncomfortable realising that no one knows I've stepped away from the celebrations.

"You're Danielle, aren't you?" Either he can see in the light much better than I or he is some kind of stalker, because I can hardly make out his face. My recent struggle with Sean replays in my mind and my hands clench.

"Who're you?" I squint against the darkness trying to conjure up his facial features. He shifts his weight, blocking a fairy light from view, which allows me to see him marginally clearer. It is the young man who was walking with my parents back at the church.

"I'm Kevin. I saw you head out before and wanted to make sure you were okay." He stares and waits for me to reply while I struggle with two thoughts simultaneously. I wonder if it is a little strange that he has noticed my movements—since he doesn't even know me—and my own parents probably haven't even realised I'm gone. Even more confusing though, is the flutter I feel deep in my core, learning that someone has noticed me at all.

"I'm fine, like I said."

"Mind if I sit for a minute?" he asks. My mind races ahead, trying to recall all possible conversation tools I have learned and might need now. *I am awkward. ESPECIALLY with people I don't know!* My panic climbs. *I have no one here to buffer me or help fill the gaps.* I try to sound calm. "It's a free country."

He sits down beside me, elbows to knees, just staring into the inky blackness of the night. He doesn't say a word for the longest time while I watch him. It is one of the strangest things I've ever seen anyone do and I'm the master of strange!

"Perhaps I should be asking if *you* are alright?" I mutter, half under my breath. He hears me. We are far enough away from the party that I can hear crickets singing among the shrubs and I mindlessly imagine butterflies tucked in for the night alongside them.

"I'm great. Was a lovely ceremony, don't you think?" he pivots around to face me in the darkness. My eyes have adjusted and I can make out more of his features.

"Yes. Lovely." *Do boys like weddings? I thought they were a more girly thing. Well… except me, of course.*

"What was your favourite bit?" He has a grin on his face. *Is this a test? If it is, I'm going to fail.*

"Favourite bit? Ah, I don't know. Maybe the part when they walked out together." My voice is full of uncertainty. Even I can hear it. *I was happy that we could get up out of our seats then and move. Even if only for a minute. Does that count?*

"Really? I thought every girl liked the kiss the most. Shows how much I know." He chuckles quietly.

"Oh… yeah. That's probably what I should've said. I'm not an average girl, I'm afraid." I begin to pick at my fingers. *What are you doing? Why'd you say that? That last bit? Oh well, it's not the first time I've said the wrong thing. Chances are strong, it won't be the last. Here comes the awkward moment where he tries for a quick but polite getaway. Three, two…*

"You're far from average! That much I've already worked out, but I'd like to learn more." *Huh? He wants to learn more? About me?*

~ Huh, maybe he has a laboratory! He wants to learn about your weirdo-wired brain. Wait 'til he figures out you never actually wear dresses OR make-up OR have your hair done up all girly. You're a total fraud! She's a nutter, Dude! She flaps her hands like a duck if someone dares touch her teacup! Run, Dude, run! ~

She-Devil screams to the stranger from inside my brain, making it hard for me to concentrate on anything else. "I'm sorry. I don't actually know who you are. How do you know Luke? Since I've never seen you before, I assume it is not my sister you know?" She-Devil is laughing at me. She thinks I look stupid. I crack my neck from side to side in an effort to ignore her.

"Oh, of course. Sorry. I'm one of Luke's many cousins. We're all *pretty* close in age, but I'm a couple of years younger."

"That must be nice… Being close, I mean."

"It has its moments! You're not close with your cousins? Or you don't have any?"

Did I say that? Damn! Nice… You should've just said nice! I make a mental note of his acute listening skills. He's far more observant than most people I meet, a stimulating but nerve-invoking change.

"Um, no. We have cousins. Not as many as your family perhaps, but enough. Most of them are close… I think." I cross my arms and tuck them into my lap, trying to remember if I'd ever heard Michelle talking about our cousins. I think she has every now and then.

"Them? Not you, too? I feel like I've missed something."

Oh, where do I start? And honestly, why would I bother? It will end the same way it always does. Just tell him outright and let him run. Shame, he seems nice. Different, somehow.

In the end, I can't bring myself to say the words I know will scare him away.

"Ha, how long have you got?" It isn't actually a question; I'm trying for lighthearted humour. I want to stay here and talk with him more, which is exactly the reason I decide that it is time to go back to the party. Before I say the wrong thing that gives me away or I start flicking my hands because something's pissed me off. For reasons I don't understand, I want to keep my autism a secret from this man. No, that's not right... I want to *be normal* for him, even if only for tonight.

Standing, I dust my rump for any marks. Kevin rises as well. Standing so close, I see he is a good head taller than me. Before I can take a step, he rests his hand on my arm. I flinch away like he's burned me, caught off guard.

For a minute, I feel disorientated and vulnerable. Memory of Sean grabbing me flashes brightly in my mind. My traitor hand flaps several times while I take a steadying breath to find my equilibrium. I grab it with my other hand to hold it still, but it's too late. *Yep... he looks weirded out. Head bobbing back and forth between my stupid hands and my... whatever my face looks like. Got to get out of here!*

I want to run. I want to cry. I want to scream. I want to beg him to understand, but mostly I want to go back five minutes in time and not be surprised! I want to enjoy this man's company a few minutes more. Our eyes lock in the bleakness, his reflect the dim glow of the fairy lights, but I can't tell their colouring. Mine sting with hot tears and I look away. If I blink, they will fall. I turn and all but run back to the party, clutching my shawl tightly around my shoulders as I go, despite it now resembling a 'crown of thorns,' rough against my skin.

The rest of my night is long after that. I force myself to mingle with relatives, remaining amongst a solid crowd at all times. I spot Kevin a few times across the marquee doing the same. Each time I look his way, his attention shifts to me as if I've called him. The mingling is tiring but I don't dare go outside again and risk him following me. He'd want answers and I don't have the strength to explain it tonight.

~ HELLO!! You couldn't explain it right anyway! Do you actually think you'd be in this situation if you did?! None of the others left because 'It's me, not you.' Nope… they left because of you. You're an awkward weirdo! ~

I down the last of my fruit punch in a bitter mouthful as She-Devil's words ricochet around in my mind.

I really hate her!

12

Danielle

The day following the wedding is a quiet affair. Mum, Dad and I packed up and brought all the gifts home with us last night while Michelle and Luke spent the night in some city hotel. Why they would spend money on a hotel room when they live by themselves is a complete mystery to me, but Mum reckons lots of people do it.

After the late night, the house is silent long past its usual hour of activity. Even before my eyes open, my mind starts dissecting my conversation with Kevin on those steps in the blackness. I've got no idea what to think about any of it—if anything—but I have butterflies in my tummy. Looking for a distraction, I check my watch. Eight o'clock. I pick up my current novel. The land of fiction is so much easier than reality. Rebel stretches out by my foot with a yawn and wanders up the length of the bed. His purr is loud as he nuzzles into my neck.

By nine am, he is swatting at my book and getting vocal. He's had enough. I get up and open my door for him to toddle off. Picking up my pyjamas from the floor— Mum finally conceded defeat over making me wear clothes to bed when I was about nine—I put them on and head for the kettle.

Mum and Dad rise shortly after they hear me moving around. We all work pretty well together and have a smooth routine. I make the cups of tea—well, coffee for Dad. Dad does the toast because he always gets mine perfect, just a blush of gold. And Mum puts out the plates and spreads along the breakfast bar—because she does so many other chores around here—so breakfast is mine and Dad's thing.

Everything comes together at about the same time and we sit along the bench like three pegs on a clothesline, spreading, sipping and eating. We tend to swap schedules and plans during this daily ritual, so everyone knows what's going on. Today I learn that Michelle and Luke are coming over for lunch and to open their gifts.

"Dani, can I put you in charge of writing the gifts on the cards? I want to take photos and your dad's handwriting is terrible."

"'Tis not! I work in an office, thank you very much." Dad says indignantly. Mum is laughing at him.

"Darling, working in an office doesn't mean you have good handwriting. Don't worry, I'm putting you in charge of the barbecue. You're much better at that." She winks at him with a smile. He frowns but I don't think he's really angry.

"So, will you scribe for me, sweetie?"

"Yeah, Mum, sure." I climb off my seat and start gathering up the empty plates and coffee cups. Mum puts away the jars while I wash up the few dishes. We take that bit in turns, though there's no official roster sorted.

When Michelle and Luke pull into the driveway, Mum races out to greet them. Luke's parents are with them and climb out of the backseat. Luke's mother struggles to open her door as Mum crowds close, hugging Michelle. *She only saw her yesterday!* She's mushy and smothering them as they get out of the car. I am SO glad she isn't like this with me. I'd hate it. Poor Luke, he looks uncomfortable. *Maybe he's overwhelmed? That wouldn't be hard… what is Mum doing?!*

~ He isn't overwhelmed you dolt! He is embarrassed because your parents know they've had sex now! ~

She-Devil's interruption hits me like a slap to the face. *Oh, yuck! Do you have to be so graphic? And anyway, go away! I have to sit with them all afternoon while they open presents and the last thing I need is you screaming in my ear. Go away!* I stomp my foot hard and then go back inside to wait for the others.

Lunch is simple. Dad cooks up patties on the barbecue with Luke at his side for conversation while Michelle, Mum and I prepare salads and bread rolls in the kitchen. The two of them keep up a steady stream of chatter about the wedding.

"Weren't the lilies beautiful? I was so happy with them."

"Oh yes! They made the whole church smell absolutely beautiful! And did you get a look at Luke's face when he first saw you in your dress? I thought his eyes were going to fall out." The two women giggle like schoolgirls.

"No, I missed that. And several people commented on your beautiful butterfly drawing, Dani. What did you like best?" I pause and look up from the slicing of tomatoes. Unsure what to say, Kevin's words resound in my head.

"Doesn't every girl love the kiss?" *Not this girl... but technically, I haven't lied.* I return to my slicing. My mind races along at a hundred miles an hour, analysing if my response is appropriate or not. Yet, only a second in real time passes. There is stilled silence around me in the kitchen. Again, I stop what I'm doing and peek up to see both women staring at me. *Nope... Apparently that is not the correct answer.*

~ That's all you are... incorrect and on your own! ~

Not now! My brain does tug-of-war with itself.

"What?" I ask quietly. Michelle and Mum trade glances. I get the distinct feeling I am missing an unsaid conversation of sorts.

"Nothing," they mumble and spring back into buttering bread rolls. *What an ironic twist of roles!* I am just about to challenge them for an explanation when my dad calls us.

"Patties are ready. You want them in there or out here?"

"Leave them out there. We're just finishing now. Can we get a hand to help carry out the salads, please?"

After lunch, Michelle is bursting with excitement to open gifts. My dad insists on cleaning up the lunch mess while we all go and get started. I offer to give him a hand but Mum reminds me, I'm required in the lounge room for the gift recording.

Amongst the presents are ornaments, towels, tea towels and other kitchen paraphernalia. The standout pieces are an expensive looking free-standing antique mirror from Luke's grandma; a family heirloom which was delivered to their apartment prior to the wedding. The other, a dinner set of fine bone china, illustrated with baby blue forget-me-nots and gilded with yellow gold trim, from us. Mum bought the set weeks ago and had been very excited to find me home so she could show me straight away. She gave me the option to go in with them and after no luck coming up with anything on my own, I'd given mum the cash.

Dad joins us after the cleanup. He watches on from the couch while Mum snaps photos of every new item they open. Finished, scrap paper and sticky-tape litter the lounge room floor, I retrieve a garbage bag from the kitchen and start to gather it all up.

Dad rises and stretches his arms high. "I need a cuppa coffee. Who else wants one? Tea, Dani?" We all agree in unison. Luke's parents follow Mum and Dad towards the kitchen, chatting easily about the reception.

"How about I go put these in the car? That way it's done later when we want to go." Luke puts a load together.

"Good plan. I'll give you a hand in just a sec, babe," Michelle agrees. Luke is nodding as he leaves with his arms full.

"So... Luke got a message from his cousin Kevin this morning." My hand pauses briefly before carrying on collecting rubbish.

"He asked if you were okay and wants to know if he can see you. He didn't... hurt you or anything, did he?" Michelle touches my hand gently but I flinch away. She releases it, understanding my reaction and gives me time to process. I grant her a quick, flickering glance sideways and shake my head, no.

"You want to tell me what happened then?" *Happened? Nothing happened.* I have to untangle my thoughts before I can actually speak. I stare at the carpet, trying to do so.

Michelle mistakes my silence for subject closure and sighs in annoyance, I think.

"Wait," is all I can manage. It comes out as a mumble but straight away Michelle seems happier. The wedding and meeting Kevin have been at the fore-front of my brain all morning. I have analysed every minute, every detail one hundred times over! In truth, I could do with the advice. Or some inside information, at the very least. Confiding in Michelle though still feels odd.

Until the whole work incident a few weeks ago, we've never been very close. Michelle gets easily frustrated with my quirky tendencies. We just don't understand each other very well. Since the incident though, she does seem different. She has a look in her eyes that makes me want to trust her.

"Nothing. I went outside for some air and Kevin found me. He introduced himself and we talked for a bit."

"Hm, he seems to feel like more went on. He's *desperate to see you again'*. That's a direct quote, actually!" Michelle smiles.

"He doesn't even know me," I whisper, more to myself than to her.

"That's usually the exact reason *why* people keep meeting. To 'get to know' one another," Michelle points out softly. I sigh.

"I can't keep my autism hidden. Once he knows, he will run, like all the others." She looks at me with a strange expression and I have no idea why. My ignorance frustrates *me* even more than it does others— I'm sure of it—I crack my neck from side to side. If she would just say what is on her mind! I realise now, this is why we are not close. There is too much guesswork involved for me when I am talking to Michelle. My head hurts from all the *unsaid*.

"Why are you looking at me like that?" Her scrutiny makes me nervous, and I start picking at my fingernails.

"I'm sorry." She raises her hands in a surrendering fashion. "Look, I just don't believe that's true. People don't run from you, Dani. You run from them!" *Huh?* "You push people away. And as for your ASD… You shouldn't want to hide it, it makes you who you are." Her words surprise me.

"Sure, you're a little quirky sometimes, but none of us are perfect. Luke tells me he's a good guy, though. Maybe you should give him a chance to get to know you." I open my mouth to argue but she halts my words and continues… "I'm not saying you should date him or anything. I know you've had a rough couple of weeks. But wouldn't it be nice to have a friend? Somewhere to go that isn't the library! And someone to talk to, other than Mum and Dad. Just think about it, that's all I'm saying. I better go help Luke finish packing the car." She finishes and collects up two handfuls of gift bags.

The rest of their visit passes in a bit of a blur. They all talk about the wedding, of course, and the antics that went on at the reception. I try to pay attention, but my mind is back at my conversation with Michelle and all that she's told me about Kevin. *I really enjoyed his company, too. Why would he want to hang out with me, though?* I half expect She-Devil to jump in and destroy my calm, but she stays blissfully quiet, for a change.

13

Danielle

In the weeks following the wedding, life returns to normal. Michelle and Luke are on a two-week honeymoon in South Australia, a place neither of them has been before. Michelle sends us pictures every couple of days. My phone has never been so busy! I'm even starting to expect them.

Working in the kitchen, I'm making cookies when I hear my message tone ping. I know it's from her. They've been away for a week and I didn't hear anything yesterday. Opening the message with a semi-clean pinky finger, I see two pictures. One is the most amazing rock—more like a boulder— I've ever seen! And the other is two seals lying together. One looks to be giving the other a kiss. I smile and read the text.

Michelle: Hi Sis, we're having a great time. You would love the wildlife here. 1st pic is The Remarkable Rocks and they're incredible! The other is 2 seals we saw when we visited Admirals Arch. Absolutely loving it! The weather has been fantastic! So many photos to show you when we get back. Kevin is still harassing us. Can I please give him your number?

My hands halt, the cookie dough forgotten. I am standing in the middle of the kitchen, staring blankly. *What do I say to that?* Unsure, I return to my task. *I'll reply later.*

Flattening all the cookie spheres with a fork, I put the tray into the oven, still racking my brain for something to write back to Michelle. Part of me wonders if she is trying to be funny. Mocking me. After tidying the entire kitchen and making myself a sandwich, I open the message and read over it again. My brain is in default mode; *avoid, avoid, avoid.* I key my reply and hope she is too busy having a great time to notice my evasion of 'Kevin'. *Neuro-typicals' almost never follow up on questions they ask. I don't even know why they bother asking them in the first place usually.*

Me: Hi, that boulder looks amazing! Is it carved like that? I look forward to seeing the other pictures you have taken. The seals are so cute. Are you standing that close or is the photo zoomed in? :)

Saturday morning finds me back at the library for my weekly book return and collection. As a regular, most of the staff address me by name. They know how familiar I am with the layout of books—probably even more than some of the staff are—so they leave me to do my own thing. Stalking the spines with my index finger, I look for titles that grab my interest. I find none. This has never happened before. Sometimes I like to read non-fiction books on autism and giggle at how wrong the 'experts' have it. But I know most of them by heart, so the idea doesn't allure me today.

~ *Hey, Nigel no-friends! Let's read something saucy for a change. Who knows... maybe you'll find a 'magical book' that you accidentally fall into and everyone there will love you and you can live 'happily ever after!' Course... I doubt you'd fit in anywhere!* ~

She-Devil! Rolling my eyes, the sound of her laughter is like nails against a blackboard. I ignore her. Despite her harsh words, I find myself drawn to the romance section. In minutes, I'm building a pile for borrowing.

Walking out, I'm greeted by pouring rain that wasn't here upon entering. *Terrific!* My umbrella is in the car, which is parked up on the roadside. The water is streaming down the hill towards the large stormwater grate. *I'm in my good ballet flats!* I head back inside.

"Excuse me, Sarah, would you have a plastic bag I can put my books in? It's pouring outside and I don't want to get them wet."

"Oh really? Sure… here you go." She hands me a clear plastic bag from under the counter. *At least that's one problem sorted.* I subconsciously chew my fingernail, considering how to get up the hill and into my car without ruining my shoes. *All I can do is make a dash for it.* I focus on moving quickly but carefully. I HATE that my shoes and I are getting soaked in the process!

Jumping in the car, I dump the plastic wrapped books in the passenger footwell. I don't want *that* seat wet as well. Absolutely drenched, my hair sticks to my forehead and neck like octopus tentacles. The feel of it has my breath accelerating with anxiety and I do my best to scoop it up off my skin. I tie it up in a rough bun to keep it from touching me, pulling the hair band from my wrist with my teeth. Turning on the ignition, I wind up the heat to dry everything out and leave after two shoulder checks. The dreary weather fractures my nerves. My shoes squelch with every push of the accelerator. It darkens my mood to reflect the hellish clouds above.

It is still bucketing down when I reach home. I pull into the carport, thankful to have some cover. At least the water here is draining away better, I notice. I decide to take off my shoes and carry them alongside the books. In Michelle's old parking space, I open my umbrella and brace myself. *Ready… Go!* I dart out into the rain and up the steps to the covered front verandah where I finally manage to take in a full breath. Resting the open umbrella down to dry out. I shiver, my cold, wet clothes stealing the heat from my skin. A warm shower awaits, I remind myself. *What a horrible day.* About to tip-toe my soggy form inside, I nearly bump straight into Dad, who's coming out.

"Whoa! Sorry, Dad." I leap backwards to avoid an awkward touch. "It's pouring out there."

"I know! The skies have definitely opened up. Hey, I'm glad I caught you. I left a note on the bench. I'm heading around to

Rob's to help him work on his new tinny. Your mum's gone to lunch with someone. She did say who, but I can't honestly remember."

"Oh… sure, Dad. Well, I'm just going to hang around here."

"Okay, well… have fun, sweetie. I don't know when your mum'll be back, but I'll probably only be a few hours. See you in a while." He smiles and darts out into the rain.

Warm and dry, I toss-up between watching a movie—since I have the house to myself—or drag my doona out and curl up under it with one of the new books.

~ OR…. *We could go to the shops and buy a whole new wardrobe of cool clothes like a NORMAL person would! We can get a cream doughnut and splurge!* ~

Agh, I don't even eat cream! With She-Devil around… I pick a movie. *Hopefully, I can drown her out with the volume control.* I like animated movies. Their depth and graphics fascinate me. I push 'Brave' into the player. I secretly think Merida might be on the spectrum too, even if she doesn't know it. My phone vibrates with a message, not five minutes in. *That's odd.*

Unknown Number: Hi, it's Kevin. We met at your sister's wedding. I hope you don't mind. I got your number off Michelle. I was wondering if you'd like to hang out together sometime? Maybe we could go to the movies tonight?

Oh crap! Double, no... triple crap! What do I say? I'm going to kill *Michelle!* I am deep in thought when—on the tv screen—a giant bear jumps out of the forest to kill Merida's father. The loud roar makes me jump and my phone tumbles to the carpet. I grab the remote and hit pause before reaching for my mobile.

Wishing Michelle were here right now so I could yell at her about the breach of privacy of giving out someone's number. He could be a stalker or psychopath for all I know! The image of Sean's stubble at close range comes to mind and I physically recoil from the picture and shake my head. *No, Kevin isn't a psychopath or a stalker.* I'm just angry because I hate it when Michelle surprises me like this.

I don't know how to handle this, or myself. What if I don't like the movie he chooses? A heavy sigh escapes me. Pinching the bridge of my nose and squeezing my eyes closed tightly, I take a deep breath in and release it slowly. Then I surprise myself and hit 'reply' to start drafting. After typing and erasing three attempts, I re-read it and hope I sound casual.

> Me: Hi Kevin. Yes, I remember. A movie sounds good. Which cinema were you thinking of? I'll meet you there. What time?

My finger hovers over the send button before I finally push it. *Did I seriously just do that?* Before I even have time to dwell on it, my phone vibrates again, still in my hand.

> Kevin: Really!?! Awesome! I'll check what's showing and session times and get back to you soon. I was thinking we could grab a bite to eat beforehand if you want? :)

What'd I say about NT's not answering questions… I roll my eyes. *I hope he doesn't pick a cinema too far away.*

An internal war breaks out for my attention. Excitement about seeing Kevin again leaves me giddy despite echoes of She-Devils negativity bouncing around in my head. She calls me an idiot and is muttering something about me stuffing everything up. I try to block her out. The more immediate concern clutching for my acknowledgement, however, is the nausea that fills my core. Anxiety. My relentless nemesis!

Watching the movie is now a complete waste of time. I can't concentrate on the screen and fidgeting has been declared a survival mechanism. Ejecting the DVD, I put it back away and return to the kitchen. It's already in order, nothing to do. I feel strange. Restless. I flick on the kettle but don't want a cup of tea, so flick it off again, opening the fridge instead. *Nope, don't want food either.* I close the door and begin gnawing my fingernail. My brain divides. Separating me from itself and my eyes, I get a third person viewing of myself. I'm an outsider watching. The girl I see—me—is the caged animal you've seen at the circus. Pacing the kitchen, full of nervous energy… I appear twitchy and unpredictable. My muscles are tight, my movement's jerky.

Still connected, however, I know that behind the exterior, my mind races with all kinds of scenarios regarding the impending 'date'. Tripping over and falling on my face. Bumping elbows in the cinema. *What if he tries to hold my hand? What if he tries to kiss me and I smash his face with my forehead?* Awkward silences. *What if I misinterpret a vital part in the movie?* My brain does somersaults. The louder my thoughts and fears get, the more my stomach churns.

My phone vibrates against the bench top. It's him. He's given me the choice between a popular action film and a comedy. If only he knew. I'd prefer to fall into a sinkhole and never be seen again! *NO! Don't do that! Remember what Michelle said.* Of course, it is easy for her to say; she isn't the one always misreading people and looking like a fool!

Movies, I like. Watching them with strangers, in a cinema, not so much! I've already agreed though, so I type a reply and take a deep breath for the strength I will need in the coming hours. *Providing I don't chicken out and cancel under the pretence of gastro!*

The next few hours are a blur of nervous tension and I feel drained before I've even got there. I've chewed three fingernails down to the skin and I can feel an ulcer forming inside my cheek, so I must have been biting that too.

~ Only boys chew their nails! Better not let him hold your hand... he'll think he's dating a dude! ~

She-Devil laughs. She is pure hatred. I really don't want her in my head tonight! I think of a fast-paced song and hum loudly, trying to drown out her obnoxious narcissism.

In my room, I am just about finished getting ready. It isn't as cool tonight as it has been, but I am in my comfy wide-leg jeans and my usual, layered singlet tops. Tonight it is purple over white. I like the contrast of the dark over light and two singlets always feels tighter against my skin. It helps me feel safe.

Rebel is sleeping on my bed. I lean in to kiss his head before grabbing my jacket. Mum and Dad are still nowhere to be seen, so I send them both a text letting them know I am going to the movies. They will reply in a nanosecond, I'm sure. I never go out! I also leave them a written note on the bench explaining that there are freshly cooked sausage rolls in the fridge, and macadamia cookies in the container. With my little over-the-shoulder bag and jacket in hand, I head out to the car and suck in a shaky breath. *You got this!*

14

Kevin

She said yes! She said YES! I haven't stopped thinking about that beautiful girl in the navy blue dress with the painfully shy smile since the night of Luke's wedding. His darling new wife, Michelle, *finally* relented and gave me her sister's number this morning and now... *I'm seeing her tonight! Just the two of us!*

With a heavy pounding on the bathroom door, I hurry Mick along. "Mick, if you aren't outta that bathroom in three minutes, I'm coming in! I have a hot date and I need to get ready!" I give the door an extra fist pounding for good measure.

"Yeah, yeah. Hold on to ya hat, I'm almost... hey... what? With who?" I hear the door fly open, but I'm already in my room, pulling clean clothes from my wardrobe to keep busy. I'm too excited to stand still and wait outside the bathroom door.

15

Danielle

Parking is easy at this time of night. The shops have closed and the restaurants and bars won't start filling for several hours yet. Walking towards the complex, I realise we never mentioned exactly where we would meet. Thinking about what I'll do if I can't find him, I'm almost in a tizz. *I have my phone, so I guess I can message him.* The problem never even surfaces and I sigh in relief. He's standing outside the main doors, looking off in the opposite direction with his hands tucked into the back pockets of his black denim jeans. He is bouncing softly on the balls of his feet. A smile creeps along my mouth. *I think he's nervous too!* That or he is cold, and it isn't cold tonight. He looks my way and spots me. His smile is immediate as he steps away from the wall, sending flutters loose in my tummy.

"You came! I wasn't sure you were going to."

"I came." I'm just as shocked as him and struggling for something else to say.

"Shall we go buy our tickets now? Then we won't have to worry about the movie selling out while we eat."

Wow! it is like he knows me and all my anxieties. *Wouldn't that be nice… If we'd just known each other since forever. He knew everything already and still wanted to be my friend.*

A darker thought rises.

What if he does know? Michelle gave him my number. What if she told him already? Would she do that? Surely not. I am going to be sooo pissed if she has invaded all my privacy! I shake off the internal chatter and return my focus towards Kevin as we make our way to the ticket counter.

"—So, all that being said… I was hoping you might let me buy your ticket, as way of thanks?"

Uh oh… thanks for what? You have to pay more attention, Dani! You aren't good at this on your best day, with people you're comfortable around. You got to focus!

"I'll agree. But... only on the understanding that I buy the tickets next time!"
*Where the hell did that come from? You just locked
yourself in for another movie date with him. She-
Devil's right... you are a dolt!* "Ah, what I mean
is—"

I feel the sleepy witch stir, as if I summoned her. She sits up, yawning with disinterest. Tormenting me, apparently, isn't as
much fun when I agree with her.

"Definitely a deal!" Kevin cuts me off
with a huge smile on his face. I think I've
made him happy. That at least, feels like a
good thing. Since he is buying the tickets anyway, I excuse myself to the ladies' room
while he lines up.

In the cubical, I rush to fish out my
phone and message Michelle. I have to
know if she told him.

Me: Michelle, did you tell Kevin
about my ASD? How much does he know?

I press send and worry how long I can
hide in here before he thinks I'm doing the
unthinkable—pooping—in which case I
will have to stay in here all night until he
gives up and leaves and I will slink back to
my car and escape. My mind is preparing a
story with exit-plan text messages when my

phone vibrates in my hand. Not even one minute has passed and I let out the breath I've been holding. *Exit plan aborted… for now anyway.*

Michelle: No. I would never! I only gave him your number. Why!?! Are you seeing him!?!

Agh, I don't have time for that now! I have my answer though, which is good, I think. Stuffing my phone back in the bag, I leave the cubicle.

"All good? I forgot to ask if you have a favourite spot to sit. Hope you don't mind… I put us up the back, in the middle." He smiles and all I can think to do is the same.

"So, where would you like to eat? We could get burgers or there is this awesome place around the corner that does wood-fired pizzas, pasta, nachos, risotto, you name it."

"Um, I think the second place sounds good, but only if that suits you, too?"

"For sure. I love that place!"

There isn't much foot traffic around yet, but there are two other small groups eating when we arrive. Kevin leads us to a table for two in the front corner of the restaurant, away from the others. The enormity of being here, with a man, on my own, crashes down on me. Hands under the table, I flick my fingers against my pant leg subtly for a few beats. I can feel my heart thumping in my chest. Kevin hands me the menu and leans back in his seat, his hands in his lap. As I read through it, I feel his eyes on me but continue to browse. Once I've decided, I peek at him.

"Why're you staring at me?" He ignores my question and counters with one of his own.

"Have you worked out what you're going to have?"

"Oh, yes… Here." I hand him the menu. Naturally, he'd want to have a look too.

~ *You're such a loser!* ~ She-Devil chants.

"I don't need it. I already know what I'm having, Tandoori Chicken Pizza. It's the best! I don't suppose you'd let me push my luck and buy you dinner as well?"

"No, I don't suppose I would!"

"Well, it was worth a try." He says with a grin. "Why don't you go and order first then, and I'll go afterwards."

"Or… I could buy yours, since you paid for the movie tickets?"

"Hah! And miss out on doing this all again with you at our next—already promised—movie? Not a chance!" His smile is infectious. All I can do is laugh. He is cheeky and fun. Even though I feel, behind his grin, he means exactly what he is saying.

Both times I've been around Kevin now, it has come easily and that is something new for me. Throughout the meal, he peppers me with questions about work and family. I have to remind myself to keep eating. He has—by some unknown miracle—finished his enormous pizza and finally run out of questions, so sits silently watching me as I put my fork down.

"Aren't you going to eat the rest?" He asks.

"No, I'm full. I ate most of it."

"Was it good? I always say I'm going to try something different but I always end up back at pizza."

"I do that too. Yes, it was delicious! I highly recommend it." I am smiling and I have no idea why.

With his eyes glued to mine, Kevin reaches over and runs his finger around the edge of my bowl. As he pops it into his mouth to taste the creamy sauce, my gaze follows. I should look away, but my eyes are transfixed. It is one of the strangest things I've ever witnessed, but has my blood running hot in my veins.

"Mmm, you're right. That *is* good! Are you ready to go?" And just like that, he gets up and offers his hand to help me out of my seat.

I blink, trying to regain some composure. The thought of his touch unnerves me and I fuss with my jacket as I rise. He notices the gesture, I'm sure. But he doesn't say anything about my rejection.

Walking through the theatre foyer towards the usher, Kevin claims my elbow and tows me towards the candy bar.

"You can't honestly expect me to see a movie without lollies?" Suddenly he looks boyish and his eyes crinkle at the sides with a wide smile. The moment would be fantastic. If only his hot hand wasn't on my arm, singeing the wires within my brain.

"Oh? I thought most people liked popcorn at the movies." Gently stepping out from under his touch, I'm smiling too. I mentally add his child-like excitement for lollies to the list of things I like about him.

"Eeew! Not this person. I've never cared much for that stuff. No, I like lollies! But I can get you some, if you want?" He screws up his face at the mention of pop-corn, making me burst into laughter. I have to wait for it to pass before I can speak again.

"No, thank you. I actually don't like it either! I will have a packet of plain M&M's, please."

"Sure. Hold these. I'll be right back." He hands me the tickets and frees his wallet from his jeans as he leaves for the sweets counter.

Inside, the theatre is quiet. There are a few couples already sitting when we enter. The screen is black and the wall lights are on. Kevin leads the way to our seats. We sit, placing our jackets in our laps.

"Your M&M's." He hands me the packet.

"Oh, thanks."

"Now, I should confess... I'm not very good at sharing when it comes to lol-lies, but for you... I'll try." He flashes me a smile. "Nuh, just kidding... Help yourself." He chuckles.

"Never get between a man and his sweets. My dad's the same. Besides... I'm happy over here with my chocolate." My smile mirrors his.

The screen comes to life with an over-sized choc-top ice-cream and the lights fade out. Kevin, beneath the glow of the lit screen, is staring at me. A strange look on his face that I can't understand. It reminds me of a time with my mum when I was small. I'd told her I wanted to feed the wild parrots. She'd said they wouldn't come that close but bought me the seed anyway. I sat outside for three hours but eventually claimed the trust of three parrots that ended up coming each afternoon to eat out of my hands. She would give me the same funny look every afternoon as Kevin is now.

Unsure of what to think or say, I turn my attention to the screen where movie trailers have started to roll. My eyes dart back to him every other minute as he continues to stare at me. His white teeth shine brightly as he smiles—in amusement—I can only guess. Before I have the chance to ask him, the opening credits begin to roll and I am forced to focus on the movie. *I will have to ask him after.*

As the movie draws to a close, I am relieved that it has been a lighthearted film with only one awkward moment, when the characters on screen had a brief burst of passion amongst the comedy. I think it'd always be weird to watch sex on a first date though. *Surely that isn't just me? Is it?*

The wall lights return and people begin to rise out of their chairs and move off. Collecting my jacket and securing my rubbish and bag, I too, start getting up. Kevin stills my progress with a hand on my arm. His touch feels hot. I flinch. You idiot! *How many times are you going to do that and wind up in trouble before you finally STOP IT?*

Falling back into my seat, I rub my arm where the warmth lingers. My thoughts are scattered. I let my hair swoop down around my face, creating a shield as I look to my feet. I should say something but words fail me. I close my eyes, sealing out the world. Just sitting.

"Sorry, I didn't mean to hurt you." Kevin's voice is soft. He's worried. Once the immediate fright has passed, I regain some level of control over my body again.

"You didn't. You just startled me, that's all." Looking into his eyes is the last thing I want to do right now, but I know it is the 'normal' thing to do. It's expected. Pinning my hair behind my ear, I raise my head and glance at him quickly with a half smile painted on, for added measure. I can't hold the pose for long. Fidgeting with my jacket button is an acceptable distraction.

"Come on, we better go. The man wants to clean the theatre." Kevin's voice is low, barely more than a whisper.

Sure enough, the man is waiting at the base of the steps with his broom and bin to clean up before the next showing starts. This time when I stand, I put on my coat. Another layer to hide beneath. We leave our seats and join the other patrons who loiter in the corridor waiting for friends and loved ones using the restrooms. I want to leave now. Things were going so well, but his touch has left me twitchy and uncomfortable. I don't know 'the rules' and what comes next. Words don't come easy because I am nervous again and I can see this is where it will happen. He will make his polite good-byes and won't call again because I'm 'strange'. I'll just be the 'weird chick' he took out once. The thought saddens me. *She-Devil was right again; I'll just end up living with a bunch of cats.*

One half of my brain yells at me to prolong the emptiness that awaits me, but the other half tells me to run back. Enjoy the quiet and predictable way of my life. Between the two fighting, I'm exhausted.

The night air is chilly now and I am glad I put my coat on. Kevin matches my steps and we walk in silence. *Which one is his car?* It looks as though he is walking me to mine. Either that or his is the blue SUV beside mine and I doubt that "This is mine." I point. Pulling the keys from my handbag, I hit the keyless entry. The indicators flash twice in the darkness. Silence.

"Hey, um… I had a really nice time tonight." Kevin's face looks pained. *Here it comes…* The promise of a call that won't eventuate.

"Yeah, me too. I guess I'll see you around?" I give him the easy out. He can just go now, without promises.

"So… how long do I have to wait before you are going to take me out to our next movie?" He is grinning and our eyes meet for a second. He drops his gaze before I do. *Wow, that's a first!* Confused, I try to search his face for clues while he isn't looking. *Is he teasing?* He continues to inspect his shoes. *I swear… all the dictionaries on body language, throughout all the world, could* not *help me decipher 'the rules of dating!'* I shove my hands into my coat pockets in an effort to dispel my frustration.

Before I can work out what to say, he steps closer, into my—unusually large—personal space zone. I try to back away, except I'm up against the car. There's nowhere to go. My muscles tense. He looks into my face, trying to find something that I'm sure isn't there. The countless social lessons and therapy sessions don't mean anything when someone is in my space. I can't think straight and my body goes into overdrive. The recent altercation with Sean only fueling that further. My breath quickens. I can hear it rushing in and out of my lungs.

"You look worried," His voice is so soft, I wonder if it isn't just my imagination talking. A nervous chuckle escapes me. A foreign noise in place of words that are impossible. I take a deep breath to help myself recover.

"Anxiety's one of my most dominant features," I reply, humourlessly.

"Well, I don't want to startle you again… so get ready. I'd really like to hold your hands. May I?" He asks. My voice is locked tight. I feel the warmth of his hands apply gentle pressure to lift mine up, out of their fabric hideaway. *Please, don't let me be in trouble again. Please, let him not be like the others. I should be able to stop this.* My belly does somersaults.

He claims them the minute they're free. His are wide in contrast to my own. They feel strong. They have the potential to be forceful, however; he keeps his touch light. *How does that feel so... nice?* He runs his thumbs across my knuckles a few times with deliberate slowness. Allowing me to get used to him. He watches my face—*for signs of change? I'm not sure*—though I doubt he sees anything other than 'blank'.

My limited ability to decipher his expressions is now completely overridden by the feel of his touch. My head droops forward and my eyes slide closed, absorbing the sensation. He lifts them to his lips and kisses their backs gently, then guides and holds each one to his shoulders until he knows I won't pull away. With no more than a feather touch, he rests his hands on my waist and inches closer. There are only a few small centimetres of cool air between us.

"I'd like to kiss you. May I?" He whispers at my ear, stirring the hair and sending goosebumps down my arm. *He does? Do I?*

His hands feel so good… maybe his lips do too? Somewhere between excited and terrified, my heart thunders in my chest.

My breath rushes out. I hadn't realised I'd stopped breathing. Lifting my head takes effort. Everything feels heavy. I struggle to understand how it is that I feel so comfortable with him and how quickly that has happened. His kiss, like everything else so far, is gentle. He moves slowly, letting me adjust to each new feel, smell, and taste. Soft, warm lips caress my own, sending a ripple of heat straight through my veins. It only takes two whisper-like passes before I am wanting some pressure. I lean into him on the third and his lips are there to meet mine with equal urgency. The smell of his soap and aftershave are strong but not unpleasant in our close proximity.

My hands itch to explore him. The firmness of his body, taut muscles. My hands find his chest and rest there, absorbing his warmth. His heartbeat races, matching my own. Tentatively, I allow my tongue to probe at his sealed lips. His heart pounds even faster against my palms, and a small moan escapes his lips. His excitement is instantaneous, and we explore the warm, slick confines of each other's mouths. Leading then retreating. Kevin's body crashes into me with a groan of desire, leaving me pinned to my car.

The feeling of it sends a quick stab of pain to my hip. The memory of Sean flashes again behind my closed eyelids. This time, however, it goes as quickly as it arrives. My skin is alive. A tingly sensation runs from my scalp to my toes. I've kissed a few guys, not lots, but enough to know that I have never experienced this reaction before. I wiggle to free my arms from between us. Kevin is strong and resistant to let our kiss end. He moves only enough to grant my arms their freedom.

The sound of nearing footsteps becomes clear to us both, and Kevin's lips reluctantly break away. His body, however, continues to hold me protectively. He looks towards the direction of its source while I hide in the valley between his neck and shoulder, trying desperately to catch my breath.

Wow! That was freaking amazing! Why has it never felt like this before? Two patrons pass by and we are soon alone again. The intensity of the moment though, is gone. Good sense and reality creep back in, crowding my thoughts. Returning his attention to me, our cheeks touch. The heat radiating between us is like standing too close to a fire on a cold night; It's so nice but too intense all at once. He kisses my cheek, a soft touch that contains the power to close my eyes again. *How did we go from holding hands to me being pressed against the car... kissing?* Before he has time to cloud my better judgment, I need to go.

"I need to get home. My parents will be wondering where I am. Thank you. I've had a lovely night."

Kevin sighs and reluctantly pulls back. I'm swamped by the cold night air as it rushes in to steal the warmth left from our combined bodies.

"I wish I'd kissed you at the start instead of just now. I don't want tonight to be over yet. Can we do something tomorrow?"

"Um, Michelle and Luke fly home tomorrow, so I'm not sure if my mum has anything planned." I reply mechanically.

"Can I call you then? Or message you? You could let me know and I can be your backup for something to do." His eagerness makes me smile and sends flutters through my core.

"How about I let you know in the morning once I know what's happening?" Kevin's face lights up like a kid on

Christmas morning. It makes me chuckle. I have clearly pleased him and knowing that makes me happy.

"Okay. Now, I do genuinely need to go. I'll talk to you tomorrow." We have been standing still for so long that my car has re-locked, I find and press the remote again. Kevin holds the door for me like a gentle-man. He gives my hand one last squeeze be-fore closing the door and watching as I back away and head home.

The lights are still on when I pull in. I can hear the television as I reach the front door. It's unlocked.

"Hi, Mum. Hi, Dad." I can't tell what they're watching. It appears to be on a com-mercial. Dad is filling the sugar jar and I can hear the kettle boiling.

"Hi! How was your evening?" Mum puts her crossword down on the coffee ta-ble between the recliner chairs and looks up.

"It was good. Probably not a movie I'd see again, but it was funny enough. You and Dad should go sometime. It might be one for you guys."

"Yeah, maybe we will. Did you go by yourself or with somebody?" There it is. *Why does she have to talk 'around' what she wants to know?* I can't often tell with other people, but with my mum, I have learned over the years that she gets a specific pitch when she is hunting for a specific answer.

Through my powers of analysis, I can understand that in this case, I don't think she wants to know if I went with 'someone,' she wants to know *who* I went with. Sometimes I tell her what I think she wants to know, but other times—like tonight—it annoys me and I deliberately use my weaknesses to hide behind. On the rare occasion that this happens, it feels *so* great to be in control of my ASD rather than 'it' being in charge of the control panel.

"No, I drove myself. But there were several of us at the movie." *Not a lie!* She looks at me perplexed for a minute, trying to understand my response, but I don't wait to see if she figures it out. I head through to the kitchen where Dad offers me a cup of tea.

"No thanks, Dad. Think I'm just going to have my milk and head off to bed." I reach into the cupboard to retrieve my tea cup. I pour my milk and drink it there in the kitchen, like every other night. Then, just the same as every other night, I wash it, hand dry it with a clean towel and set it back in the cupboard, in the same place. I have done it for so many years now that my parents don't even look twice anymore. Once in the sanctuary of my room, I turn on an instrumental CD softly and revisit my night. A screen by screen breakdown, for analysing.

Rebel is curled up where I left him. The glow of lamplight filling the room stirs him and he looks up through squinted eyes. Yawning and stretching out, he takes up half the length of my bed. He sits up, looking for a scratch and purrs loudly when I oblige.

In the quiet, my mind is busy with memories. *Should I've let him kiss me? He felt so nice against me. Safe. Why did it feel awful and wrong when Sean leaned against me, but perfect when Kevin did? What's the difference?* My thoughts jump around like a pinball.

Should I have held his hand when the sex bit came on in the movie? Maybe. His lips were so soft when he kissed me. I shouldn't have let my tongue roam. Maybe he was intentionally waiting... for me to make the move, instead of pushing? He does seem to be very understanding. Almost too understanding. What if he only wants sex, like the others? What if he thinks I only want sex? He wouldn't think that. Would he?

I roll onto my stomach and groan into my pillow with exasperation. *This is so pointless! There is no way to know any of these answers unless I ask him outright and since I'm definitely not about to do that... please mind, be still! I need sleep! A distraction. That will help!* I get up in search of my phone. I wonder what time Michelle's flight arrives tomorrow. I know she sent me an email—that I never got around to opening—It was titled 'Our flight details.' Opening the phone, there are three new messages. They are all from Kevin.

Kevin: Thanks for a great time tonight. It was fun. I still can't believe we only live ten minutes from each other… That makes hanging out together tonnes easier to organise.

Sent 8:27pm

Kevin: Confession time. I really hope I haven't scared you off. I promise I don't make a habit of pinning girls to their cars in carparks. :) I promise to be on my best behaviour if we catch up tomorrow.

Sent 8:55pm

Kevin: Did you make it home ok? Let me know hey?

Sent 9:09pm

The time on my phone now reads 9:13pm. I quickly type a reply. I know how much I'd be worrying if I was the one waiting.

Me: Hi, sorry… just talking to Mum and Dad. I'm home. Just about to go to bed. Good night.

Kevin: Good night. xo

16

Danielle

With the light of morning, I'd hoped to have magically gained some clear perspective on what'd come over me in the past twenty-four hours. If someone told me yesterday morning that I would go and see a movie with *anyone*, I would have laughed at them. But that is exactly what I'd done, and with Kevin, no less. Of all the strangeness in my life! My head spins remembering I may even see him *again* today. Maybe.

At breakfast, Mum announces that she is going to get Michelle and Luke from the airport and they'll bring pizzas home with them for lunch. They want to hand out souvenirs, so Mum suggested the get-to-gether before she drives them back to their place.

After everything is away and the kitchen is clean, I text Kevin as promised.

Me: Hi. I should be free after 2pm this afternoon if you still want to do something? Any ideas?

It isn't long before I have a reply.

Kevin: Sounds awesome! How do you feel about dogs? I was planning to take my dog for a walk down by the creek near my house but we can do something else if you'd prefer? I can organise her walk around any plans.

Me: I didn't realise you have a dog. What sort? What's her name? A walk sounds perfect. Where will I meet you?

Kevin: There's lots you don't know about me. ;) Lol. Patch is a Staffy. She's my best friend. There's a carpark by the playground, straight off the big round-a-bout. You know the one I mean?

Me: I think so. Is that the one near the service station?

Kevin: Yep, that's the one. Meet you there around 2:30?

Me: I'll be there. I look forward to meeting your furry friend. See you then. :)

The house is quiet.

Mum's car is gone and Dad is out in the shed, so I use my time wisely. I pack an old knapsack with things I might need. A towel, in case I get wet—since Kevin mentioned the creek—suncream, band-aids, a bottle of water, a plastic container for Patch to drink from. A hat and two muesli bars. Next, I pull out what I'll wear and place it on my dressing table—Rebel will have it covered in fur if I leave it on my bed!

Deciding 'less' attention is best, I take the bag and put it in the boot of my hatchback, just in case the others are still here when I need to leave, I can walk out with only my keys and phone—keeping suspicions and *questions* to a minimum.

From my seat in the lounge room, I see Mum's car pull up. Luke emerges with the pizzas, reminding me about lunch, and I go to set out plates and glasses for us all. Dad ushers them inside, and we all take our seats.

"So you had a good time then, honey?" Dad asks Michelle.

"Oh, Dad… it was so incredible! I feel like I need another holiday to recover, though. We crammed so much in."

"That's great. And you liked it too, Luke?"

"Yeah. It's a gorgeous place. We barely scratched the surface, though. There was lots more we wanted to see." Luke lets Michelle take over the conversation in preference of downing his lunch. *Maybe he is keen to go home?*

"I want to get all the photos printed tomorrow, but I have so much washing to catch up on first. When I do, I'll have to bring them over to show you all!" Michelle is hardly eating, she is talking so much.

"When do you go back to work, hon?" Mum asks her.

"Agh. Back to work Wednesday, I'm dreading it!" I don't understand. Michelle loves her job.

"How about you, Luke, when do you go back?" Dad asks. I make a mental note to thank him later for keeping the conversation flowing before Michelle ramps up her dramatising.

"I'm back tomorrow. It's been awesome and I don't think I'll like my alarm in the morning, but I'm looking forward to catching up with the guys. I'm sure they'll want to hear about our trip." Sitting across from them, I can't help but think how different Luke is to Michelle. Luke seems so quiet, sensible and down-to-earth, whereas

Michelle's always been so dramatic. *What would a guy like Luke see in her? Sure, she's pretty… Is that really all it comes down to in a match? There has to be more to it than that? She does seem different lately, though. Genuinely caring, if I am being totally honest!*

"Hello… Danielle!" Michelle clicks her fingers in front of my nose.

"Sorry, what?" I reply, snapping back to reality.

"Can you please pass me the Orange?" Despite my best efforts, I still have no idea what she is talking about. My face must confirm this because she points to the soft drink bottle beside me. "The Orange, please. Geez', you're miles away. You a bit scattered still? Have you thought about going back to your Psych for a chat?" She stares at me.

"I'm fine." I grind out. *Does she have to bring this up in front of Luke? When will my family learn that I'm quite capable of deciding by myself if I need to go running back to the professionals? I'm a big girl! Why do they keep pushing me? Honestly, they all seem far more affected by the whole Sean saga than I am anyway… Maybe they all need to go see someone! I wish they'd all just leave me alone.* My leg begins to bounce, annoyed, under the table. I release the death grip I have on my drinking glass.

"Dani went to the movies last night… didn't you, sweetie?" Mum says quickly. Changing the subject, I guess. Course, I'd prefer if she moved it off me completely and onto someone else at the table!

"Oh re-a-lly?" Michelle's eyes light up. *Just terrific!* I swear… Michelle can sniff out gossip like the proverbial polar bear that can smell a seal through three feet of solid ice. And once she smells it, she is just as determined to get it within her claws.

"Who'd you go with?"

"I drove myself." I say, answering the same way I did to mum last night. Hoping this closes the topic. Michelle, to my annoyance, has always been more intuitive than Mum. I'm not sure if it's because she was the one always trying to get me to play with her as a child. Or because she was the one 'looking out for me,' in our junior years at school. Of course, after about fourth grade, I wasn't 'cool enough' to be allowed near her. Regardless, she's always known how to get the most out of me and this is the precise moment I remember the text message I sent her last night.

Sitting across the table from her, she stares at me intently. My leg picks up its pace and I give up eating in preference of destroying the skin around my thumb nail.

"You went with Kevin, didn't you? That's what the message was about?" I feel the heat in my cheeks burn. Hearing his name brings back the memory of last night's kiss, in all its sublimity. My face is so warm. I must be the colour of my pizza sauce.

"Well? How'd it go?"

Looking around the table, all eyes are on me. Mum is watching me with equal enthusiasm to Michelle. Dad is a bit confused, I think. I try to remember if we've spoken about the wedding that much. I doubt he even knows who Kevin is. Luke is the only one who looks genuinely annoyed. *Oh, no… he doesn't want his cousin hanging out with someone like me.* Guess I shouldn't be so surprised. Childhood memories flash through my mind. I'd start talking to kids in the playground about studies that had been performed and recorded on the number of bacteria and germs found around public playgrounds for children. Parents would come and move their children away to play with the 'other kids.' I just found it fascinating and thought the other children should be aware. My mum would say...

"You just need to talk a little less. Maybe you could make a friend by just building a sandcastle with them?" She'd not appreciated it when I'd informed her that I was between fifteen and twenty percent more likely to pick up harmful bacteria or parasitic worms from playing in a sandpit than visiting a public restroom. Her face had scrunched up, her lips stuck out like they were tied together with a rubber band. I don't remember going back to the playground after that, actually. She must have decided she didn't like those odds.

Snapping back to reality, I see everyone is staring at me. I don't want to talk about my night. Least of all, with Michelle. One answer is *never* enough for her, and I know she will hound me for more details. I grit my teeth.

"Yes, I went with Kevin. No, we're not talking about this now! Next subject."

"Oh, come on! You got to tell us more than that! Was it a date? What'd you see? Was it just the two of you?" Michelle leans forward during her interrogation. I can't tell if she is excited or angry, but if she leans any further, she will get pizza on her shirt. *Her shirt, sauce on her shirt, she's going to get SAUCE ON HER SHIRT!*

"Your shirt's about to fall into your pizza!" I point my index finger towards her plate in panic and she straightens. *Finally.*

"Don't change the subject. Spill!"

"I already said 'next subject' Michelle." Reaching for spare napkins, I dump them in front of her. I can't see what she's spilt this time, so I just hope a handful is enough. My dad chuckles from behind his glass and my attention shifts to him. His smile vanishes and I realise I've misunderstood something. Yet again.

An inner frustration grows and I'm overtaken by the red film, working its way across my peripheral vision. My dad apologises, but his voice is lost through the cloud descending on me. Everything surrounding me becomes far away. Voices mute. From within, I hear my pounding heart. It is fast and loud, filling my ears like a steam train coming close. Too close! I try to push the noise aside. It's quickly replaced with inner chatter, memories and the cruel laughter of She-Devil. I once again have confirmed I don't fit! For all my efforts, lessons and fails. I will NEVER FIT!

Outwardly, not much has changed. Less than a minute has passed, but I am sitting stoic. Not moving, not blinking. My family know me well enough to understand the signs and are familiar with the outcome. From somewhere deep in my subconscious, I can hear my brain wrestling with itself, trying to gain control. It reminds me that *Luke is an outsider. Dad didn't mean offence. He wouldn't do anything to hurt my feelings on purpose.* The need to explode and release the anger still trapped inside is—for now at least—overshadowed by my need to keep control in front of Luke.

Receiving my diagnosis when I did—in my final year of school, after a complete and total burnout—has, in part, given me the ability to semi-control my melt-downs. It's exhausting and has terrible repercussions on my mental health, but the need to 'blend in' makes me sub-consciously sabotage any chance of a healthy headspace. It is both a blessing and a curse. My calm may have returned outwardly—for the moment—but this is only a temporary solution. If I do not find a healthy way to dispel my anger… Eventually, it will escape. It will find a weak spot and erupt whether I try to stop it or not.

The haze that penetrates my mind has a distinct feel to it. It is red. Like I have a filter over the camera lens through which I see. Closing my eyes, I visualise my field of flowers. Somewhere in the depths of my brain, I know I'm sitting at a table full of people with my eyes closed. *It's still better than the raging psychopath I've been known to unleash!*

Where was I? Oh, yeah… A soft breeze creeps across the field, bending flowers like a bright yellow wave. Slaves to the wind's control, they're forced to yield under its command. My anger simmers under the surface, but I have clawed back enough physical control to stand, take my plate over to the sink and flee to my bedroom.

Sealing myself inside my room, I feel calmer. Safe. Here, though, the space is quiet and the noise in my head is loud.

Too worked up to read and only interested in the kind of offensive music that Mum will make me turn off, I pace. Rebel isn't here, he must have gone outside. *Agh, I need to keep it together!* I glance at my watch, but it isn't time to get ready yet. Pacing only adds to my agitation. I spy my sketch pad poking out from under my bed. *Maybe that will lift my funk.* I grab the book, my pencils, and graphite. Opening to a clean page, I draw. One line this way. The next one, that way. All that comes initially is angry lines, but it isn't long before my true calm returns and I'm able to draw constructively. What emerges on the page in front of me is no surprise. Another butterfly. Today's is a Monarch with her impressively large wings of orange and black, her delicate features, just as important.

I learned long ago that drawing helps me quieten the internal chatter, shift focus and relax in times of stress. Although I have on occasion drawn other images, butterflies are usually within the artwork somewhere. Getting so engrossed in the detail, often I don't even realise what I am drawing until I have finished, finally stopping to look at the whole picture. Staring at it now, I ponder… for the fifty millionth time.

The simple caterpillar, so focused on its sole task, eating. For a cause, it probably doesn't even understand. Then, just like that, it cocoons itself in a safe place to transform. When it is ready, it emerges… a spectacular new creature of colour, symmetry and grace. Instinctually taking to the skies and joining its kind, to fulfil its goal of life. The cruel irony that a caterpillar is born with the ability to morph into a whole new beautiful version of itself. *Yet here I sit… waiting for a transformation that won't come to release me from myself.*

A tap at my door brings me back to the here and now, but it doesn't open.

"Come in?" A knock is only ever a precursor to my mum opening the door. The fact it hasn't now is unusual. Slipping into view, Luke's face is the last one I expect to see.

"Oh… Hi." *Why's he here? What's he want?*

"Sorry to interrupt. We're just leaving and I wanted to see you quickly before we do. I just want you to know… I didn't agree or like the way Michelle harassed you at lunch. Don't get me wrong… I love my wife, but I wish sometimes she wasn't quite so nosey. I just wanted you to know that." Luke is kind. *He must be what's rubbing off on Michelle.* What would have drawn him to her initially, I can't fathom.

~ *She's gorgeous and totally in her element playing the social games! What man wouldn't turn and follow her? She knows how to fit in! She knows how to laugh.* ~

She-Devil, geez, you always know just when to rear your ugly head, don't you?

The memory of Luke's face at lunch flashes through my mind and the words escape before I can measure them. "But you were angry when you heard I'd seen your cousin. I saw your face." It is a statement, not a question.

"Huh?" His eyebrows shoot skyward. I can't tell if he is surprised or amused. "It's absolutely none of mine—or anyone else's—business who you or Kevin hang out with. You're both old enough to sort it out yourselves." His tone softens and he continues. "I wasn't mad at you. I saw how Michelle was distressing you and even then, she didn't stop. She knows how I feel about her doing that to people." From out on the driveway, a car horn toots. "Well, I've gotta go. I just wanted you to know, like I said. Hope I didn't disturb you." Luke closes the door behind him. *Today's fast becoming even weirder than yesterday!*

There is no time to brood. The day has run away on me. Dumping my pencils and sketch pad on the bed, I jump up and quickly throw my clothes on. Thank goodness I got them ready this morning!

My drawing materials are still strewn all over my bed when I snatch up my sneakers from the floor and race out, pulling the door as I go. Peeking through the front windows to make sure the others are gone, I pull my car keys from the hook and exit.

"Where you off to?" The house was so quiet, I thought they'd all gone together. Dad's swinging gently on the verandah swing chair.

"Dad! You scared the daylights outta me! I'm going for a walk." His gaze drops to the keys in my hand, not missing a thing.

"I'm meeting Kevin down by the creek to walk his dog." My watch ticks away the seconds. If I am to get there on time, I can't afford twenty questions. Fortunately for me, Dad is the complete opposite of Mum and Michelle. He is direct and easier to talk to. Gossip doesn't interest him, so unless he feels concerned or is genuinely stimulated by the topic of conversation, he won't bring anything up.

"Nice day for it. You sure you're up to it? Just be careful, hey? Keep your phone on you."

"Will do. I shouldn't be gone too long." Leaving him waving from the swing, I select first gear and get going.

Kevin is waiting when I pull in. Patch sits by his side, attached to a hot pink lead and collar. It makes me chuckle. She is a beautiful-looking dog. A steely blue colour with white running up her chest, and four white feet, giving her the appearance of wearing socks. Her face and head are mostly white, but her left eye is hidden in a circle of the same blue that covers the large percentage of her hide. I'm drawn to her almost faster than I am to her owner… almost! Before I've got my car turned off, Patch stands beside her owner, tail wagging out of control. Her entire body moves with the action and she is staring straight at me the whole time.

In my seat with my feet angled out the door, I pull on my anklet socks and sneakers. I am hunched over when two black canvas shoes with eyelets but no laces come into my realm of vision.

"Hi there." Kevin is leaning over the top of my doorframe. This morning's challenges have left me a little standoffish and shy. I fiddle with the tongue of my shoe. It doesn't feel right and digs into my sock.

"Hi." I return, my eyes on my laces.

Patch hears my unfamiliar voice and hurries around to investigate. Her whole rump is wagging in excitement. My face is low. Perfect height, for a warm, wet tongue to lick my hairline, apparently. Kevin pulls

153

back on her lead until she is out of tongue's reach.

"No, Patch! Sorry... she gets excited."

"It's fine. She's lovely." With the back of my hand, I wipe away the trail of slobber. Grabbing my knapsack from the boot, I close the hatch and lock it.

"So, which way?" I'm awkward with nothing else to focus my attention on. I can feel it.

"We normally wander that way. After the bridge, it opens up and usually has less people, so I can let her off the lead." Kevin points to our right. Walking in that direction, we have a good metre between us. Patch leads the way.

"Your sister and Luke get back okay?" He asks. Images of Michelle badgering me at lunch come back.

"Yeah. What did you do with your morning?" *Is that an okay question to ask him? Maybe that's too personal.*

"Not much. Did some washing, helped my mum around their house. It's a bit crazy there lately." Kevin chuckles. I think he looks nervous too, perhaps.

"Why?"

Kevin bends to unhook Patch's lead now that we are past the bridge. He was right; the previously narrow path has opened out into a beautiful wide grassy strip that parallels the creek. The creek itself is barely a trickle on our left. Ankle deep water flows over and around pebbles, the gravelly bottom clearly visible.

17

Danielle

Patch is a textbook example of responsible dog ownership. She scampers off with her nose to the ground, absorbing all the fresh smells. Kevin watches her intently. He scans often, looking for any sign of danger or trouble for his canine companion. At regular intervals, Patch turns back in search of him. Once she sees he is still there, she resumes her play. I feel privileged to witness this glimpse of rare beauty. The bond between this man and his dog is one of mutual respect and genuine love for each other. Watching them warms my heart.

Further along, the creek widens. The bottom, still clearly visible, is deceiving and I can't tell if it's inches deep or metres.

"Patch... ready?" Kevin hasn't finished her name before she spins toward him and bounds excitedly on the spot. Kevin pulls a tennis ball from his pocket and she leaps towards us at lightning speed. With a flick, the ball goes sailing through the air, followed by an enormous splash as Patch collides with the water. Kevin bursts into laughter beside me as water flies everywhere.

"Be warned... she'll be back any sec and she'll shake water everywhere. So if you don't want to get wet, you need to look out." His smile is big, his joy infectious. Before I can even decide, Patch returns just like Kevin said, shaking and showering us both in icy cold water that makes me gasp as it hits my skin. The ball plops in front of him and he scoops it up. Again, it sails through the air with Patch in pursuit.

"That water is freezing!" I gasp, backing up when as I see her returning. Kevin's still smiling when he sends the ball away for the third time.

"Yeah, it's pretty cold all year round. Warms up a little in full summer but still too cold for most people. I've been bringing her here since she was a pup. It's our special spot. Isn't it Patchy?" She's back, panting hard. Kevin pays no attention to her freezing, wet mass as he sits down, cross-legged, letting her bound into his lap, where he pets her. Patch—still too excited to be contained—launches out of his arms, nudging the ball towards him again. Their game of fetch continues.

I move away a short distance, not entirely sure if I'm ready for her to jump on me covered in water. *Stop staring at him!* He is even more attractive in this new light. "How old is she?"

"She'll be four next December" Kevin's face falls and he seems far away suddenly. I don't understand the cause, or if I should press the subject. *Maybe I should skip to another topic? No, I want to know why his mood's changed. If he doesn't want to talk about it, he'll say so... won't he?*

"I feel like maybe I shouldn't have asked that? I usually say the wrong thing, Kevin. So if I have, you need to tell me, okay?" I peek at him quickly, trying to gauge his reaction. *Argh, it's no use. I don't know him well enough yet.*

He surprises me and answers.

"Sorry. I got her at a rough time in my life. Thinking about her age just reminded me and I got lost for a sec." He gives me a half smile, which I take as a positive sign.

"What happened?"

~ You're such an idiot! He doesn't want to talk about it! ESPECIALLY with you, who he barely knows! ~

Shut up!

"Um, sorry… That's none of my business!"

"No, it's okay. My parents bought her for me a few months after my seventeenth birthday. Some mates took me out on the night of my birthday, but we never made it to the party they'd organised for me. It was a rainy night. My friend Alex was mucking around in the wet. The car left the road and the next thing I remember is waking up in the hospital." Kevin unfolds his legs and lifts his knees, locking his arms around them.

Is he about to cry? He looks like he might. I sit still, trying to work out what to do if he does.

More questions come to mind, but now I feel unequipped for his emotion. I think about going to him to offer some kind of comfort, but I hesitate and he speaks again.

"I wasn't too badly hurt. Some glass damaged my eye. But Alex, he… he died on the way to hospital. I never saw him and I was still in the hospital for his funeral." Kevin trails off.

"That's horrible." Unsure what else to offer, I parrot what countless movies and television shows have taught me to say. "I'm sorry for your loss."

"Things got a bit better after Patch came along. Mum insisted I talk to someone, you know... a professional. She helped me make peace with myself." Patch nudges him, tipping him sideways, and Kevin pulls himself from his reverie. "Patch and I were a perfect fit. I had to wear a protective patch over my eye for six months after the accident. The breeder said she would struggle to sell Patch because of her markings, but Mum and Dad knew she was exactly right for me. And she is!" Patch's collar and name tag jingles as Kevin gives her an all-over rub.

In the quiet earthy bubble, we lose track of time. Discovering each other's likes and dislikes. We swap life stories while lounging around on the grass with Patch stretched out in a circle of sunshine.

I learn that Kevin lives with one of his many cousins and he hates peas. Kevin learns that I have a Ragdoll cat named Rebel. What a Ragdoll looks like—when I show him a photo on my phone—and that there are *lots* of foods I don't like! He thinks I'm joking until I rattle off several foods and he starts to believe me.

Kevin is an only child, I discover. He has trouble understanding when I tell him that Michelle and I have never been particularly close. In fact, I've only been to their house a handful of times! I want to explain to him that I am not the girl he thinks I am. The 'almost normal' girl he met, the one in the long dress with makeup and hair done neatly for her sister's wedding. The one who went to the movies and laughed over dinner. That's not the real me. The me who loves reading more than making friends. The me who needs music constantly to shut my brain up. And definitely the me that wants to scream nerdy butterfly facts from the highest mountain because I think they're so freaking amazing!

In the end, though, I can't bring myself to crush the illusion. Once it's done, there will be no going back, so I sit quietly, listening. Smiling.

Kevin is part of a very close family, even his cousins are more like friends. He works as a plumber for his dad's plumbing business and his mum takes care of the 'family home', as Kevin calls it.

The trill of my mobile breaks through our banter, and I rise to retrieve it.

"Hi, Dad. Yeah, I'm fine. Oh, wow. Sorry, I lost track of time." Kevin rises and dusts his rump for grass while I continue. "Yeah, no worries. I'll be home soon." I hang up and slip the phone in my rear pocket.

"Everything okay?"

"Yeah. They just thought I'd be home by now. Just checking I'm alright."

"Sorry, that's my fault. I completely lost track of time."

"It's fine. They're just not used to me being out."

"Why?" Kevin is frowning.

"Cause I don't go out much, I guess," I say matter-of-factly.

"Your dad must have to fight them all off with a stick!" Kevin is chuckling, but he has lost me. I have zero idea what he's talking about!

"What do you mean?" I mumble. His laughter unsettles me. Like he can read my mind, he stops abruptly and frowns.

"Huh? Sorry. I just figured your dad has to be fighting off a long line of guys chasing after you."

"I can assure you, there's never been a long line of any kind for me!" Retrieving the knapsack, I fidget with the zipper to occupy my hands before slinging it over my shoulder. "I don't make friends easily." My voice is so low, I'm not sure if I've actually said the words or just thought them.

"I don't believe that. You're so interesting and the more I find out, the more I want to know."

"Me too. I mean... that's how I feel about you." My face feels hot again.

"Come on, we better head back." Kevin takes my hand for the first time all afternoon and we stroll, Patch back on her lead in Kevin's other hand.

At the cars, I place my bag on the passenger seat. Kevin stands beside me, hesitant, I think.

"So... my hours with Dad can get pretty crazy. Can I see you next Saturday?" He has his—fast becoming familiar— cheeky smile in place.

"I'm not sure. I go to the library on Saturdays. And there was talk of a possible interview with my mum's friend's son." *Did that even make sense?* His smile fades quickly.

"Oh. I guess I'll text you then? Through the week, maybe?" Kevin tacks on the end.

"I'd like that. But right now... I have to go." To reaffirm the fact, my phone rings. 'Dad' flashes across the screen. I contemplate not answering it. I *could* be driving. But in the end, I can't do that. Kevin watches on.

"Hi, Dad. I'm just getting in the car now. Oh. Yeah, I can do that. No, no... It's no problem. Okay. Yep. See you soon." I hang up.

"He needs me to pick up tomatoes on my way home... I better go." I lean in gently and kiss his cheek before sealing myself in the car and reversing out, waving as I pass him.

Once at home, I head straight to the kitchen with the tomatoes. Dad is cooking his famous steak in tomato and onion gravy while Mum puts together a salad and her home-made coleslaw. They have music playing and both seem to be in a cheery mood.

"Do you need a hand with anything?"

"Nope, all sorted. Did you want to go have a shower? Tea's still a little while off."

"Thanks, Mum, that sounds great." I'm amazed she hasn't crash-tackled me for information the second I walked in, but I'm eager to escape to the shower—I smell after having a soaked Patch, jumping on me. Under the hot water, I focus all my attention on the feeling of it hitting my skin and running tracks down my body to the drain below. It has an almost hypnotic effect that calms and stills my mind's chatter. A result I am very happy to achieve after the completely unexpected twists that have shaped my whole weekend.

Having stood under the stream for long enough, I wash quickly and turn off the taps. Steam lingers in the small room and clings to the mirror. It is thick, and I watch it swirl and stir as my drying movements cut through the air currents. I am simply 'in the moment,' something that rarely happens. I'm always so caught in the past, analysing situations… or the future, worrying about what's going to happen. Here, in this moment, though, I am focused only on drying my limbs and watching the tiny moisture particles dance.

Dinner is almost ready when I exit the bathroom. It smells delicious! I end up leaning against the breakfast bar. Rebel is quick to find and preen himself against my leg. He leaps up onto the barstool beside me.

"UH! Hop down! You know he's not allowed up here near the bench, Dani." He leaps off the stool. Rebel is pretty well behaved, but like all cats, he'll push the boundaries if he thinks he can get away with it.

"He knows, Mum. He just hasn't seen me all day. Have you, buddy?" I bend to stroke his long, silky coat at my feet. He flops down onto his side, purring loudly. He's an affectionate little man.

"Well, dinner's ready, so wash your hands and come get your salad," Mum orders. Giving Rebel a final scratch under the chin, I rise and do as I'm told.

Dinner ends up being a disjointed affair. With a call from his colleague and something about a report due tomorrow; Dad leaves to eat in the study. Mum and I continue eating at the table, but Dad's voice travels through the house from the other room.

"Did you have a nice afternoon with Kevin?" Mum asks. *Here we go...*

"Yeah, it was nice. He has a Staffy. We took her for a walk and swim."

"You… went swimming?" Mum's eyes look like they are about to pop from their sockets. I laugh.

"Absolutely not! Patch did. The water was freezing!"

"Oh… I was going to say. She isn't vicious, I hope?"

"Not at all. She's gorgeous! In fact, she didn't even chase after a butterfly that I saw there! She's really well trained."

"Oh, that's good then. You were gone for a long time."

"Yeah, I guess. We lost track of time. It was just so beautiful by the creek."

"Did you do anything else?"

"No. Should I have?" *What else would I've done?*

"Ah… no. I just want to make sure you're being careful. Don't put yourself into a vulnerable situation. Especially when you're still getting over your last traumatic experience. It's only been a month. You can never be too safe, you know? Promise me you're being careful after everything that's happened."

"You mean sex, right? Is that what you think we were doing? We were in a public park, Mum! You don't need to worry. Kevin is one of the nicest guys I think I've ever met. We're just hanging out. He's not the type who goes around having sex with girls in bushes." My face flames with both anger and humiliation.

Mum's mouth drops open and I watch a piece of coleslaw fall out. Seriously disgusting!

"Mum... chew with your mouth closed, you just dropped coleslaw."

"I'm sorry. I didn't mean it like that. It's. just... well, you've been through a lot this year and I wanted to make sure you understand some of the danger signs so you don't get yourself into trouble again." *If only you knew. Sean isn't even the one you should be mad at. You have no idea.* "Everyone needs to be careful of their surroundings, but girls especially and because of your autism... social struggles—whatever you want to call it—you're even more susceptible to fall victim. You need to be extra cautious of what's going on around you and who you're spending time with. Do you understand what I'm saying? You can't talk about sex and rape so flippantly. It's serious."

"Agh! Mum, Sean didn't *even* rape me! I think you're more upset about the whole thing than I am. Nothing happened! And Kevin isn't like Sean. Kevin is nice and... and he seems to really get me. He's friendly, Mum." I smile.

"What do you mean by 'friendly'?" Mum looks at me strangely.

"Huh? I mean, he isn't afraid to talk to me. And he tells me stories about when he was younger, even sad stories. And he doesn't talk in circles. I can understand him. He makes me feel kinda calm, Mum. It feels... nice." Mum's face is getting weirder the more I say, so I stop. I think maybe she is a mix of happy and suspicious, but I could be completely off-track.

18

———

Danielle

Side by side, we all sit at the breakfast bar discussing plans for the week. Dad is expecting a relatively quiet week at the office, as is Mum. She mentions a few appointments for herself and that she'll be home late.

"There's still plenty of leftover sausage rolls in the fridge, thanks to Dani. And bread and cup-a-soups in the cupboard, so we'll just have scratch for tea tonight. If you go out today, Dan, can you please pick us up another bottle of milk? If not, send me a message and I'll find a servo on my way home." She smiles and stacks up our plates, rising.

"Sure, Mum. I have to get petrol anyway, so I'll be able to get it." I jump up too and start packing away the spreads back into the pantry.

"Thanks, sweetie. That'd be great." She pulls me in quickly and kisses the top of my head before running to their ensuite to get ready. *That was weird. Why'd she kiss me?*

Knowing I will end up reading the day away if I don't make a plan, I decide to clean the house. Since I'm not paying board.

The house looks great when it's all clean and tidy! I save the shower for last and clean it while I'm there for myself.

Clean, dried and dressed, I go to make myself a sandwich for lunch when the house phone rings. It surprises me and I drop the butter knife. *Damn it, butter on my clean floors!* I wet a piece of paper towel and answer the cordless phone.

"Hello?"

"Hi, sweetie, just me. I just got off the phone with Barb. They want you to go in for an interview tomorrow at two o'clock. I said you'd be there. Isn't that great? I have to get back to work, but we can talk more about it tonight. I'll get the address and everything for you. See you tonight."

"Okay, bye, Mum." *Why didn't they ring me? I put my number on the resume. Shouldn't they have called me for that?*

Having argued with Mum over whether jeans are appropriate for a DVD shop interview and losing… Here I sit. In my car. Outside the shop front, rehearsing my answers. These black pants feel like they have itchy caterpillars crawling in them. This awful shirt feels like it is sewn together with barbed-wire. *Just stop and breathe. You're anxious because of the interview, and that's revving up your sensitivity. Breathe.* Reasoning with myself when I want to rip my skin off is hard, but I know I need to try.

The interview is short and after fifteen minutes, I'm back on the street climbing into my car. I have no clue if it's gone well or not, but he said he would get back to me this week sometime. I can't wait to get out of these clothes. Stereo up loud, I head for home again.

Mum is already there when I pull in. Rocking softly on the swing chair, she flips through catalogues on the verandah.

"How'd it go?" She looks up from her page.

"Yeah, pretty good, I think. I think I answered everything right. Said he'd let me know this week."

"Well, that's great news. Just have to wait and see now."

"Yep. Any ideas on dinner?" I ask.

"Not exactly. I've got chicken out. Thought I'd do some roast veggies and maybe crumb the chicken in pieces. What do you think?"

"Sounds good. Want some help after I get out of these awful clothes?"

"Sounds great, thanks."

We're both cutting away when the phone rings. Mum answers it but soon extends the receiver to me. "Hello?" It's the man from today's interview. In the space of one quick phone call, my buoyant mood is lost. Instantly I feel myself spiralling out of control, plummeting towards earth with unrecoverable speed. Course, this is all metaphysically. Outwardly, I'm still vertical and robotically responding to the voice down the line. "No worries." It's all I can think to say.

Concentrating on his explanations becomes too much. She-Devil embraces the moment to get loud. Very loud!

~ Well, well, imagine that. They found someone more 'engaging!' It's hardly surprising. Can't even get a job stacking DVDs and covering people while they eat! That's a new low, even for your broken arse! ~

Her words are harsh, and they cut straight through me. Tears sit on my lower lids as I hang up. Mum's smile fades when she sees them.

"I didn't get it." I say, two tears fall to my cheeks. Mum opens her arms to me and I let myself be hugged.

The destructive self-talk has picked open the unhealable wound on my heart and it bleeds afresh. The pain of it reaffirms that no matter how far I think I've come, no matter how many things go right for me in a day. It only takes one negative pattern haunting me, to send me back down the dark path. Where self-worth and positivity run out.

Unable to hide my hurt, I pull away from Mum and make my excuses. "Are you okay if I go have a shower instead, Mum?"

"Of course, sweetie. There'll be another job. Try not to let it worry you, hey?"

All I can do is nod, not trusting my voice to hold steady and seeing my vision blur. *Escape!*

Grabbing my clothes up from my wardrobe, my phone blips on the bedside table. I swipe at my stubborn tears and have a look. Kevin's name lights up the screen. The message he's sent remains unopened. I can't handle anything right now. I clutch my clothes to my chest and lifelessly aim for the bathroom.

19

Kevin

Pulling the shifter one last rotation, it slips off the tap fitting and smashes into my knuckle.

"YEOW!" I give it a rub along with a few curse words.

"Hey! take it easy. You don't want to scratch the finish."

"Yeah, 'cause I meant to smash my hand and scratch the bloody fitting, didn't I?" I spit back, throwing the last couple of tools into an old towel, I scoop the lot into my arms and dart past my dad.

At the van, I pull open the side door with enough force to send it flying from its guides. Towel unfolded, I see blood leaking from my hand and wipe it on the rag. I am still slamming tools back into their correct spot when Dad leans casually against my front passenger door.

"So… you going to tell me what's eating you today or are you gonna make me guess?" He casually cleans his glasses with the bottom of his shirt.

"It's nothing, Dad. Just hurt like hell and annoyed me. We heading off to that shop fit soon? It's three thirty now. Didn't you say we could get in at four?"

"Oh, I forgot to tell you, I got a call just before. Apparently there was a stuff up with the order or something so the other guys have been delayed. They don't think they'll be ready for us until the start of next week. Possibly longer. Reckon we call it a day."

"Really? That sucks about the order. Someone'll get their butt kicked for that, I assume."

"Yeah, but not us, so it's all good! Go on, you head off. I'll finish this."

"Thanks, Dad. Think I will. Can't wait for a nice hot shower this arvo." With a flick of the thumb, I awaken my phone, still nothing.

"*And…* you're going to leave your crap at home tomorrow, right? Uncle John mentioned you've got a new girlfriend? Is she the cause of these tantrums today?"

"Uncle John? Bloody Mick! She isn't my girlfriend. We've just hung out a couple of times." *Why did I think that living with a relative would work? Everyone knows everyone in my circle!*

"Hmm. Well, sort it out, hey. I much prefer working with my happy-go-lucky son over this sour one. Yeah?"

"Yeah, Dad. Sorry." With a solid shove, I send the van door rolling home until I hear a click of the latch. I chuck my phone and wallet across onto the passenger seat, next to my trusty esky and pass my boots carefully over and into the passenger footwell onto the old towel that is now a permanent fixture there for exactly this purpose. My phone comes to life and pings with my message tone. *Finally! Please let that be Danielle!*

20

Danielle

3.34pm—I wake up groggy and stiff-limbed. Searching my room with confusion, reality creeps back in. *I didn't get the job.* Rebel is nowhere to be seen and the house is silent. I stare at my ceiling, thinking. *How long have I been asleep for?* Counting it up, I realise I've been out of it for the best part of nineteen hours.

Shit, I don't think I ever got back to Kevin last night. I should message him. But what do I say? Should I explain why I never replied? Tell him about the job interview? What if he thinks I'm a loser? I pick up my phone from the bedside table. *One missed call from Tom and a voicemail… I'll get to that after.*

    Me: Hi Kevin. Sorry I never got back
to you yesterday. Had a rough day.

That's an understatement and a half, but I spare him the full pathetic story of my life.

It doesn't take long before he replies.

    Kevin: Hi. I was starting to think I'd scared you off. I hope everything's ok?

    Me: Not exactly, but it's a long story. Did you work today? Are you still at work? Should I let you go?

I can ask those questions, right? I push send.

    Kevin: Nah, just finished actually. Sounds serious. Can I take you out for dinner tonight and you can tell me about it? I'd love to see you. :) xo

Do I want to go out for dinner? I haven't been hungry all day. Am I up to it? Do I want to tell him what happened?

Still staring up at my white ceiling, Michelle's voice comes to mind... *'but wouldn't it be nice to have a friend? Somewhere to go that isn't the library! And someone to talk to other than Mum and Dad.'* With a sigh, I start typing.

    Me: Um, ok. I guess there are a few things I probably need to tell you. Stuff I should've mentioned before. Stuff that might scare YOU off. We could discuss it tonight, maybe?

Nervously, I hit send. *Moment of truth. No backing out now... You're going to have to tell him.* Minutes tick by and I read and reread my words, waiting for a reply. I start to fear that he won't write back. *That's it? He isn't even going to let me explain?* My mind races. Blip-blip.

```
     Kevin: Uh, ok… now I'm nervous. Is
this where you tell me you're a serial
killer and you want me to come see you for
conjugal visits and bring you magazines in
prison? Lol. Xo
```

```
     Me: Heavens no! Nothing like that.
Just think you should know the rest before
we keep seeing each other. Well, anymore
after tonight, that is. Where do you want
to go?
```

With the specifics locked in, I race off to shower and get ready. Kevin wants to pick me up like a *real* date and he will be here soon! I hear Mum's car coming up the gravel driveway, but I don't wait. I dive in and get cleaned up. She looks cautious when I come out dressed in my good jeans, hair neatly brushed.

"Hey, Mum. Kevin's taking me out for tea. I'm telling him everything. He'll be here shortly. No time to talk."

At ten to five, I am pulling my black cardigan from its hanger and stepping into my good ballet flats. One of which still harbours the faintest stain from the day in the rain. Sliding the second foot in, I hear tyres crunching up the gravel driveway. *He's early, unbelievable.* I can't think of a single person who has ever put as much importance on punctuality as I do. *Don't overthink it, Dani… it's probably just coincidence.*

I barrel down the hallway towards the front door. The cut on my hip pulls and although it no longer hurts, it feels weird and I slow my steps slightly to keep from drawing attention to it, but I also want to avoid the whole 'awkward parent meeting' thing.

Grabbing my house keys from the hook by the front door, I yell back to Mum that I'm leaving and wait for her distant response of acknowledgment. I give Kevin a timid smile as my nerves increase about revealing my secret to him.

21

Danielle

I can't tell you what I thought the inside of a guy's ute should look like, but somehow, it isn't what I expected. I guess I thought it would be messy. Maybe half-empty drink bottles or burger wrappers scattered around the floor, but I am pleasantly relieved to find it as spotless as my own car. All I can do is smile at my naivety.

"What?" Kevin asks as he clicks his seatbelt into place. I follow suit and put on my own belt.

"It's nothing. Let's get out of here, away from all the eyes." I wave from the passenger window to Mum, watching us from the verandah, confirming my point.

Tension builds as we sit silently in the small space, with houses flashing past the windows. The only noise to be heard is the steady hum of the engine and the indicator ticking as we turn this way and that. If I wasn't so nervous, I might even laugh at us, tonight however, I am much too anxious to see the funny side. It is only now that I remember the unheard voicemail that I never got to. *Damn! I'll listen to it later.*

"So, where are you taking me for dinner?" If we were in a movie, it would have sounded cool, maybe even flirtatious. On my lips, though, it comes out fact finding and flat. I curse myself.

"Well. I thought since my cousin's watching the footy at a mate's place, we could go back to mine and I could cook us dinner. Or we can grab something easy and close by if you'd prefer that?" Kevin wears a strange expression. One I don't know or understand, making me uncomfortable. I start to fidget with a crease in my top. His eyes dart to look at me… twice.

"I kind of need to know before the next intersection. So I know which way to turn."

"Oh, right! Um, maybe we'll just keep it nearby tonight. Subway?"

"Subway, it is." He frowns, creasing his forehead unnaturally. "So… did you want to start? Whatever it is you wanted to talk to me about." He sounds different. There's a tone to his words. The fact that I have even noticed it tells me I am starting to decode his essence. He is not his usual teasing self, tonight. I wish he was. Cheeky Kevin loosens my brain, helping my words flow easier. I chicken out. It doesn't seem sensible to risk upsetting him further while in charge of a vehicle.

"Are you alright, Kevin? You seem... different tonight. More serious."

"Me? You ignored me for a day, then you finally write back and ask me how my day is going. Only to be followed up with something about needing to tell me stuff I should know before we see each other again... Geez, I don't know why I'm stressed." He lets out a large rush of air before continuing. I look down at my hands, fidgeting. He isn't yelling, but I feel uncomfortable. I don't know what to do. *This was a bad idea.* "Look, Dani... I know you've got something to say, and if it's okay, I'd like to go first." I nod for him to go ahead. The power of speech, no longer one I possess. *Here it comes... 'I don't think we should see each other anymore.' I've heard it all before.*

"Dani, I really like you. I've loved hanging out with you and getting to know

185

you a little, but I've had my share of dead end relationships. Girls who seem to think I'm only here to take them to dinner when they don't have a better offer. Girls who think it's fun to string me along, like some cruel game. So... If you're breaking up with me, can you please just get it over with? So I can go home, rather than potentially humiliate myself in a public arena." He sighs.

Arriving at Subway, Kevin Pulls into one of the empty car parks, and as soon as the car is stationary, he leans forward, resting his arms on the steering wheel. I think I see his eyes close.

Me? Breaking up with him? Why would I want to do that? I must have this muddled up. I'm sure he said 'Me... breaking up with him.' Huh?

"What?" I am so confused right now, I don't know what to think. *Am I breaking up with him? I ask myself again... When did we become 'together'? Is this why he's acting odd? What have other girls done to him? People are mean!*

He rolls his head to stare at me, mirroring my confusion. I know he wants me to say something, but I have to untangle my thoughts.

I raise my hand, signalling him to give me a minute before resting it on his arm. "Are we together?" I have so many questions pulling for my attention that it's hard to make sense of them all. This is the only one that makes it to my tongue with clarity while I sort through the rest.

"Aren't we? I thought we were heading that way." Poor Kevin looks even more confused than me, his face all creased up. A half smile creeps up my cheek, a completely inappropriate reaction to the moment, but my relief is so great that I suddenly feel confident enough to tell Kevin everything! I am laughing. Kevin's honesty about his feelings gives me the strength to do the same. He frowns at me, of course. Firstly, I need to explain my laughter, it seems. *Must stop laughing.*

"I'm sorry. Give me a minute... I'm not laughing at you. Please... give me a sec." Finally, I gain control again and take a deep breath to steady myself. *Please let me get this out without going mute! Please brain, let me get through this.* I rush ahead as if rattling off like word vomit will keep the momentum going before the axe falls and my tongue's rendered useless.

"Kevin, I'm Autistic. Please don't be mad. I know I should've told you right back at the start, but I didn't want you to freak out or laugh at me. No, I don't want to break up with you. No, I didn't know that you thought we were 'together' but yes, I do like that idea. I like you too.

"A month before Michelle and Luke's wedding, my boss forced me into a corner to rape me or whatever. I'm not exactly sure why he'd choose me. Anyway, long story short... I got a deep cut that needed stitching. Everyone found out about the incident and blew it way out of proportion. My mum made me go to the police and said I had to quit, so I did.

"I haven't had a job since. Getting a job isn't easy for me. I went for an interview on Tuesday at this DVD shop who needed some help. I got a call last night to say I hadn't got it... So, I spiralled and I tend to push people away when that happens. In any case... I need time to regroup after an episode or spiral like that, so... I'm sorry."

I suck in a big breath of air and wait patiently, watching him for a reaction now that I've successfully got all that out without losing my tongue.

"Wait, slow down... Your boss did what?" Kevin shouts. "Oh, my god! Are you okay?" His eyes are big. The white is visible all the way around his irises. Before I get the chance to speak, he covers his face with both hands and mumbles into them, "Oh, my god! Oh, my god!" He leans forward again, still clutching his face. Panic sweeps through me.

"What? What's wrong, Kevin?" My heart pounds in my chest with fear.

"In the carpark! I pinned you up against your car and kissed you in the damn carpark!"

The memory returns of him leaning against me in welcome pleasure. The desire it brings with it flushes my face, and I'm certain I must look the colour of ripe strawberries. *I knew I should've been more guarded that first night.*

"Yes. I'm sorry about that. I realised after I left that I shouldn't have maybe… you know… my tongue." I cough uncomfortably and pick at a non-existent thread. "But it's not contagious, if that's what you're worried about? I would never do that to you."

"Huh? No, that's not it. Here you are recovering from a rape and then I come along and act like a damn animal! Probably scared you to death! Dani, I'm so sorry. I had no idea, but that doesn't excuse my behaviour, regardless!"

"Kevin stop! I wasn't raped this time. *That's* what I'm saying! He didn't get that far because one of my colleagues caught him before he got the chance. I'm fine, honest. I don't want this to change things or make you weird." Dropping my voice to a whisper and with cheeks still aflame, I admit, "I liked it when you kissed me. You made me feel... normal."

"Hold on... What do you mean *'This* time'? Have you... have you been raped before?" He squeaks, his voice higher than I've ever heard it. Frowning, a deep groove forms between his eyebrows. *Agh! How do I keep doing that? Foot in mouth again!*

"Ah... technically, yes—"

By the time I've finished answering Kevin's questions, the Subway staff are turning off the last interior light to the restaurant. There is a single flood light at each end of the small parking lot so we are now thrown into semi-darkness. We sit longer, absorbing all that has changed here tonight.

"Well... I guess we've missed dinner. Any chance I can interest you in a lousy drive-thru meal instead?" He has his cheeky smile back where it belongs. It sends my heart fluttering in a wholly new and rather strange way. *Am I falling in love with him?* I can only nod in agreement. A wad of emotion in my throat threatens my speech. *He still wants to hang out.*

Kevin starts the car and backs out of the space. He takes my hand and we travel like this to the McDonald's further down the road. I am very aware the whole way that he should have both hands on the wheel, but I know how much it annoys my family when I tell them how to drive. Kevin is probably the same. Not wanting to wreck this, I keep my lips buttoned. At the speaker, he asks me what I would like and I'm tossing up between chicken or beef. I opt for a plain cheeseburger and chips meal. Kevin orders the same, but in a bigger size, and I giggle. *What is it with men and 'bigger is better?'* He leaves the drive-thru and we park again to eat it rather than drive home where it will be cold. I think he is happy to steal more time with me before dropping me home, which is perfectly okay with me!

We are sitting quietly, side by side. This time, however, there is no awkward-ness. Our silence is only due to the need to eat. We both devour our burgers and I'm shocked to discover that I am ravenous. It seems my appetite is back since talking everything over with him. *He is like a kind of therapy, how awesome! Mum is going to be so relieved to see me eating again.* Kevin finishes his burger a few large bites ahead of me and moves onto his chips. He has a thoughtful expression on his face. At least, I think that's what it is.

"What're you thinking about?" I ask him.

"Um. It's probably really late to be asking this, but I think I have overlooked another a large part of what you said before…"

"Mmm, what's that?"

"You mentioned… you're autistic, I think?" His brows furrow and he looks almost scared. My chewing stops and I swallow my mouthful. *If he can handle everything else we've talked over tonight… surely he can handle this.*

"Oh. Um… Yeah. I have autism. Though I refer to myself as an Aspie. To me, I feel it fits better even though it isn't technically accurate." I sit unmoving, waiting for him to say something, anything to give me a hint at what he is feeling or thinking of this news. I can see in his eyes that he has more questions forming. It's a look I've look a hundred times. As soon as new people learn this of me, it appears. I give him a minute to process what I've said. I'll know soon enough how much he knows about it, once he starts asking questions.

"Okay... And what does that mean, exactly?" He is unsure but doesn't want to hurt my feelings. Another look I have seen a hundred times. *He is an ASD virgin. Back to the basics we go.*

"Okay. You eat, I'll talk. Firstly... I'm not dying. People hear disorder or syndrome and always think the person is on death row. I'm not. I didn't get it from vaccines and it's not curable or contagious... despite what you might read on google. I presume you've heard of the word autism?"

He nods yes... "Well, it's a spectrum disorder. ASD. This means all of us who are on the spectrum vary greatly in our strengths and challenges, severity and functionality. You're probably aware of the stereo-typical 'non-verbal' institutionalised, possibly rocking in the corner description. Or the genius variety. Like Rain Man? A lot of us, however, fall somewhere in between. Me... I'm awkward enough to struggle socially and in life skills, but without the genius that might make it 'cool' or acceptable." I frown at the words I've thought so often.

"I was diagnosed at fifteen. Mum kept pushing when I was little, but no one would listen to her. There just wasn't the knowledge back then. Especially not for girls.

"In very basic terms, my brain is wired differently to say… yours. You're what I call Neuro-Typical, AKA… 'normal.' They tell me I have a unique view of the world, compared to other NTs like yourself. I solve most problems differently to you, and on a bad day, I need more space than others do, both physically *and* mentally. I don't handle 'busy' very well and I can be weird… well, pretty much all the time. For you, I guess the most important thing to know is that I can be very literal. I say stupid things at wrong times, I often mix up what people's body language is saying and sometimes I muddle up my own as well. Like before when I was laughing. It wasn't funny, but I couldn't stop either. I shy away from people when I'm stressed out. But the worst is when I flip out completely. Especially in public! That's the worst! There is a tonne of other weird stuff I could tell you, but to be honest, it's just something you will pick up over time. Well, if you want to keep hanging out with me, that is?" Kevin's stopped eating his chips and is staring at me oddly. I can't tell if he is taking the information well or not.

"So... I hope this doesn't sound ignorant or anything, but... what can I do to *not* cause you stress? I'm not sure if that even makes sense, sorry."

"No... it does. This isn't something I want you to worry about." I place my hand on his. The gesture feels a little strange, but not terrible. Most NTs use touch to comfort, I've learned. "If I do something you don't understand, ask. I'll try to explain it. It's more about me learning 'you.' Your essence, as I call it... Your feel, your mannerisms, your facial expressions. Everyone is different and I don't have an instinctual radar for the unsaid. For me... I basically learn each person individually that comes into my life."

Kevin's looking at me like he is confused. I continue to try easing his mind. "Tell you what. How about a deal? If you promise to ask questions when I do something you don't understand. I'll promise to try and explain when something upsets or triggers me. Yeah?" *Ah, that face looks more promising.* I think I'm getting through to him now.

"Deal. I'm sorry if I drive you crazy with questions, though. I'm a very curious person, you know." He smiles lop-sided.

"You won't drive me crazy as quickly as I probably will, you. So don't worry about it, I'd rather you ask and know, then get frustrated and leave." I become sad momentarily and his face shifts, no doubt resembling my own.

"Hey, I'm not the type to scare easily. You'll have to do better than that if you want to get rid of me, okay? You finished with those?" He packs our rubbish into the large bag.

22

Kevin

Mick is snoring on the couch when I get home. The lights and television, still on. Quietly, I place my keys on the side table by the front door and head to the kitchen. Patch's nails click against the timber floorboards as she comes to greet me.

"Hey, girl," I whisper, pulling out what I need to make myself a couple of sandwiches for tomorrow's lunch. Despite my best efforts to be quiet, I hear Mick shuffling. He wanders in, hand up his shirt, scratching his belly.

"Hey. You're home late. Kind of expected you a while ago. You got a late start tomorrow?" He pulls a water bottle from the fridge and sculls half its contents before catching his breath and recapping it.

"Nuh. Actually got to be up in too few hours. Just putting some lunch together before I hit the sack."

"You out with Danielle again? For someone who said it wasn't working out, you're home mighty late. Or maybe you just got in one last go for the road 'eh? Oh… or was it a nightcap with Ange?'" Mick is grinning, his eyebrow dancing. I am not a violent person, but I could take a swing at him right now. It's that kind of mentality from a jackass that hurt Dani.

"Go to bed, Mick. You're still drunk and your revolting is showing. I don't ever want to hear you talk about Dani or Angela—or any other woman, in fact—like that again, or I'll knock your block off, got it? Now go to bed!" I let the butter knife clang into the sink and walk around him, shouldering him as I pass.

"Hey, I was just joking. Sheesh, talk about touchy…" He mutters something else, but I close the bathroom door on his words.

Lying in bed, I can't stop thinking about everything Dani told me. *How does one poor*

girl get raped by an ex-partner and then almost endure another at work? Her boss, of all people! That's the type of thing you see on the news or in the movies… Not to people you know. Least not that I've ever heard.

Oh god! I pull the pillow up over my face and ball my fists into the stuffing, remembering leaning against her. My hard-on pressing into her through my jeans and mauling her. Jesus, dude… you're a jackass too. Not okay, man!

Despite the steady stream of thoughts, exhaustion wins and I eventually drift off. Before I know what's happening, my alarm screams into my ear from the bedside table, scaring the wits out of me.

Agh. Too early! Before I fall back asleep, I pull myself to the side, upright on the edge of the bed, and scrub my face. Sleep in my eyes and a two-day-old growth gives me an unkept look but I don't have time to care this morning. A quick shower and piece of toast is all I can get through before running out the door to meet Dad for our first job. Luckily for Mick, he is gone before I rise. I don't know how he manages all the socialising and early starts, but I'm glad for his sake he is out of my way.

23

Danielle

Kevin is insisting on taking me out for a proper, traditional date. He won't tell me where we're going or what type of food to expect. All I know is that it is dinner, and he's checked the cuisine with Michelle to make sure I will like it. As someone who hates surprises and not knowing what to expect; I take slight comfort from knowing Michelle has okayed it. But still, I wish I knew where we were going!

Nervous, but completely dressed and ready, I'm turning inside out while I wait for him to arrive. Catching myself picking my fingernails, I pound my fist against my thigh. *Stop it! Think about something else.* I bounce my leg at speed. Tom's voicemail from yesterday comes to mind. I haven't told anyone about it. I'm not sure it's a good idea when things are finally getting back to normal. I don't want to wreck that. Tom sounded so mad. He wanted me to know that Sean got off on 'Good Behaviour' since it was his first offence, he said. I don't know how he found all this out. I haven't called him back.

Mum looks up from behind her reading glasses to stare at me. *Definitely better off NOT telling them!*

"You're shaking the whole lounge room. Why don't you take out your book? He'll be here soon enough." I shake my head no. *As if I could focus!*

I hear a car slow down, out on the main road, and jump up and check the front windows. A neighbour's blue sedan turns into our street and cruises past. I watch it disappear around the bend at the far end. *Exhale.*

Headlights flash through the window, making me squint. Gravel crunches under tyres. Kevin's ute crawls up the driveway. I don't know if my heart races or stops all together. All I can feel is sickness churning in my stomach and a light-headed wooziness like I should sit down. *Don't let me faint.*

"Dani!" Mum shouts, startling me. I'm flicking the window glass repeatedly with the back of my finger.

"Sorry, Mum. Better go. Wish me luck."

"You don't need luck. It's supposed to be fun." Her voice gets louder to compensate for my leaving. She has been way more chilled out since talking to Michelle and finding out that Kevin is a decent guy. *Surprise, surprise! Didn't I tell her that? No-one ever trusts my judgement. Although perhaps with good reason.*

I jog down the couple of front steps. Worry and excitement, a competitive cocktail running through my veins. Kevin holds my door for me at the car like an old movie. A moment of weirdness passes between us, but I ignore it. Sliding into the passenger seat, I watch him angle around the bonnet and climb in beside me. I'm hyperconscious of every turn and bump in the road as my mind scrutinises the directions we're going, desperately trying to calculate our final destination. It's so frustrating.

On the outer fringes of the city, we pull into the carpark of a small set of restaurants. There is a Thai place, A Turkish place and the mysterious one directly in front of us. The sign doesn't hint at its origins. I chew on my lip. *Please, let there be just one thing I will eat!*

Walking through the main doors brings total surprise. What I thought to be an older, possibly oriental flavoured restaurant, is actually an open-plan and modern cafe-type style. High-top tables and barstools line the perimeter of the building while restaurant-style tables and chairs are dotted sparsely in between.

A live band plays in the rear corner. They have a grungy style but it's muted enough to still be hear over comfortably. The menu is casual, continuing to surprise me. Nothing so fancy that it is daunting. I order a chicken schnitzel and Kevin gets a chicken parmigiana. We chuckle together as the server walks away.

Halfway through our meal, Kevin is talking about his mum, but my attention is drawn to movement when a couple walk in.

"So… my mum wants me to take you around for dinner. She can't wait to meet you." Kevin smiles his cheeky half grin. "I'm not—" He halts. "Shit. Angela? What the hell're you doing here?" Kevin asks of a woman now leaning against our table. A second glance reveals she's the woman who entered a minute earlier.

"Who the fuck are you?" The woman demands. *Why is she yelling at me? Who is she? I don't even know her.*

"Angela! You need to leave! Now!" I hear Kevin, but my eyes transfix on the marble swirl of the floor tiles.

"Oi, I asked you a question, slut." I hear her yell again. Suddenly everything is too loud. The band. The sizzle of food cooking in the kitchen hisses angrily and every knife and fork in the building squeaks against plates like they're shattering glass! A loud clap sounds and instantly my cheek flames. The heat of it stings my eye and tears blur my vision. My heartbeat pounds so loudly that my ears ring. All the noise from a second ago fades far away as I slip into my own bubble. Unable to move. Unable to climb out. The burn of my cheek, scratchy seams and strands of my hair caught in the creases of my neck make my skin crawl. It is as though I'm covered in insects and takes all my concentration not to jump up and flail around like a lunatic to shake off the infestation.

24

Kevin

Are you fucking kidding me?

"Shit, Angela. What the hell're you doing here?" *Of all the people, honestly!*

"Who the fuck are you?" she challenges Dani. *Jesus! She's tanked!*

"Angela! You need to leave! Now!" I grab for her hand to stop her from toppling our table in her uncoordinated state, but she arches away and I miss. A second later, she leans heavily on the table to steady a sideways stagger.

"Oi, I asked you a question, slut." Before I can grab her, her hand strikes out and connects with Dani's cheek, snapping Dani's head sideways. I shove Angela backwards, sending her staggering into an unoccupied table. Not wasting a second on Angela, I go to my knees beside Dani's chair.

Before I can say anything, Angela tries to pull me out of the way. I feel her nails peel away layers of skin along my forearm. Our table is crowded now. Staff members are closing in on us from all sides as a man—he must be a patron 'cause he isn't in a uni-form—and the manager pulls her off me and leads her away. *Shit, even the band's stopped.*

"Dani, are you alright? Come on, I'll take you home." I say. Dani doesn't move. Several staff members escort Angela out-side. The rest hover and ask questions.

"Excuse me, sir, madam. Would you like me to call the police?" It's a young man in work slacks and a button-up shirt.

"Would you like some water, miss?" asks another one. I can't concentrate on any of them. Dani makes no acknowledgement that she's even heard me. Or the staff. I'm not normally a panicky person, but if ever there was a time, now was it.

"Dani? Danielle?" I say as calmly as I can. Nothing. It's like she is stuck in a trance or something. Her eyes, glued to the floor. She is humming something. It sounds vaguely familiar, but I'm too scared to focus on that right now. *Shit, what do I do? Maybe I should just give her a minute? What if she's hurt, though? Agh, I don't know.*

Angela's loud protest ceases as she is finally shoved out the restaurant door. *How could you've been so stupid to think she was a nice girl? You gotta call Michelle, dude!*

"Dani? Dani, I'm just going to call Michelle, okay?" I ask. Still no response. I grab my phone. *Please pick up!*

"Hey, Michelle! Something's happened with Dani and it's like she's totally frozen. I don't know what to do."

"What happened? Tonight's your date, yes?" comes her business-like response.

"Yeah, we're at the restaurant. We had a run in with a girl I was seeing. Anyway, Angela was harassing her and things escalated super fast. Angela... Angela slapped her." I finish, ashamedly. *God, I'm a total jerk!*

"Jesus! Well, I'm out with a friend but I could be there in say, forty-five? What's she doing, anything at all?"

"Just staring at the floor, humming. I'm really worried." Glancing around, most patrons have gone back to their meals. A few curious eyes continue to sticky-beak. Blood is drying along my arm, sticking some hairs down in a matted mess.

"What's she humming, 'Bullet with Butterfly Wings' or 'Titanium?'"

I stare at Dani in confusion. "Um, I think it's 'Titanium.' Yeah, it's definitely that. What the hell does that mean?" Thank Christ for older cousins or I'd never have known how 'Bullet with Butterfly Wings' even goes! *How did Michelle know she was humming or* what *she would be humming?*

"That's good! She'll be fine. Listen, Kev, I've gotta go. Just stay with her. Don't touch or talk to her, she'll recover faster. Please tell me the other chick is gone?"

"Yep, she's gone. What if she doesn't come around?" I begin to panic at the thought of not having Michelle on the other end of the line now.

"She will. Listen to me. Dani shuts down when she gets overwhelmed. She just needs to sit. Think of her right now like a computer that has to reboot when it's gone haywire. Dani's the same, she's rebooting. Is it noisy there? I can't hear much through the phone, but it will take longer if it's noisy. You'll be fine. See you soon. Call me if anything changes."

"Okay. Thanks. Keep your phone near you!" *What a mess! Please, Dani. Please talk to me.*

"Sir, is there anything I can get for you?" Pesky servers linger close by. I shake my head.

I've been kneeling so long that a cramp screams through my calf muscle. I must stretch. Fearing it will come straight back if I go down on my haunches again, I decide to sit back in my seat across from her. My eyes never leave her closed posture. Our dinner goes cold, sitting forgotten between us. I watch Dani blink. It is the smallest thing but restores a glimmer of relief after seeing absolutely nothing for the longest seven minutes of my life!

After another two minutes, Dani's humming fades, and her eyes slowly look around. Initially, its different sections of the floor, but then I watch her scan the table-cloth and our plates. I want to talk to her. I want to know if she's okay, but I'm scared she'll freeze again. My mouth feels like a desert. It's so dry. I don't know what to do.

"Dani?" I ask softly. My lips are the only thing that moves as I mirror her stiff form. She blinks and slowly her eyes meet mine for the briefest of seconds. She blinks a few more times. I think I hear her sigh.

"I want to go home." She says, her eyes drop to her lap.

"Sure. Just let me get the bill." I signal over one of the four staff still in earshot. "Can I get the bill, please?" The woman nods and makes her way to the register.

Pulling out my wallet by feel, my eyes never stray from Dani as I extract my bank card from it.

"Excuse me, Sir." It's the manager. "My name's Troy. Your meals tonight are all taken care of. We hope that despite what's happened, you enjoyed your meals and will visit our restaurant again soon."

"Oh. Thank you. That's very kind of you. The meals were lovely, thank you." *What we got to eat, anyway.* Troy smiles and moves back behind the counter. Turning back to Dani, I speak softly, "Okay, let's go. Here, let me help you." I reach for her hand, but she darts sideways, avoiding my touch. Her cold rebuff stings, but how can I blame her? She heads for the door and I fall in behind her, disappointed at the night's turn.

Climbing into my seat, the tension in the car is suffocating. *Shit. I need to let Michelle know we're leaving now.* I turn the car on to get some air circulating but knock it out of gear and grab my phone. Waiting for her to pick up, my eyes are trained on Dani. I don't know whether to expect a reaction or not.

"Hi, Michelle. Just keeping you in the loop. Dani wants to go home, so we're just leaving now." Dani looks up, surprised when she hears her sister's name, but doesn't say anything.

Michelle responds, "Yep, she'll be embarrassed. Take her home. I'll call Mum and let her know what's happened, so she's there when Dani walks in. You head over to our place after that, and I'll meet you there shortly. We'll have a cuppa and go over a few things. I'm sure you've got some questions and Dani isn't able to answer them tonight. See you soon."

"Thanks. Bye." Just like that, I'm on my own again. Feeling helpless. After several seconds of hoping Dani will look at me, give me any kind of sign on what she's thinking or how she's feeling, I realise she isn't going to. I put the car in gear and drive her home.

Her mum is waiting when we arrive. Lights are on around the front verandah. Dani opens her door before I have time to get it for her. Her mum rushes down to meet her. Dani shakes her off when she tries to hug her. "Mum, I'm fine. Just let me go in." Dani turns back towards me, her face cast into darkness against the lights beyond.

211

"Goodnight, Kevin," is all I get before she turns back to the house.

"You! You were supposed to take care of her! What the hell was all that about tonight, huh?" Her mum is furious, as expected. I have no excuses. Before I can say anything though, Dani cuts in from the verandah. "Mum, it wasn't his fault. Leave him alone and come inside. Just go, Kevin. I'll talk to you later. Come on, Mum!" It's the most words Dani has spoken all night.

Dani's mum scowls at me, her lips pinched tight in anger. Finally, she marches after Dani. I sigh heavily as the bitter feeling of finality sinks in.

Luke opens the front door at his and Michelle's place. Without a word, I wander in and fold myself into a dining chair, suddenly weary.

"Shell's just ducked in for a quick shower. She won't be long. What happened? Shell said Dani got slapped or something?" Luke takes a seat on the opposite side of the table. "That a part of it, too?" He points to my bloodied arm. I just nod, seeing it myself for the first time in decent lighting.

"I think I've stuffed it. You should've seen her mum's face when I dropped her home just now."

"Did you think she was gonna wrap you in her arms? Geez, Kev. It's pretty up there, you got to admit."

"I know! I know. But it's not like I planned for Angela to be there. I didn't even know she knew about the place." I finger-comb my hair in annoyance.

"So you two never went there together then? You and Angela, that is?"

"Never. We never even talked about it. Hell, we weren't seeing each other long enough! Only a few times. I realised she only wanted someone to call on when she was bored, so I ended it. She started acting a little weird. Desperate, you know? Sent me a few grotty text messages, so I blocked her. Then she shows up tonight, hammered, and starts in on Dani. What a mess." Leaning forward with elbows on the table, I put my head in my hands and stare at the woodgrain running through the timber dining table.

"Wow. Yep, that's a doozy!" Luke replies.

"What's a doozy?" Michelle joins us, her face scrubbed clean and her hair stuck together in a soggy mass.

"The mess ol' Kev's landed himself in." Luke says, a smile pulling at one corner of his mouth. *I guess it would be funny… if it wasn't my life!*

25

Kevin

Watching Michelle sit down next to Luke at the table, I prepare for the onslaught of criticism and accusation I know I deserve. Unlike her mother, Michelle is remarkably calm.

"I'll make us a cuppa," says Luke and moves into the adjoining kitchen to switch on the kettle.

Michelle slams her open palm down on the tabletop, startling me. "Stop looking like you're the one who slapped her! You didn't and there was no way you could've predicted that Angela would be there, so just stop it! I can guarantee you, that's not what Dani is worrying about right now, okay?"

"No? Well, I know your mum is. Not that I blame her, of course."

"You leave Mum to me! The only one you need to worry about is Dani and I can promise you… she's *way* more worried that you saw her in 'meltdown mode' than anything Angela did or said."

"You can't know that. You didn't see how bad Angela was. She was out of control," I finish meekly. *Dani's never gonna forgive me.*

"It doesn't matter, Kevin. Not to Dani anyway," Michelle says matter-of-factly. Her words make no sense. Luke returns with three cups of coffee.

"Thanks, Luke." I take a tentative sip while I think. "I don't get any of this! How did you know what song she was humming when I rang you?" I ask.

"Because they're her songs. Songs that she picked up from god knows where. Look, I wasn't there tonight, but I've seen it all before. Every birthday. Every Christmas. Every time she out-grew her school shoes and Mum would drag her to the shops for new ones." She takes a sip of her coffee before continuing. "She's gotten better over time, in some ways, but still… when she gets overloaded or just can't cope, she either melts down, or shuts down and reverts to humming her songs. When she was little, she would throw herself around and kick and scream. Usually injuring herself in the process. Whenever that happened, she would fall into a negative spin for days after. One day she just came out and said—totally left-field—that she was sick of her body taking over. Told us she'd come up with an idea that, instead of acting out… she would completely shut down from the outside world. She didn't want to look like a crazy person all the time."

I stare into my coffee, wondering what it must have been like for Dani.

"It took her a few years of meltdowns to perfect it, but what you saw tonight was exactly that." Michelle pauses for another sip of her coffee. "She realised later though that—unfortunately—shutting down often brings equal attention from society as a meltdown. It's still very noticeable. Her recovery, though, is faster, only wiping her out for a day or two instead of three or four like it used to be."

"You keep saying that. Wiping her out, falling into a negative spin… but what does that actually mean? What happens?"

"It depends on what's triggered the episode. Sometimes it's migraines. Other times it's just pure exhaustion. I think it probably brings with it a level of depression or shame, I guess you'd say. She gets very flat and anti-social. You'd have to ask her that, though. I don't *live* it like she does, obviously."

For every answer I get, more questions arise. My head is spinning. I swallow down the last mouthful of my coffee, knowing it's time I left. Before I go, there is one more question I need to ask.

"I'll go and leave you guys be, but what do I do from here? I'm pretty sure I've completely stuffed it all up but… If I have any chance of working this out with her, what should I do next?" *God, I must sound like a total douche-bag.*

Michelle pauses, like she's choosing her next words carefully. I feel nerves jittering in my stomach when she speaks again. "Firstly, you need to seriously think about whether that's what you want. Dani isn't your average girl. A relationship with her is going to take a lot of patience and learning. For both of you. She can be very rigid, so she needs someone who is either in sync with her quirks or very adaptable. If you don't think you're up for it, then just break away now. She's very used to it. Probably expecting it even, I'd almost guess. That is her protection mechanism, but the more time you two spend together, the harder it will be for both of you. I'll go around this week and have a chat with Mum and see what I can get out of Dani and let you know. I wouldn't text her until then. She'll be tired. Certainly… if you *do* text her, don't expect to hear back from her. I doubt she'll answer. She doesn't do it to be mean or drive you crazy, she just shuts off when she needs time. But I know it will drive *you* crazy 'cause it used to drive me crazy!" Michelle chuckles.

"Thanks, Michelle. I really appreciate you letting me come around. And thanks for helping when I rang earlier too. Feels like forever ago now," I say, trying to lighten the mood. I give her a parting hug and then follow with a brisk man-hug for Luke. "Thanks for the cuppa, bud."

"Anytime. You're always welcome here, you know that." He claps me on the back.

Wandering back to the car, I watch them standing together on their small front landing, wrapped in each other's arms. Sleep is going to be impossible tonight. My brain's bouncing around inside my skull like a pinball game.

26

Danielle

I detect the sound of a car pulling up out the front and Mum and Dad's distant greeting of the visitor. Mum sounds talkative, so I know it's not Kevin. She is still snarling at anyone who mentions his name. I return to my scribbling. I've been trying to sketch all day but I can't make my pencils work their magic on the page. First, I tried my coloured pencils, then I tried my charcoal set but even the mono's didn't call to me. With a sigh, I grab a lead pencil and slash lines across the page. Using too much force, I cut through the thick paper.

~ *Can't even draw now, well done dummy! Mummy and Daddy will be sooo proud!* ~

Tears blur my vision as She-Devil's words ricochet through my soul. She's right. I am worthless. My anger rises like water coming to the boil on the stove. I see it. I taste it on the back of my tongue like bile about to explode from me. Gripping the pencil with both hands, I snap it in two before pegging it across the room. The point of it slams straight into my cupboard door and clatters down onto the metal wardrobe track beneath. I yank up my doona and crawl in underneath it, plunging myself into solid blackness. The dark magnifies the chatter inside my head and I slam my hands against my ears. *Shut up! Shut up!*

I register a heavy feeling from beyond my cocoon. A small window of light begins filtering through. A muffled voice calls to me. I untangle my twisted limbs from the foetal position, slowly allowing more light in at a time.

Still covered from the nose down, I squint up to find Michelle leaning over me. Her weight pins me tightly beneath the bulky cover. It's calming in my heightened state of frustration.

"I forgot you used to hide in the doonas. Never realised you still did it. You remember that time when we were kids, and we were playing hide 'n' seek? You were hiding in Mum and Dad's wardrobe under Mum's dressing gown. They were so worried. We looked for you all afternoon. Mum was so mad at you that day."

"That's not how you play the game!" I roll my eyes. This argument is a life-long difference of opinion that arises now and then, so I know the day she's speaking of. "Anyway, not much has changed. You should've seen her face when we got home the other night." The memory of her pursed lips and frown lines, clear in my mind.

"Yeah. I heard a little something about that. How're you?"

"From who? Mum? Or have you been talking to Kevin?" I swallow.

"He came over that night. He was so worried. Still is. He asked me to see how you're going. Since you won't answer his calls."

"I can't talk to him. Not after that. He knows I'm crazy now."

"Yeah? It's funny you say that because I've been talking to him a lot and he's never once said he thought you were crazy. He feels terrible. Perhaps you should give him a chance to apologise? He's coming to our place for dinner tomorrow night. I wondered if maybe you'd like to come too?" Michelle asks. She must read the hesitation on my face because she continues. "You don't need to decide right now. Just think about it."

"Mum will flip if I see him again. She said so."

"Listen, if you want to come to dinner, you just tell her you're coming to my place for tea. She doesn't need to know who else is coming. Mum means well and we're all a little guilty of thinking we know what's best for you, but this is *your* life. You need to live it. Sometimes we have to do things that are right for us and not everyone else. Do you understand what I mean? We aren't lying as such. We're just not going to tell her *all* the info." She smiles at me. I nod.

"Like that time we rehearsed the right wording for my job interview?"

"YES! Exactly like that! Just leaving out the bits they don't need to hear. Hey, what's this?"

Agh, my files. "Um… they're just files I keep on certain butterflies. Pictures, facts, eggs and plant info. That sort of thing. Nerdy, I know, but you know how I am with butterflies." I shrug.

"I sure do! Alright, I'm gonna go. Let me know, okay?" Michelle stands.

"I'll have a think and let you know in the morning."

"Of course. See you."

"Yeah. Thanks, Michelle."

Pushing send, I release my breath. I've agreed to go. Understanding that idle hands are bad for my anxiety, I head to the kitchen. *At least cooking will restock the 'freezer-meals' so mum doesn't have to do it.*

By the time I'm finished, there are only a couple of clean containers left in the drawer. Everything is washed, dried and back in its rightful spot.

Michelle and I have it all planned. I'm going to get ready and head to her place before Mum gets home from work. That way, I won't have to worry about facing her. I'll just leave a note. Luke will be home to let me in and I've asked to start on dinner for us, because we both know I'll be crazy nervous there too.

After a shower, I dress, write my note, 'Gone to Michelle's place for dinner. Love Dani' and pop it on the kitchen bench by the phone.

Reaching her house, there are cars lined up and down both sides of the streets. I scan for any sign of Kevin's but of course

I can't see it; he's probably still working. Luke opens the door in his work wear, his feet clad in thick woollen socks. Stepping inside, I see his steel caps standing neatly by the door and worry that he expects me to take my flats off. Remembering past visits though, I have never taken my shoes off here, so I keep them on and wander in.

"Hi, Dani. Come on in. Shell says you're staying for tea. That's great news." Luke smiles. He reminds me of Kevin. They're very similar in so many ways. Since getting to know them both, I feel comfortable around them. Like it's okay to be myself.

"Hi. Michelle said I could get straight into the kitchen to start. I know what she wants done. That okay with you?" I can feel my words are scripted. They aren't flowing freely, probably because of my nerves about tonight, when everyone is here.

"Oh, sure. Go right ahead. I was just gonna take a shower. You need a hand to find anything before I go?"

"No, she keeps most things in the same layout as Mum does, so I'm good." I smile at him. He just nods and disappears down the hallway. Digging into my bag, I grab out my iPod and flick through until I find a decent song. Earbuds in, and I'm ready to start.

In my music-filled bubble, I take out cutting boards, knives and fresh ingredients from her fridge. Dicing and slicing everything individually, I keep them all separate in different bowls, like you would see on a cooking show where everything is pre-prepared for the chef to use. Every time I'm cooking, I remember back when I first started, my mum would flip out about all the dishes I was dirtying. Slowly, she learned that it didn't matter because I always clean up everything I use, anyway. The memory of her face all scrunched up in irritation makes me chuckle now.

Spinning around to grab the spring onions, one of my earbuds falls out. It's one of my favourite songs, so naturally, it annoys me "Stupid things!" I mutter to myself, frowning.

Less than two minutes later, I feel a tap on the shoulder and it jolts me upright from my measuring. Luke is standing close beside me. Closer than I'd like, but I see his lips moving as he holds up a pair of headphones. I remove my earbuds so I can hear him.

"Sorry, I didn't mean to startle you. I tried to get your attention before by waving, but you were pretty focussed," he grins. "Saw you struggling with your ear things and wondered if you wanted to use mine? I have narrow ear canals so those things never work for me. I use the old-school variety. You're welcome to give them a go if you'd like?"

"Thanks," I say, turning the kitchen tap on. "I'll just wash my hands."

With clean hands, I swap my earbuds for Luke's over-the-head ones and feel instantly happy. The head band isn't too tight across my skull and no more painful buds stabbing my ears. The sound quality is just as effective as well. Luke is watching me when I look up. He gives me a thumbs up. I return the gesture with a smile and without removing the headphones, I say "Thanks," before getting back to my task.

Dinner is cooking away in the oven and I'm finishing up the dishes when I see movement from the corner of my eye. Luke is talking to someone.

That's when our eyes lock. Kevin is standing there, a bottle of wine in his hand.

Crap! Is it that late already? Michelle was supposed to be home first, so I'd know when to put my iPod away! The music feels louder suddenly, now raging in my ears. I slip the headphones down to rest around my neck. The music, still clearly audible through the exposed speakers. I wonder if the guys across the room can hear it, too. I pluck the device from my back pocket and switch it off. Everything goes quiet. No one speaks.

"Hi," says Kevin, breaking the silence. My brain and tongue are frozen. I just smile.

"Smells fantastic in here! Shell just messaged. She's only about ten minutes away. Beer, Kev? You want another drink, Dani?" Luke asks.

"Thanks, bud. I'd love a beer if you've got one."

"Too easy. Dani?"

"Another juice would be great thanks, Luke." I pass him my glass.

The two men exchange an odd expression, but I can't follow what's happening, so I return to clearing away the last of the clean dishes.

Murky memories of the restaurant carpet play over and over in my mind, like a stuck record player. *I must've looked so stupid that night.*

~ Yep, you totally did! ~

Agh, I wasn't asking you! I cringe.

"How've you been?" I hear Kevin ask. When no reply follows, I look up to find Luke gone and Kevin staring at me. *Where's Luke gone?* I need to answer Kevin. *How have I been?* The truth tumbles from my mouth. "Annoyed. I can't draw anymore. I've tried everything." Looking down, I fiddle with the tea towel. Kevin just stares at me.

Before either of us can say any more, Michelle barrels through the front door and the place fills with chatter as she hands grocery bags to Luke. She's apologising for being late. Released of her burden, she joins Kevin and I in the kitchen, Luke closely behind her to unpack the bags.

"Thank you so much, Dani. It smells amazing! I'm sorry I took so long." She hugs me. It's awkward; her touch is too light. I gently shrug her off.

27

———

Kevin

Seeing Dani's car in the driveway hits me like a fireball to the chest. Michelle mentioned she'd invited her, but I'd not heard any more. I guess I didn't believe she would actually come. She's unpredictable. I sit and stare at the little white hatchback for a minute.

The adrenaline that spikes when I knock on the front door quickly shifts into a giant lump in my throat. It threatens to block my airways as I enter and see Dani working in Luke and Michelle's kitchen. She moves gracefully, confident even. With headphones on, she glides around like it's her own. She is unaware of my arrival.

I see a new side to her and am mesmerised. Observing her unguarded like this sends a rush of joy through me. Luke is saying something about last week's footy match, but I can't even pretend interest. My eyes are glued to the girl floating around the room. Finally, she turns and our eyes meet.

Her learning of my arrival coincides with the return of her rigid movements. Realising that I am the cause makes me want to try all the harder to help her feel comfortable with me. I hate the idea that she is afraid or nervous around me. *Though I certainly can't blame her after everything.*

Luke wanders off towards the lounge room looking at his phone. I use the opportunity to try making amends with her before he returns.

"How've you been?" I ask her.

My heart pounds in my throat while I wait patiently to see if she will answer me or just walk away. Just when I think it is the latter, she replies.

"Annoyed. I can't draw anymore. I've tried everything." She tugs so hard on the tea towel in her hands that I fear she will rip it in half. Her answer confuses me. *Am I supposed to know what she means?* She leaves me rattled and I'm not sure how to respond. I don't want to make things worse between us.

Fortunately, Michelle arrives, and the awkward moment between Dani and I is broken. *You're such a coward! Maybe you're not cut out for this? Should it be this hard?* I resign myself to the fact that since I can't escape dinner now, I just have to enjoy the evening as best I can and not over think things with Dani. *Easier said than done.*

Tension hangs in the air as we all try to talk about anything other than 'the incident.' Michelle again saves the day and asks for Dani's help to serve in the kitchen, instructing us boys to 'chat amongst yourselves in the lounge room.' I suck in a deep breath, one it feels like I've been holding for far longer than advisable.

"Mate, you got to loosen up. You're tighter than a fish's arsehole tonight." Luke grins.

"I can't help it. I don't know what I'm doing here. Maybe I should just go?"

"You can't go now. Shell will kill you for one… if you ruin her matchmaking plans. And secondly, I can tell you like Dani. I've known you all my life, so don't deny it. You're just nervous."

"I'm not sure it's supposed to be this hard so early on. Maybe it's just not meant to be and we're trying to force something that won't work, you know?"

"Come on… no relationship's easy. Shell's a total pain in the arse, but I love her. Some days it's great and other days you could choke each other. You just gotta remember—in that moment, when you wanna choke her—all the things you adore about them. That ought to keep you out of jail at least." Luke winks at me. I smile in spite of myself. "Look, I know Dani a little better than you do. Not much, but a little. From what I've seen… I think you guys could be awesome together. You're always saying how you hate all those fake barbie dolls you keep meeting in the clubs. Dani's the real deal. She just needs someone who believes in her and who will be patient enough to really get to know her."

"Whoa… okay Mr Psychoanalyst! Geez, man." I roll my eyes.

"Well… I'd hate to see you give up on someone that might actually be worth sticking it out for." Luke finishes the last mouthful of his beer. "Another one?"

"Nuh. I'm driving."

"Okay, dinner's ready… let's eat," Michelle calls.

Dinner is quiet compared to most cousin catch ups I'm used to, leaving me to hash over everything Luke said. *Could we truly*

233

get past everything that's already happened? What if I invest all my time and she still doesn't let me in? She might never let me in! Some of those blog posts make it sound impossible. My heart pounds heavily in my chest. I feel sick just thinking about it.

That's when it hits me. Everything Luke said earlier is exactly true. I want to laugh with her. I want to share secrets with her. I want to be close to her and I want her to be close to me. Happy with me. *God help me… am I? Nah, can't be. Could I?*

Luke does his best to start up conversation around the table. The first few topics fall short and everyone looks dismayed except for Dani, who eats seemingly unaware. Michelle lights up with enthusiasm. Clearly a fresh idea upon her.

"How's your mum? She got many critters at the moment?" She throws me an encouraging look across the table, like she wants me to get where she is going with this. I'm lost but answer, hoping I'll stumble upon it.

"Um. Yeah, she's good. Things have been a little quiet for her for the past few weeks, but it never lasts long. I'm sure she'll have a house full again soon. And she's still got little Prickles. She's coming along nicely, now that she's gaining weight, I believe." I say, nodding awkwardly, running out of things to say on the subject.

"Who's Prickles?" Dani asks. An intense look creases her brow.

"Huh? Oh, Prickles is a baby echidna that my mum's rearing. Some hikers found her on the side of a road after her mum was hit by a car. She's the cutest little thing. I think even Dad's got a soft spot for her. Which is kind of odd for him. The animals are definitely my mum's thing."

"I've never seen an echidna up close before. Only at the zoo, once, when I was little." Dani states. I look to Michelle for help. *What do I say now?* Her smile is huge, and she gives me a discrete nod to go on.

I venture, "Maybe I could take you over there sometime. You can help my mum feed her, maybe?"

Dani drops her fork against the china-ware with a clatter. She cringes at the loud noise.

"Sorry," she says. "Can we go now?" Dani looks up from her plate, eyes wide with excitement. Michelle breaks into laughter, seeing her sister so enthusiastic. I finally understand her plan. With Dani's love of animals, I guess she knew it would draw Dani out into the conversation.

I struggle to find the right words, but Michelle dives in to save me. "It's a bit late for visiting now. Besides, we haven't had dessert yet."

All the excitement falls from Dani's face.

"Maybe we could go on the weekend, if you'd like?" I ask, trying to recover her buoyant mood.

"Yes! Thank you… I'd like that."

"Great." I smile hesitantly. "I'll find out when's a good time so you can help Mum feed her."

28

Danielle

After two slices of chocolate mud cake with ice-cream, I am beyond full and it is getting late. Together, we all take dirty dishes and left-overs back to the kitchen. On my second trip, Michelle blocks my path to the sink, leaving me confused.

"I was just going to start the dishes," I say.

"No, you cooked. I'll clean this up. You guys head off. Kevin, can you please walk Dani out?"

"Sure. You ready, Dani?"

"Um. I'll just get my bag." I frown—hopefully subtly—towards Michelle. Willing her to read my annoyance.

Checking I've got everything, I see my iPod. It still has Luke's headphones attached. I disconnect them and wind the cord up neatly. "Thanks for letting me borrow your headphones. They're great." I hand them to him.

"Keep them. I bought them to study online ages ago. I haven't used them since." He smiles.

"Are you sure? What if you start studying again and need them?" I ask.

"Tell you what… if I need them, I'll let you know. 'Kay?" Luke winks at me.

"Wow, thanks. I'll take good care of them."

"I know you will. Was lovely to see you tonight. Oh, and thanks for the delicious meal," he says.

Kevin arrives at my side. "Yes, thanks, Dani, it was awesome."

"No problem. It was Michelle's idea. Thanks, Michelle. Thanks, Luke."

"Yeah, thanks for inviting me, guys. It was a lovely night," Kevin adds.

I receive a hug from both Michelle and Luke while Kevin holds the front door open for us. The smell of his cologne hangs in the still night air as I pass him. I like that it is mild.

"Night, guys," we say in unison.

The front door closes with a click but they leave the verandah light on for us.

Kevin and I bump shoulders, walking away from it. His hand claims mine. The firm clasp he uses feels nice.

"Did you have fun tonight?" He asks.

"Yes. I'm really looking forward to meeting Prickles."

"Yeah, I'll check with Mum tomorrow and text you to sort out when." Kevin smiles.

The previously crowded street is now quiet and empty of vehicles.

"I had a nice time tonight. It was great to see you again," Kevin says.

Unsure which social script I'm supposed to be utilising, my anxiety elevates and I struggle to say anything.

"I've missed you, Dani. Our texting chats, hanging out." He claims my other hand—now that we're at my car—urging me to face him. I peek up at him, shyly. *No one's ever said they missed me before.* He frowns. A small crease down his forehead. *Is he upset? Is he angry because I'm not saying anything? I can't talk when I'm nervous. Have I told him this yet? I can't remember. I'm so confused!* I close my eyes and breathe steadily.

"If you've missed me, why the frown?" My fingers have a will of their own and I draw circles on his skin with the pads of my thumbs. The action and sensation it provides my thumbs is soothing. Melodic even.

"Have you missed me, Dani? I'm sorry. You don't have to answer that!" Kevin stumbles over his words. His own apparent nerves loosen my tongue.

"I never have to answer anything I don't want. So that seems a weird thing to say. Yes, I've missed you. I miss talking to you. I miss the feel of your lips when you kiss me and I miss how normal I feel around you, even when I'm doing something weird. Most people are mean when I stuff up."

I have to work hard to keep meeting his gaze. The feeling of it while I'm trying to think and speak clearly is uncomfortable. Similarly to how some people would have trouble keeping their mind on task while someone else ran fingernails along a blackboard, I presume.

"You miss my kisses?" His half-smile is back.

I squirm under his penetrating gaze. "Yes… yes, I do." In the glow of a streetlight, I see Kevin's cheeks are red. "Are you blushing?" I ask.

He shrugs and drops his gaze. This reaction confuses me after his direct questioning a moment ago.

"You're hiding from me. I thought we were being direct? Remember, you need to tell me when I do tha—" I'm cut off when his lips claim mine.

A soft meeting of warmth. We're barely touching. Like he can read my thoughts, he leans in, applying more pressure. A deep sound escapes him.

Shaking my hands free, I slide them around his waist to hold him tightly. His scent is familiar to me now and has this magical ability to both calm and excite me simultaneously.

Tonight's kiss feels guarded and fragile. Too soft for me to really enjoy. My tongue incorrigibly inches beyond my teeth to taste him. Again, comes a groan from within him. His tongue meets mine passionately, fulfilling my need for a more rugged reunion.

Kevin breaks the contact all too soon with a gasp for air. I refuse to release his body from my grip. He wears a strange look on his face. His eyes grow intense again, shifting between my eyes and mouth. His stare makes me uncomfortable, and I look away. "What?" I ask.

"You drive me crazy when you do that."

"I'm sorry… I struggle with direct eye contact sometimes," I reply automatically.

"No, not that. When you kiss me like that. When you surprise me with your tongue."

I look up in confusion. *What's wrong with how I kiss?* I go into default mode, *must appease!*

"I can learn. I will try harder," I almost shout.

"No, no!—geez, you don't have a high level of self-confidence, do you?—It's good, Dani. It's TOO good! I never want to stop." He pauses but quickly adds, "Of course, I always would, though. I mean… you know… I'd never… do that. Force you, I mean. I'm not—" he stammers to a halt.

Still close and in my arms, I rest my forehead in the valley of his neck. He is warm and masculine in both shape and smell. He encloses me in an embrace and my eyes drift closed. I can feel his breathing and hear his heart beating in his chest. I feel safe here. Loved here. I've always known my family love me but it comes with the deeper understanding that they 'have to love me.' This obscures its impact.

This beautiful man, though, is different. He doesn't have to like me and yet he does. He has a special heart. Not just for the normal, but for the quirky, abnormal and often awkward, that I am. *I want to love him. I want him to love me. Please, let him be patient enough to see I'm worthy.* Words that weigh heavily on my heart. Hasn't that always been the question? *Am I worthy?* A single tear rolls down my cheek. With a quick hand, I swipe away the moisture undetected. I have to believe…

I am enough.

29

Danielle

Today is the day! I'm so excited I can't sit still! Kevin's mum received two baby magpies into her care this week and still has Prickles. Kevin is taking me to meet them all. *An added bonus to escaping home.*

Mum's taking every opportunity to remind me of what happened at the restaurant. She wasn't even there, but she's acting as if she was. I'm so sick of hearing 'that boy is bad news.'

With an hour to get through before I need to get ready, I try to think of something to do. Pacing the lounge room floor—and giving mum any more reason to unleash her opinions—isn't appealing. I put on a mix CD of 'Golden Oldies' and take out Rebel's brush to give him a pamper session. He laps up the attention and purrs loudly whilst bunting against me. I croon to him as I glide the brush along his body, smoothing his coat. The action is rhythmic and touching his silky fur makes me feel peaceful. Not just on the outside, but on the inside, too.

The CD clicks back around to the first song. Looking around my bedroom floor and over my shorts, the place looks like a snowfield. I give Rebel a quick scratch under the chin, a kiss on the head, and race for the vacuum cleaner. *Glad I included time for a shower.*

When Rebel spots the vacuum, he takes off from the room, his bell ringing as he goes. In just a few minutes, the floor— and my shorts—look clean again, sort of. Remembering to empty it first, I put the unit back away and start getting ready.

Not knowing how Mum will act when Kevin arrives, I am ready and waiting on the verandah swing chair well before he is due. The minute I see his car, I'm up and have one foot on the steps. That's when Mum calls from behind me, "Just a sec, Dani." I pause. My second foot in mid-air. "Have you got your phone?" she asks.

"Yes." I reach the next step with the foot that was hovering. She nods.

"Call me if you have any trouble. Anything at all. I'll come get you, okay?" she says. I just nod and restrain myself from running the rest of the way to his—now familiar—truck.

"Hi!" I blurt out excitedly.

"Hi, yourself. You're cheery today. Should I be worried that you don't get this excited to see *me*? I should hop out and say hello to your mum."

"No, I think we should just go. And no, I've just never seen a baby echidna before. I love most animals." I say. Kevin chuckles.

"What kind don't you like?" he asks, backing out of the driveway with a raising of his hand in silent farewell to my mum. I wave too.

"Huh? Oh, um… I don't like most insects. Especially ants and spiders. Though technically spiders aren't insects, they're arachnids, but I love butterflies!—but everyone says I shouldn't talk too much about that… side-tracked, anyway—I don't love bats either. They're a little creepy. So how far away do your parents live?" My fingers drum against my thigh.

"Not far. About fifteen minutes if we get every red light along the way." He's smiling at me. I wonder silently if he sees the fireworks going off inside my body. The happiness radiating from every pore in my skin right now. His words are so simple, but the understanding behind them is what's special to me. No one new ever gets it, but Kevin does. It's as if he's known me forever. Realising that giving me the 'worse-case scenario' is what I need, so that anything above that is a bonus. I'm so caught up in my excitement, I haven't noticed he's still talking.

"—with the maggies now, she's pretty busy. She wanted to do lunch, but I said not to worry. We'll go back to my place. It's only around the corner from theirs. It's my turn to cook *you* a meal, anyway."

The thought of seeing Patch again makes this day sound even better. I'm curious to see his house. *Is it clean? Does it smell like him? Will his roommate be there?* Remembering his cousin, I frown. My hand switches from tapping to finger picking with the rising anxiety.

Once again, it is to my pleasant surprise that Kevin notices the change. He gives my hand a gentle squeeze.

"What's wrong? We don't have to go to my place, if you don't want? We can just go somewhere quiet for lunch if you'd prefer, or I can take you home?"

"Will your cousin be there?"

"Mick? No. He's away for the weekend with a mate."

"Oh, cool then." I smile in relief.

"You… don't like Mick?" Kevin frowns.

"I haven't met him. I get nervous around people I don't know. Especially those around my own age. Older people are more forgiving in my experience. Cramming 'meet the parents' into the same day as 'meet your cousin—and flatmate' would be a lot for me."

"So… you aren't worried about meeting my mum then?" he asks.

"I'm always worried about new people, but your mum looks after animals, so I know I'll have something I can talk about. That makes it easier."

"Awesome." He smiles at me, interlacing his fingers through mine.

Turning into a long driveway, all I can see are overgrown trees until the very top where it opens up. A large, circular vegetable garden acts as the centre of a round-a-bout styled driveway. The house sits on the far side of the circle. Sandy coloured brickwork is accentuated by a deep verandah running the length of the house frontage.

Kevin pulls on the handbrake and turns off the ignition. My nerves now bubble to the surface. I sit quietly. Kevin stays in his seat, watching me.

"Can I do now what I was too chicken to do in front of your mum?" Kevin's cryptic question confuses me. "Can I please kiss you?" he continues. Relief floods through me and I nod in agreement.

We lean across the space, and our lips connect. His are warm and soft. He is chewing gum. The smell of peppermint is strong on his breath.

"Mmm, thanks. That was nice." Kevin smiles.

"It was okay… I don't like peppermint much."

"Oh. Is there a flavour you do like then?" he asks.

"Um, I like fruity flavours like 'juicy fruit'. Spearmint is better if you have to use a minty one. Just not cherry; I can't stand anything 'fake-cherry' flavoured. You don't have to accommodate me, though. It's your choice. I just… might not kiss you while you're chewing it." I fidget. Worry creeping in again. "Hey, do I have to take my shoes off at your mum's house?"

He chuckles at me. "No. No need to take your shoes off here. It's actually probably safer if you leave them on." He smiles again.

"Okay." I reply.

We meet at the front of Kevin's car and I clutch his hand like a lifebuoy.

Prickles is too cute. Cuter than I ever could have imagined. She is cheeky and full of mischief. The baby magpies resemble their quilled foster sister, their spiky feathers not yet fluffy.

Helping Kevin's mum feed them with a syringe fascinates me. They're so vulnerable. Together we feed, clean and toilet the bald babies. After they're settled quietly back in their artificial nest, it is Prickles' turn for some lunch and outdoor play time. Kevin, his mum and I all take her out the back along with her crate for a cleanout.

So intrigued by the spiny marsupial, I lay down on the grass, chin resting on my hands—which are folded beneath me—and just watch her waddle around. She sniffs me, and everything around us fades away.

Unaware of if it's five minutes or fifty that's passed, the others return to my peripheral brain. The rustling of dry leaf litter penetrates my ears. I look over my shoulder, following the noise. Kevin and his mum stand together, reconstructing the echidnas crate. Their eyes are on their work, but they are quiet and I get the feeling they've been watching me.

The crate is clean.

"Would you like to put her back in for me?" Kevin's mum asks.

"Really?" I return excitedly. She nods, yes.

"We have to be careful; her quills are sharp. If you carefully go in from the sides and gently scoop her up from underneath." She demonstrates with her hands before guiding mine beneath Prickles' soft belly to the spot that my inexperienced hands don't know. "Gently now… okay, now slide your hands back out. Slowly. There you go. You're a natural!" She praises me as Prickles begins rearranging the fresh leaf litter with her snout. "You're out of work, yes? You should put your resume in down at the refuge. A lot of it's on-the-job training. Seems you're good with critters and that's what they need down there."

"Seriously? I'd love to do something like that! I will, thanks."

"Anytime. I'll let them know to expect it." She winks at me.

30

———

Kevin

Turning the car towards home, I question if I've made a huge mistake. *How could I've been so dumb? She's never been here before and now I'm bringing her when no-one else is home. Worse still, she doesn't even have the security of her own car either! She's probably scared out of her wits!*

I park behind the work van and leave the engine running in the driveway. "Hey, um… I guess you'd probably feel more comfortable with your own car here. I'll take you home. Sorry, I just didn't think."

Dani unclips her seatbelt. I curse myself for not thinking this through.

"What? No way. I want to see what your place looks like and I definitely want to say hello to Patch!"

Dani's mention of my Staffy brings her barking into focus beyond the idling engine. *It wouldn't be very fair to her if I was just to drive off again now that she's seen the car. I could just get her. Patch would love to come for the drive to drop Dani home.*

"You sure?" I'm torn. I want Dani to feel safe here.

"Mick's definitely out?" she asks.

"Yeah. He left right after work yesterday." *Is this Mick thing gonna be an issue?* Before I get a chance to voice my concern, Dani jumps out of the car with her little handbag slung over her shoulder.

With an unsteady breath, I turn off the ignition and retrieve the keys. Dani waits patiently by the front door. A dandelion twisting to and fro between her fingers. She looks childlike but sexy at the same time. Such a simple gesture.

Inside, Dani eyes the room. She scans everything from the 4X4 magazine on the coffee table to the photo of all my cousins and I hanging on the adjacent dining room wall.

I can't tell if she likes it or not. With a critical glance, I wonder if I've done enough. If it's tidy enough. I shake off the feeling. *It's just a house! A house doesn't make the man, right?*

"So… what do you think?" I ask, unsure if I truly want the answer.

"It's lovely. I can't imagine living away from my parents. I doubt it'll be a good day when I try to get that past my mum. She thinks I'm still a child. It's hard for me to imagine. Is it good? Do you get lonely?" she quizzes me.

"It's pretty good. It's nice not to have to explain your every move or change of plans. I guess I see my folks so often, though, that most days it still feels like I live with them." I chuckle. "And there's always Mick to liven up the place." Fond memories of our brother-like antics flood my mind's eye.

Patch whimpers and scratches at the locked door, reminding us that she's still outside. I move to open it. My hand hasn't finished turning the knob before Patch barrels through the gap, pushing the door wide as she runs straight to Dani, her tail audibly smacking furniture as she passes.

"Hi there, beautiful!" Dani goes down on a knee to pet the boisterous pooch. Patch is enthusiastic and jumps up, licking Dani's face, knocking her to the floor.

"Patch!" I yell.

Dani's laughter is hearty and surprises me. *Huh? Can Patch break down her walls? Help us bridge the gaps?* My heart fills with love and a newfound excitement of my own. I go to them. My two beautiful girls. Patch has Dani pinned to the floor, showering her in slobbery kisses. Dani's continued laughter is the only thing keeping me from rousing on Patch again. She knows I don't like her jumping on people.

"Patch, off. That's not very lady-like, is it? I'm sure Dani doesn't want a slobber bath from you." I reprimand her like a naughty child. Patch backs up off Dani but only far enough to still be within reach of her out-stretched hand. Patch flops down to the floor.

"Sorry, she is not usually quite this excited or I'd have warned you. Here…" I offer her a hand up.

"No, it's fine. My fault for kneeling down. I was asking for trouble." She chuckles and pushes her hair back from her face with a forearm. I guess, the only thing not covered in slobber.

"Oh, here… let me get you a face washer and towel. Bathroom's just through here." I open the small linen cupboard while directing her. "Feel free to wash your face and hands and anywhere else she got you with her, um—" my words fade as I hand her the clean towels.

Patch interrupts the moment. Her nails click along the floorboards. "I'll… I'll give you a minute." I finish lamely and escape back to the kitchen. *You're such a goddamned idiot! Stop looking at her like that! Get your head on straight! Have some restraint and stop acting like a schoolboy who needs a cold shower. Geez, man!* In the kitchen, I pour myself a glass of cold water just to cement the self-motivated lashing. I take a solid swig of the cold liquid.

Dani and Patch make their way out of the bathroom together. I can't help but feel a little betrayed by the canine who is supposed to have my back. A dog's loyalty doesn't discriminate, though. They seek out the purity of surrounding hearts and trust those instincts. *How can I begrudge her that? She has remarkable taste… I'd pick Dani too.*

"Um… there weren't any spare towel racks in the bathroom. Where should I put these?" she asks, wet washer and towel in hand.

"Oh here. Let me take those. I'll hang them over the back railing." When I try to take the towels from her, Dani doesn't release them straight away. Her reaction forces me to look back at her.

"Can I... please hug you?" She asks. Her voice, barely a whisper as she drops her face. I'm so confused by her. My heart is ready to burst and I don't know how to explain to her what she's doing to me.

Fear and excitement grapple within me as I contemplate our future and the steps that lay ahead. I'm falling in love with her. I want to explore a sexual relationship with her. Her past, though, combined with her autism, makes this whole situation more complicated—*not to mention terrifying!* The level of responsibility I feel for her is very strong.

Dani steps close and slides her arms around my waist, resting her cheek against my chest. Her hair smells like berries. For the longest minute, we just stand together. Her arms locked around me. As I lean away to drape the damp towels over the closest dining chair, Dani must mistake my movement for leaving. She clutches tighter and stretches up to place her lips on mine. Her tongue swipes gently along my top lip. Enticing. My resolve wanes, but I fight against my own carnal instincts. *Easy Kev, you gotta take this slow.*

"Please kiss me. I mean *really* kiss me. I need pressure." Dani whispers shyly and starts fidgeting.

My dick swells at her words, and I curse him silently. My jeans are so tight, they're uncomfortable. I desperately try to distract myself from her soft lips and warm curves in my hands. The hint of something floral comes off her heated skin, teasing me. If she were any other girl, I would take her signals as an invitation. With her, though, all the usual rules don't apply. I don't know what she's thinking or how far she wants this to go. *The only way you're going to find out is to ask her.*

She kisses the side of my neck. My eyes slide shut with desire. Her actions make me crazy.

"Um, Dani... I don't want to scare you or anything. But you're, um... winding me up pretty good right now. I... I'm trying to keep my cool here, but you are just too good at that. Can you maybe... um... give me a sec?" She continues to kiss sweet circles along my neck and jawline. I clench my jaw and suck oxygen in through flared nostrils.

"Um, Kevin..." she parrots, breaking free of my neck. "Do you know you...

um… stumble over your words when you're nervous? Hmm? I've had a great day and I… um… want to explore you further."

"Are you mocking me right now?" I pull back a fraction to search her adorable face. *Oh my god, she is! Cheeky minx!* "It's a good thing you're gorgeous," I tease and rest my chin back on her shoulder while I try to process her words. *What'd she mean? Does she want to… go there? Don't get ahead of yourself. Focus, Kev! Did she just sniff my hair? I think she did. My quirky little minx.*

I can't stop the smile that creeps up my face.

31

Danielle

"**D**ani, listen to me... you don't have to do this. Us guys... we can be pretty primal, but I want you to know I'm not like those other guys. I'm not going anywhere, and I'd never force you to do anything you don't want. We can wait however long it takes. However long you need. You don't have to do this because of anything I've said or to *please* me. I need a minute, yes... but I wasn't meaning to rush you. I never want to hurt you. You know that, right?" Kevin tips his head, trying to make eye contact, I think. I continue staring at his chest.

Why do NTs always want eye contact in the heavy moments? The same ones I really don't *want to. Does he not want to be with me?* Suddenly confused about what I'm supposed to do next, thoughts swirl around inside my head.

I open my mouth, but no sound comes out. *Great… perfect time to lose the of power speech, NOT! Why does this always happen?*

~ Because you're a weirdo! I told you you'd stuff it up. ~

Oh god, haven't you died yet, you vicious cow? You need to leave; I'll never get through this with you in my head like a poisonous weed! Poor Kevin is still waiting for me to answer him. Knowing this only makes it worse. With words tangled around my tongue, I shove my finger into my eye socket and rub it with frustration. The pressure soothes me, and removing my sense of vision helps me to focus on my internal chaos and calm it down.

"Dani?" Kevin touches my cheek and I hold up a finger, hoping he'll understand that I need a minute. I lead us towards his couch to sit down while I unscramble my thoughts.

Kevin follows me but kneels down in front of me instead of sitting beside me as I'd hoped. He looks worried. The more I want to tell him to wait, the tighter my tongue binds up. *Agh, Please!* I close my eyes and breathe. *Focus on your happy place.*

I'm in my field, flowers and butterflies everywhere. Kevin is there this time. No one's ever entered my imaginative place before. His presence surprises me, and my eyes fly open. I lean forward, hugging him fiercely. The warmth and smell of his skin calms me, and I try for words.

"Need a minute." It comes out in a mumble. Kevin nods and the worry lines denting his forehead relax a little.

"Take your time." He releases me but holds my hand in his, rubbing the back with his thumb. I take another slow breath. Thoughts form into words. I focus on his thumb's movement when I can speak again.

"Sorry, my words got all stuck. Look, I'm no good at all the social games and mating rituals that other people play. You have to say what you mean with me. If you don't want to have sex, then you can't hint at it with me, you just got to say it—" Kevin waves his hand to interrupt, but I shake my head at the floor and rush on.

"I'm not like other girls. I'm not going to get all pissy. You *must* be honest with me. I know I'm not supposed to say this either, because it's *too soon,* but I think I'm falling in love with you… You don't have to say it back just because I did. I'm hard work, I get that. It's just… I just want you to know how I'm feeling. And that *is* how I feel. I'm not sure if I'll freeze up and back out, but I know I want to try. You're special to me. But if you don't want to, then please just tell me."

The last of my breath rushes out. *Thank god I got all of that out without clamming up again!* He is silent and his thumb has stopped. I'm forced to peek at his face. He has his familiar half-smile tipping up one side of his mouth. His cheeks are red, but I can't understand why.

"I definitely want to, Dani. But I'll admit, I'm a little scared. You're different and you're very special to me, too. I want to tell you something too, but I want you to believe me when I say that it's not just because you did. Yeah? I am falling in love with you too, Dani." He leans in to kiss me and my eyelids slide shut. With my sight gone, my thoughts become so loud with elation. *He loves me too! He loves me too!* I struggle to keep still. His kiss is nice, but I'm too happy to remain seated and contained. I need to move. I tap him on the chest and break free of his kiss. Happy energy buzzes along my limbs. He looks at me, a frown on his face… confusion maybe, I'm not sure.

"I need another minute. Sorry, I know I'm confusing." I wiggle out of his arms and climb to my feet, looking for a 'normal-looking' way to release. There's no music on, so I can't dance or bounce. My hand drums against my denim shorts while I glance around. I spot Patch lying by the open front door and inspiration strikes. I skip over to her and indulge her in an over-excited rub down. She wakes and joins in the excitement immediately, happy for the attention. I would whisper, but I'm too full of joy. I need to make noise.

"He loves me, Patch... did you hear that? He thinks I'm special! Which is great because I think he's super awesome too!" I jump up to my feet again and shake my hands loosely, bouncing on the spot a time or two, finally giving up any pretence of who I am.

Sensing that the fun has passed, the dog wanders to the kitchen where I hear her have a loud drink of water. I turn to Kevin. He wears a cute but odd look on his face. *Time to explain myself, again.*

"Sorry. There was so much happy in my brain that I had to move. I do that. Is that too crazy?" I bite my lip, nervous of scaring him away still.

"Maybe a little... but I like it. Can I get in on some of that affection, though?"

His playful smile is back, the one I love the most.

"Sure! Maybe I'll quickly wash my hands again, though first. Two seconds." Still happy, I half skip, half bounce my way to the bathroom.

Oh my god, oh my god! Okay, calm down. Try to play it cool. Calm down! The internal monologue is loud. I take two quick breaths before turning off the tap and remembering that I took the towel out to Kevin already. I turn to leave the bathroom and that's when I see him. Kevin's leaning against the bathroom door frame, watching me.

"Oh, hi." *Did he see me peeking at the boxer shorts on the floor just now?*

"Hi." Kevin pushes off the doorjamb and slowly comes to me. Placing his hands on my hips, he tips his head and kisses me. My mood quickly switches from hyperactive to ardent.

With eyes closed, my senses are heightened and everything intensifies. The smell of his usually subtle, soapy aroma, the one that's so familiar to me now, is stronger here. My head flops sideways to accommodate him. He nips softly at my neck with deliciously plucky kisses. My body comes to life, one nerve ending at a time. I spiral into a vortex of sensation and passion as my hands roam over his clothing, looking for an inlet. Someone lets out a moan, but I don't know who. It doesn't matter.

With a firm grasp, I feel Kevin's hand on my rump before he squeezes it affectionately. Crushing me against his length. The pressure feels amazing and suddenly I want more. This time, I know the moan is my own. I grab him around the neck and press my mouth to his in need of firmer contact.

Somewhere in the back corner of my mind, I acknowledge that we are moving together through the house. I'm content. Not dwelling on the specifics. It isn't long before I am lying down on something soft. Kevin's bed, I presume, because the smell of him is all around me now. In my current state, it is intoxicating, and my whole body is tingling with lust for this beautiful man.

Everything gets hazy. Just like when I am in the throes of a meltdown, I am overtaken by an epic visual filter. This time, however, instead of red, it is blue green. Everything beyond us fades away into the distance, or maybe it's me being sucked away from reality? My limbs feel heavy and disconnected, like the strings of a puppet that have been cut. Landing like a pile of jelly. My hearing is muffled—probably from the sensation overload—leaving me feeling as though we're completely alone inside our perfect, sensual bubble. Everything is so amplified that I can't even make sense of whose hands are where and who is doing what. I vaguely notice that Kevin's shirt is gone, but if I removed it, I don't remember it.

Something is pulling me back towards reality, but I fight against it mentally, not ready to leave the quiet realm of pure sensation. It comes again and I realise it is Kevin.

"Are you sure?" His face is beneath my own, surprising me. *How long have I been straddling him? How can I be on top when I don't even feel like I have control over my limbs?* As I try to move off him awkwardly, to clear my head of the heavenly fog, I feel the searing heat of powerful hands on my hips. High above him, in only my bra and underwear, I struggle to make sense of my surroundings. The blue haze hovers provocatively in my peripheral vision and I'm eager to let it suck me back into its vortex, where my mind is blissfully hushed.

"Dani... are you sure? We can stop." Kevin asks again.

"God no, I don't want to stop!" I succumb to the desire to kiss him and fall forward, almost head butting him in the process. *Whoa, get some control, Dani. You don't want to give him a concussion!* His warm, wet tongue has me back on the cusp before he interrupts again.

"Okay, hold that thought." Kevin shuffles out from under me and my limbs feel robbed, away from his firm body. With a groan, I roll onto my back and move the pillows aside to lie flat. Suddenly self-conscious with him gone and out of my haze-filtered bubble, I climb under the cotton sheet just as Kevin returns.

"What's this? You changed your mind?" He asks. A look of what I think is concern etched on his face.

"Nuh-huh." Is all I can manage. Nervousness threatening to wreck everything as I watch him strip out of his jeans. I don't know where to look. Panic rises in me, that I won't be able to go through with this after all.

My panic, however, is short-lived. Kevin slides in under the cotton sheet, his trunks still on. Carefully, I let out a controlled sigh of relief. I don't want anything to wreck this.

"You're so beautiful. There isn't really an *easy* way to do this bit, so maybe we should just get it over with? Can I take your pants off, beautiful? Or would you rather stay under the covers and do it yourself? I don't mind."

My anxiety is escalating, threatening to ruin everything and send my delightful blue haze far, far away, forever. I can't answer. Kevin's deep and loving eyes look to mine for a response. I do the only thing I can... I reach down beneath the covers and shimmy out of my underwear, hoping he doesn't get offended. Kevin follows my lead and rids himself of his own. Resting the small foil packet on the mattress beside him, he leans up on one arm and strokes the hair away from my face. I'm grateful for the distance he's intentionally left between our bodies, giving me time to adjust. *How did I ever find such a man? He's more patient than I could've ever hoped for.*

Together, we build up to where we were. Our kisses and need for one another starts slowly and grows to a monumental carnality. The blue filter returns to linger on the fringes of my vision, waiting impatiently. I love seeing it there, ready. Like the first taste of a powerful drug, I am hooked on this new and delectable state of my mind. Where the chaos is muted and my senses tingle with anticipation.

Kevin's weight shifts on the bed. The fog moves in. He is whispering something to me but my eyes are closed again and I just smile at him, comprehension fading.

Lying together, tangled and sated, my brain returns full force, trying to sift through and organise my memories. Standing out the most is a point, early on, when Kevin touched me intimately. It had brought a deep pressure and tightness to my belly that required equal force. Like in the animal world, no words were necessary. We ran on instinct. The sensation of Kevin sliding inside me sent me over the edge in an earth-shattering way that I've never known before. Somewhere amidst my pleasure and the sensations, I vaguely remember apologising about it. Had Kevin hushed me or was I already in fantasy-land by then?

I guess that was an orgasm? No wonder people love sex so much. How could anyone relate what we just did to anything remotely similar to rape? The two are as opposite as ice from steam.

Kevin shifts his weight off me and slides to the edge of the bed. My eyes follow him of their own accord. The crease of his pale backside is accentuated by the dark tan line that runs low from hip to hip. As he pulls on his shorts from earlier, I study him, pondering. He is a contradiction. His smooth skin is soft beneath my fingers, but I know from moments ago that against my body, he is muscly where I am soft and his lean body felt firm and strong yet safe. Always safe. *Stop trying to wreck this beautiful moment with an analysis!* I reach across the bed to pull him back to me, but he darts towards the bathroom before I can grab him.

I look around at his bedroom. His private space. A wardrobe door rests open, a rogue piece of clothing peeking out from an open draw front. Loose change sits idly on his bedside table next to a photo of some young people I don't recognise, and a simple reading light.

"Whatcha thinking?" Kevin returns, disturbing my scrutiny. He's wearing an odd expression. One I don't recognise.

"Not much. Just letting my brain catch up. I'm having some trouble putting things in order. You?" His bare chest and fine spattering of hair that trails down before disappearing beneath the waistband of his shorts stirs my insides afresh. I pull the sheet up to cover my budding nipples.

"Just how incredible you are. And how amazing I feel right now." He chuckles lightly and I feel the bed move again with his return.

He has the most inviting smile. Looking into his eyes is the easiest it's ever been. I feel so connected and safe in this moment with him. I could stay here forever, just the two of us.

Kevin breaks our eye contact before me. Another first for the book of amazing moments in my life. He rolls to his back with a full-body stretch.

Not having received my fill yet, I follow him and lean on his chest for more. His eyes shift from feature to feature. My lips act on their own and connect with his. Several minutes later, we are both short of breath and well on our way down the blissful path again.

32

Kevin

If someone told me that Dani and I would reach the next step this weekend, I would never have believed them. It seems so far from where we were a week ago. Yet, only a few nights after dinner with Michelle and Luke, we have closed the gap, know each other intimately and feeling that much closer because of it.

We played in bed all afternoon together. When her phone buzzed to life with a text, reminding us that reality was right beyond the bedroom door. I reluctantly drove her home, where we shared a chaste kiss of goodbye—thanks to her parents in plain sight on the verandah.

Dani invited me to join her family for dinner—since Mick won't be home for company—but I declined. Dani's mum is still frosty and making it clear she doesn't share her daughter's warm feelings for me. *It's going to take a lot to win her over. You better come up with a plan. Soon. Avoiding her isn't an option.*

The thought of calling Luke up for a few beers crosses my mind but, in the end, I chicken out. Sisters always talk and if Michelle's heard what we've been up to, god only knows what she'll have to say.

Looking around, the house is mostly tidy. I pull out the dirty clothes and chuck the few things into the machine. *Now what?* My mind revisits the fresh memories of our day together. The way she looked at me, twisting that yellow dandelion around in her fingers. Her laughter as Patch jumped all over her in the lounge room. Her beautiful eyes looking up at me with complete trust and passion in them.

I feel like such a schoolboy, catching myself smiling like an idiot. *How long has it been since I felt this way? I can't even remember. Maybe Vanessa? Nah, it's got to be Lacey, back in high school. But shit, that was kids' stuff. Have I never?*

A darker memory creeps in. The car accident. Losing my best friend. *Is that why? Have I been pushing people away before they get too close? That can't be it… can it? Nah, I'm close to Mick and Luke, and all the others.*

I shake it off and force my thoughts back to Dani. I decide to strip my bed and change the sheets. Mum made sure when I moved out that I had spares of everything, clearing out her own cupboards to do so.

With a clean set, I remake the bed and do the 'wet, clean clothes out… dirty sheets in' swap of the machine. Patch stays beside me the whole time and follows me outside for one last run around while I hang everything out. She brings me every toy, stick, and stone she can find. She wants to play and nudges them closer when I don't respond.

"In a minute. You know I don't play while I'm hanging stuff out. Give me a sec." I say to the inpatient pooch, looking up at me with her *but I'm so cute* face. I chuckle.

It isn't long before we're forced back inside by the pesky mosquitoes. Three or four welts rise on my arms and neck. *Bloody mozzies!*

A glance in the fridge confirms what I already know. There isn't much here after cooking up omelettes for Dani and I at two thirty this afternoon. I grab out the milk and cereal.

My phone goes off on the coffee table. I'm smiling before I've even picked it up.

Dani: What did you end up having for tea?

I can't tell her I'm eating cereal! Not after she invited me to stay for dinner. Her mum's death glare comes vividly to memory.

Me: Not much. Still pretty full from our late lunch. ;) You?

I wait…

Dani: Mum made apricot chicken, which I hate. So I just had 2 minute noodles. Probably a good thing you didn't stay in the end. :(

Me: Haha… That's so funny. I didn't want to say but I'm eating cereal. I don't love apricot chicken either, but I will eat it if I have to. Wish I was with you, though. xx Can I call you?

Again, I wait.

Dani: Sure. :) Xo

She picks up on the second ring.

"Hi." I say. I am smiling so wide, my jaw hurts. *Idiot!*

"Hi."

"How were your folks after I dropped you off?"

"Yeah… Good, I think. They didn't say anything."

"Your mum didn't look too happy to see me. I'm pretty sure she's still mad at me." I try to make conversation.

"Oh, she just thinks I need protecting more than I do. She'll be fine. I'll talk to her about it."

Visions of us entangled in each other's limbs springs to my mind and I panic.

"No! Sorry—" I chuckle with nervousness. "No need to do that. I'm sure it will all work itself out. Hey, um… Did you tell them about… you know?" I sit forward on the couch, tense. My cereal, forgotten in my hand.

"About what?" She asks. I can hear the confusion in her voice. *Oh, my sweet Dani.* I look for the right words to ask, but she beats me. "Oh… you mean about us having sex?"

Geez-zus! Could she've said that any louder? Her mum's gonna have a hunting party out for me!

"Um… yep, that. Hey, where are you right now? Please tell me your parents aren't right beside you?" My leg bounces with anxiety.

"My parents aren't right beside me. Why'd you want me to say that? I'm at home, silly."

Depositing my bowl of soggy cereal to the coffee table, I cover my eyes with my free hand. Okay, so having a conversation with Dani over the phone is harder than I thought.

"Babe... where are you in your house?"

"Oh... I see what you meant now! No, they're out watching telly. I'm in my room. Rebel says hello. Can you hear him purring? He wasn't very happy to see me when I came home smelling like Patchy." I hear her chuckle into the phone and the image makes me happy. "Oh, I was thinking after you dropped me off. I need to be sure of a few things."

I smile at her voice on the other end and rest back against the couch, ready to hear her cat antics. *Seriously, man... you're going to break your face if you don't stop all this goofy smiling!* "Of course. What's up?" I ask.

"I think we should be boyfriend and girlfriend. Like... properly. Would you like that too? Because you said you were falling in love with me as well. I wouldn't like it very much if you still went out with other girls and had sex with them when I'm not around. I know some people do that, but I don't think it's a good idea. It spreads diseases, and it's not very nice."

I am bolt upright again. My mouth hangs open in shock. *She's giving me whiplash the way she chops and changes. We were talking about her cat. Does she honestly think I'm that kind of guy? Haven't I made it clear enough that I like her?* Suddenly Luke's voice replays in my mind 'She just needs someone who is patient enough to really get to know her.' I sigh. *This isn't personal. It's not about me. She needs confirmation. What did that article say… they like to know the rules.* I approach her questioning with a new level of understanding. She deals in fact and the spoken word.

"Yes, Dani. I want to be your boyfriend and I already think of you as my girlfriend. There will definitely not be any sleeping with other girls. You have my word on that one. I love you. I'm not a cheater." There is a long pause on her end of the line and I wonder what she's thinking. "Dani, any you still there?"

"Aha. I'm sorry. Um… I mean no sex with anyone either. I don't want women staying over in your bed but also no sex with them, anywhere!" *Huh? Didn't I just say…*

"Oh, I think you misunderstood me. Sorry, my fault… most people think of 'sleeping with someone' as meaning 'having sex' with them. I think you took it as 'sleeping beside them' maybe?" I try to be clearer. "No, I will not have any other girls… or women in my bed, and I definitely won't be having sex with any, either. Only you, I promise." I sigh. "And only if you want to, that is." I add.

"Okay," she replies. I am hanging on for more, but it doesn't come. Awkward silence fills the line, so I carry on.

"Hey, I was going to take Patch for a swim tomorrow down at the creek. You want to come? I can pick you up if you like?"

"Sounds good. I can meet you there. It's the opposite direction for you to pick me up. What time?"

"Oh… okay. Meet you there about nine, nine-thirty?" I ask. *Is she a little cold suddenly, or am I imagining it?*

"Great. I'll see you then. Well, I'm going to go. It's been a big day." She yawns through the phone.

"It was. Was a good one, though." I smile *again*. "Okay, well, good night, my beautiful girl. I'll see you in the morning."

"Good night, my boyfriend," she replies. The wording is off, but the sentiment puts flutters in my belly. As I hang up, I'm grateful not to have Mick here. I can feel the goofy look is back on my face and know all too well the smoochy faces and batting eyelashes he'd be giving me about now from the other side of the couch.

33

Kevin

Looking across the vacant carpark as I drive in, I see Dani beside her car and pull in next to her.

"Hi! Been waiting long?" I ask, glimpsing my watch, *nine-twenty.*

"You said 'nine, nine-thirty.' The middle is quarter past. I've been here since then." *Hmm, not the greeting I was hoping for.*

"Oh, sorry. I didn't realise we were being specific. Hey, um... are we okay? You seemed a little... upset on the phone last night?"

"Did I? No, I'm fine." She locks her car while I grab Patch and attach her lead.

"Great! No second thoughts about anything then? Us being together? You know we can slow down if you want to?"

"Are you kidding? No, I don't want to do that. I can't wait to have sex with you again! Oh… well, not here though, of course." She giggles. I scan around to see if people are looking at us. *She has no concept of subtlety when it comes to blurting out 'sex'. Maybe that's something we should discuss, and soon!*

Beyond the picnic area, we stroll along the creek edge, fingers laced together. I finally release Patch, and she takes off to enjoy her freedom.

"What are you thinking right now?" I ask.

"Just how much I love the smell of the trees mixed with the water down here. It's so peaceful and earthy, don't you think?"

"Yeah, I do. I never realised I did though… until you put it like that. I've always known I liked it, but hearing you say it like that, you're exactly right. You are great at noticing things. The details." Dani stares at me, a smile on her face. "What?"

"Nothing. Just… thank you, I guess. That was nice."

"You're very welcome." I lean down to kiss her, and she meets my lips eagerly, surprising me. I thought she might've retreated to shy again, reset after our time apart. The kiss ends mutually as we break for air. *She feels so right. Like we've been together forever... Wow, that sounded corny!*

Patch races towards us, in the hope of a game, no doubt. Releasing the soccer ball tucked under my arm, I give it a soft kick. Patch chases after it. I know she will play with it by herself for long stints before coming back for attention.

"What's she doing?" Dani asks.

"Playing ball. She plays with that bigger ball for ages, by herself. It's one of her favourite games."

"That's so cool."

"Yeah. Want to sit?" I motion to a flat piece of grass, dappled in shade from the high trees that line the outskirts. Dani nods in agreement. I wait for her to sit, but it seems she's doing the same.

"You first," she motions. It feels a little odd, but I comply. Dani again surprises me, taking a seat in the valley of my legs. Her butt against my crotch. Back to my chest. She twists her head to rest in the hollow of my neck. Having her nestled against me. The smell of her shampoo assaulting my senses feels so right. Perfect. I wrap my arms around her middle and we stay that way for most of the morning. Patch frolics before us, nudging and grunting with her beloved soccer ball. We laugh together at her antics.

After several minutes of silence, I decide to bring up the whole 'sex talk' issue.

"Hey… um, can we talk about something?" Realising too late that I've probably left my words too open-ended, I rephrase— "Sorry. Let me start that again… Can we talk about some… uh, I'm not doing very well here. Hang on, I'll try to work out my question." *You moron! Spit it out already.*

Dani chuckles.

"Take your time… I do that *all* the time!" She is completely at ease by comparison to my tension and lack of sentence ability right now. "But if it's just that you're worried about offending me that's stressing you out… I wouldn't think it's likely, so just say it." She waits then, no doubt wondering what it is I'm choking on. *No sugar-coating. Just dish it!*

"Okay, bear with me while I try to say this. So… you know before, back at the carpark? You said you 'can't wait to have sex with me again.' Well… you were pretty excited and said it kinda loudly. Most people don't say that word so… comfortably. Do you get what I'm trying to say?" I ask, falling short. *How could she? You haven't said anything resembling a point yet!*

"Um, maybe. I think maybe you mean... no, I've got no idea... Sorry. I'm guessing I've done something wrong? But I'm not even sure about that." She frowns.

"No... honestly, it isn't technically anything wrong. It's just... you don't have any problem saying 'sex' and aren't worried if others hear you. But most... argh, what do you call them again? Non-aspie people—"

"Oh... NT's? Neuro-Typical." Dani smiles.

"Right... most NTs either use another phrase or would say it quieter. Quieter than the rest of what they were saying. I suppose—thinking about it now—they probably think the word should be private because the act is? Which is kind of dumb, actually." I smile what I hope looks like a compassionate smile.

"Okay, I'll be sure to say—" she looks around before whispering "*sex* quietly from now on," she says. Her voice returning to normal volume.

I have to chew on my lip to keep from smiling. She is so funny but in such a sweet way. I kiss her forehead for a distraction.

"Hey, maybe we could call it 'sleeping together?' 'Sex' feels too harsh. Like there're no emotions involved." Trying not to say *'more along the lines of your previous experiences'* because I don't want to overstep a line and land myself in dark territory, I'm unsure how to word what I want to say. *Sex seems too close to the predatory act she fell victim to before. I don't think I'll ever look at it the same way. Is it so wrong that I don't want what we shared to be bundled into the same category?*

"But we aren't sleeping together. I don't understand why people call it that. It's completely separate and odd to me," Dani frowns.

"Okay, what about 'making love' then? It's a little corny and over-worked but it's softer. I think what we shared feels too special for it to be just 'sex,' don't you?"

"Yes, I like that. Making love is nicer." She leans up and kisses me. Tenderly at first, then firmer, wetter, deeper.

"Mmm… you're way too good at that!" I'm forced to shuffle and rearrange my hardening dick in my shorts. *Think about something else! Say something.* "Can we maybe… not tell your parents that we made love, please? Not just yet. I'm not exactly their favourite person and I'm worried they'll think

I'm only in this relationship for that. Like the other guy was. You know I'm not, right… only here for sex, that is?"

"Of course I do! No one's ever put up with my weirdness this long. Just so we're clear though… my parents don't know about my ex taking my virginity. They only know about the attempt that Sean made… my old boss. Michelle knows about the other time, but I asked her not to say anything. They don't need to know about the other time. It'll only stress them out more, and it was a long time ago. About us though… You do realise they're going to find out some time, don't you? I was thinking about talking to Mum, actually. How would you feel about staying over one night soon?" She buries her face into my neck, shy, maybe, or a little embarrassed. My heart aches knowing she has carried the burden alone of her virginity being taken by force and never feeling worthy enough to have gone to her parents when it happened. I wasn't raised around violence but if I find out who hurt her, I'll have no hesitation knocking out his teeth. Clenching and un-clenching my fist, attempting to push aside my anger, I focus on Dani, squirming to es-cape eye contact and hide beneath my chin.

"Why're you hiding? Look, it's not that I don't want to. I do! But... I don't think we should push your parents. Your mum, in particular. She doesn't trust me yet and I don't want to make that worse." I stroke the hair away from Dani's face. "Don't suppose you have any tips on that, by the way?"

"Mmm, I think you should come over for tea. Mum didn't really like Luke at first, but she did after a barbecue one night. You could stay over then too and we could actually *sleep together*." Dani chuckles.

A vision comes to mind. Dani's mum walks in on us together and throws me out of the house with only my clothes covering my junk. I shudder at the nightmare.

"I think we should take it slowly. Maybe dinner and we'll work on the sleepover another time. You can always stay at my house, though. If you want to and your parents are okay with it."

34

Danielle

It's all organised. Kevin is coming over for dinner with my whole family tonight. Convincing Mum has been a challenge, but she is finally listening to me and promises to be nice to him. Dad doesn't seem too concerned by the whole thing and I'd guess he's just happy that I finally have someone other than them to hang out with.

Dressed and ready with a lifetime to spare, I'm waiting on the verandah swing chair. Rebel sits contentedly on my lap. His purr is loud and the vibration of it against my thigh calms me.

Michelle and Luke are the first to arrive. I told her to get here early so they could help act as a buffer between Mum and Kevin. They approach the front steps, a sizeable cooler bag hanging from Luke's shoulder. I wave in greeting and they detour my way.

"Hiya. Mum and Dad inside? Hey, little guy." Michelle gives Rebel an affectionate scratch under the chin before pulling up a chair next to Luke. "You're quiet. You aren't worried about Mum, are you?"

"A little," is all I can get out.

"Don't be. Luke and I are here and Mum said she'd behave, so it'll be fine."

"I don't think Kevin wants to come," I mumble, fidgeting with Rebel's collar.

"Huh? It's not that he doesn't want to come. He's nervous. Meeting the parents is a big deal, and he's already on rocky footing with ours, so cut him some slack, yeah. Look, we're gonna go in. I got to get this cheesecake in the fridge. Take a breather. He should be here any minute. Go easy on him, okay? You, of all people, know what anxiety feels like." Michelle grabs for the bag but Luke insists.

"He's nervous because it matters a lot to him what your parents think… if that helps at all." Luke adds before following Michelle inside.

Only a few minutes later, Kevin's dual-cab pulls into the driveway and I watch him park on the grass, off to the side. With a nudge, I shuffle out from under Rebel's fluffy bulk. He's not impressed, and leaps down to preen himself instead.

Dusting off Rebel's fur, I try to act calm and slow my steps to walk out to meet him.

"Hi," I say with a broad smile. *Put away your creepy face! Try to be more normal and less 'yourself'.* I reign in the smile.

"Hi," he replies, drumming his fingers against his leg. Watching it, I'm overcome by a strong sense of familiarity. *Hey, that's what I do when I'm stressed!* He's dressed smartly in new-looking, dark jeans and a patterned blue, button-down shirt with the sleeves folded up to the elbows. The shirt fits him well, accentuating his toned body beneath. He drums again.

Finally! Understanding what he needs in this moment, I press my body to his, pinning him against the car door. I lean up and kiss him. Knowing it's pressure that will help him calm down, I hold him tightly. He pulls back from the kiss and glances towards the verandah. I follow his gaze. No one is there. He peels my arms from his backside and shakes them loosely between us. *Huh?*

I am—yet again—utterly confused and suddenly feel stupid. Frustration bubbles up, but I have to try to keep it contained. *I want tonight to be perfect.*

My eyes drop to our loosely joined hands as I try to figure out what's happening. Blank nothingness. Past our hands, I see Kevin shuffle from one foot to the other. A knee flexes and retracts, once, twice, before he shifts his weight back to the original leg.

"Look, I'm sorry. I just… I want tonight to go well and I'm a little afraid that if your parents see us all over each other, it might set everything up wrong. You know? Can we keep it… a little light tonight? I just… I want them to like me and I don't want them thinking I'm rubbing anything in their faces, kind of thing," he finishes.

"Okay." I try to make sense of what he's said. *What the hell does 'keep it light' mean?* The squeak of the front screen door tells me that I'm out of time to ask. We head back. Michelle and Luke are watching and waiting for us. Kevin keeps hold of my hand and we stroll together with fingers linked loosely.

Inside, Mum appears to be fumbling around in the kitchen. I have no idea what she's doing. Everything is already organised and the back table is all set because I did it two hours ago.

"Mum, Dad… Kevin is here," I say to both of them. Michelle and Luke hover silently on the far side of the breakfast bar, drinks already in their hands. They all stand awkwardly for a second while I pass glances between them. Finally, Dad steps forward, offering his hand.

"Hi, Kevin, nice to finally meet you properly."

"Likewise, sir." Kevin meets his handshake and they both smile politely. I feel my own smile mirroring theirs. This is a good start. "Oh, I forgot… I left something in the car. Please excuse me a minute." He dashes out, leaving the rest of us to swap odd looks. Everyone's eyes turn to me.

"Don't look at me; I have no idea." I reply to no one in particular. We all hear the door swing closed again and his returning footsteps.

"These are for you. I put them in the rear footwell so they wouldn't fall over, but then forgot to get them out." Kevin gives Mum a large arrangement of earthy-toned, native flowers and fronds. They must have cost him a fortune based on its size. They're beautiful.

"Oh, thank you. They're lovely." Mum says, somewhat shocked, I think.

"You're welcome. I just wanted to bring something as way of thanks for inviting me tonight." Kevin smiles. I struggle to understand him tonight. He's different. Guarded or half-hearted, almost. Certainly not the usual cheeky and teasing Kevin I'm used to. *Michelle said he was nervous… maybe when he gets nervous, he can't smile. You can't talk, so it shouldn't be so hard to believe that he can't smile.* Michelle breaks up the introductions, taking drink orders from all of us.

"Just a soft drink for me, please, if you have one," Kevin says.

"I'll have one too please, Michelle," I add.

Before long, the group splits up as it always seems to do. Luke, Dad and Kevin are out by the barbecue. Michelle, Mum and I are inside, arranging the salad and sides, ready for serving. Michelle refreshes everyone's glasses.

"Meats cooked. I'll leave it over here on the cooktop. Just be careful everyone, that dish is red hot. Alright… dig in guys and gals. Grab a plate, Luke, Kev." As soon as I hear Dad call Kevin 'Kev', I know I've got Dad's approval. I wink at Kevin and am rewarded with one of his cheeky half-smiles that I love so much. He appears to be feeling more relaxed now. *Does that mean we can turn off the 'keep it light' filter now? I guess so.*

Out the back, around the big table, we all take seats and eat our tea. Dad and Luke have found themselves again in a discussion about one of the latest political scandals while Michelle fills Mum in on the goings on at her work. Kevin and I share a silent moment. Side by side, he caresses my hand under the table and I turn to face him. The warmth from his touch is wonderful and his eyes are soft.

"Oh, my god… You two have slept together!" Michelle's words don't hit me straight away. The look on Kevin's face changes and it is only after that; her words reach me like an echo bouncing off city buildings.

"Shit, Shell! Did you have to?" Luke frowns at his wife. Everyone else has stopped talking. No one moves. I don't even think anyone is breathing. Mum's lips pinch tighter and tighter, like they're being drawn closed by a string. Her eyes seem to bulge slightly from her sockets. Looking to Dad, he is probably the calmest of everyone. Shocked perhaps, but no crazy eyes.

Kevin tries to clear his throat. A piece of something still in his mouth, distorting his cheek while he refuses to chew or swallow it down. It's like I'm inside a movie. Everyone has paused around me, but I'm able to move freely, scanning between the characters that surround me. *Finally, I'm not the mute one for a change.*

"That is the most stupid phrase! Why do NTs call it 'sleeping together' when it doesn't have anything to do with sleep?" I protest at an enthusiastic decibel. From the corner of my eye, I see Kevin's lids slide closed. He gently relinquishes the fork he's been holding to rest on the plate's edge. His actions confuse me. Turning to look at him fully, I see his eyes aren't actually closed. He is looking into his lap, his cheeks scarlet.

"Kevin, what's wro—" my words are chopped off as Mum interrupts.

"Is that true, Dani?" she asks.

"Is what true, Mum? That it's a stupid phrase or that we've had sex? Actually, it doesn't matter because they're both yes." My attention turns back to Kevin. "What's wrong? Your face is all red and blotchy." I ask him. He looks at me, a strange expression on his face.

"Maybe... I should go." He removes the napkin from his knee and moves to stand, but I grab his hand and tug him back into his seat. *The whole night is turning out wrong and I have to turn it around! Please words, don't fail me now! If anyone can say what they want, no matter how inappropriate, and get away with it… it's an aspie. Do it, Dani!*

"I don't see what the big deal is!" I shout, making sure the words make it from my brain, out into the world. Everyone around the table freezes again. *Good, I've got their attention.* "I love Kevin… and he loves me! Michelle was *'sleeping'* with people when she was in high school!" I emphasise the word sleeping for their little NT minds before going on, "I've been out of school for years now!" I look around the table for someone to challenge me.

"Your sister was not bringing boys home while she was in school." Mum hisses.

"No, but she was staying out at parties and stuff. She had condoms in her bedside drawer and that boy, Scott, used to be allowed to stay over when she was nineteen! I'm twenty-three years old! Why is she allowed but not me?"

"You're different. Every situation is different," Mum defends.

"Yeah, I'm different. I'm Autistic, Mum, not brain dead! Yes, I stuff shit up *regularly* and yes, I still have meltdowns at twenty-three, and do I hate that? YES, I do! But I can't just live with you and Dad forever with no one else to share my time with. Don't you want me to be happy, Mum?" I droop back into my chair, the heat from my previous fire now a flameless smoulder.

"Yes, Dani. But…" Mum's voice breaks. She pauses before continuing, "We're worried you will get hurt. Your close call was only a few months ago." She looks at the others around the table. If she wants backup from them, she doesn't get it. Everyone sits mute, looking at each other. If I wasn't so annoyed right now, the moment would be quite ironic. Humorous even. I'm usually the only one lacking words.

"Shouldn't that be for me to decide? Since it was *my* close call and it's *my* life." I question.

"Dani… you can't even get another job." Mum disputes, cutting a fresh wound on my soul. Only Kevin knows about the resume I've sent to the animal shelter and that I've heard nothing back yet. The more time that passes, the less hope I cling to that they will call. Everyone interjects, challenging Mum's words simultaneously.

"Oh, that's a bit har—"

"That was a low sho—"

"Now wait just a damn minute!" Dad is on his feet, cutting off the others to be heard. "That's not fair at all! We told her to quit the store and take some time off because of what happened. I still stand behind that decision and I think it's incredibly unfair for you to imply that she isn't *capable* of getting another job. Now, I'll admit that I was concerned about Dani's safety when she started seeing Kevin here," he waves a hand at his subject. "But I've seen nothing to warrant further concern. In fact, quite the opposite! Kevin's been a gentleman with us all the way and Dani has been the happiest I've seen her in... I don't even know how long! I think Dani has made several fair points tonight and I think we should do her the courtesy of accepting her decisions." Turning to Kevin, Dad finally sits back down and lowers his voice.

"Don't get me wrong... if I ever find out that you intentionally hurt my baby, there'll be hell to pay. And I'd hope you would spend *some* nights apart, at least until we know you a bit better. But in fairness, we can't get to know you if you aren't welcome here, so from now on..." Dad throws Mum a serious look across the table, "you *are* welcome in our home and we'd hope you will spend some time here so that can happen." Kevin's eyes are glued to my dad's. I scan the table to find Michelle's eyes on me, a wide smile on her face. I smile back at her in automatic response. Dad's blessing is a big step forward. I'm so happy.

"Great! So, he can stay over tonight?" I ask. Looking between my parents' faces.

"No, Dani… She doesn't mean that, sir." Kevin says to my dad hurriedly, waving a hand aimlessly. I look at him in confusion.

"Yes, I do. What do you mean, *I don't mean that?*"

Michelle bursts into laughter, and Luke appears to simultaneously choke on something, coughing quietly to himself. I look around at everyone.

"Babe, I love you. Please stop talking!" Kevin whispers to me. Bringing another round of laughter from Michelle. Luke joins her this time. Even Mum wears a small smile.

Between the 'movie freeze frames' and the laughter of the past fifteen minutes, everyone's remaining dinner has gone cold. Michelle relieves herself to the bathroom, and this signals the end of dinner. Mum and I stack plates, returning them to the kitchen.

Kevin is behind me with a pile of dirty glasses when I turn around.

"Oh, thanks." I take them from him.

"You want a hand with dishes?" he asks.

"Nuh, we'll load the dishwasher to-night. You can stay though if you want, while I rinse them." I smile up at him despite still being a little confused about everyone's laughter before outside. I can't shake the feeling that it was at my expense.

Mum fidgets beside us, wiping over the already clean counter tops. *Now* she's *being weird*. Before I have time to dwell on it, Michelle joins us and the space becomes very crowded.

"I'm going to get the dessert ready," Michelle says to no one specific. "Shoo!" She waves Mum off. "There isn't enough room in here for all of us. Go sit down. I hope you're hungry?" She turns to Kevin. "We have enough cheesecake here to feed a small army, and I'm not taking it home." She pulls the large container from the fridge and places it on the bench. "Dani, you able to get me out one of the ramekins? I've got something for you, too."

"Sure." I leave my spot at the sink.

"Here, I'll take over that," Kevin says.

Kevin and I finish loading the dishes when Michelle delicately tips the last piece of cake sideways on the plate and adds sliced strawberries to each. *Why does food always need to be 'garnished?' Why can't it just be good food that tastes nice? I'm pretty sure our bellies don't care what it looks like. Well… mine definitely doesn't, since I don't eat cheesecake, anyway. Horrible texture and taste if you ask me!*

The microwave dings and a chocolate aroma lures me over to it. Michelle rams her hand against the door of it, keeping it closed and startling me.

"Nope, it's a surprise. Those are done. One for everyone. Kevin, can you please help her carry them out? Sit down. I'll be out in a minute with yours."

All I can do is roll my eyes at her. she's so dramatic. But in a small corner of my heart, I'm a little surprised and excited that she's even remembered I don't like cheesecake. The fact that she's making me something special is nice of her. I do as I'm told, Kevin right behind me.

We place everyone's plates in front of them, including the extra one at Michelle's vacant seat. Ooh's and aah's move around the table like a Mexican wave as we take our seats.

"Where's Michelle?" Mum asks.

"Putting mine together. Apparently, it's a surprise."

I'm on the last word when Michelle wanders out with a plate that harbours the ramekin she'd asked me for and vanilla ice cream off to the far side of the plate. Once on the table, I can see the ramekin contains a chocolate cake-looking dessert. It smells delicious. Michelle takes her seat across from me, looking pleased.

"What is it?" I ask.

"It's a self-saucing chocolate pudding technically but basically, it's sticky chocolate cake with gooey chocolate fudge in the middle. I think you'll like it, but it'll be hot, so go slow." She smiles again and glances to Mum, probably for back up.

"You don't eat cheesecake?" Kevin asks. I realise this is another one of those times for explanation between his world and mine.

"Um, no. I'm a bit of a texture-phobe." I screw up my face, thinking about the incriminating dessert. "Remember, I told you that there were lots of foods I don't like? Well, usually that's because they're a funky texture to me or if they have a strong taste. I don't generally like strong flavours and I don't do spicy *at all!* I'm a pretty simple girl when it comes to food. If a little kid will eat it, then usually it's perfect for me. None of the fancy stuff. Cheesecake is like gelatinous cream to me."

I continue. "Jelly is another thing that's all wrong to me! So is cream. Unless it's in cooking—like a creamy pasta sauce—I don't eat cream. Blugh!" Kevin's fork rests idly in his hand. He is staring at me. "What?" I ask. He blinks and drops his eyes to his plate.

"Nothing, I just… I thought everyone liked cheesecake. Everyone I've ever known does." He looks back to me and races on… "Sorry, that came out wrong. That's cool… just surprising." He takes my hand and rubs the back of it with his thumb. His firm touch is heavenly after going through most of this night without it.

35

Kevin

Chucking my keys on the side table by the door, I hear the shower running and Mick's off-key rendition of 'Working Class Man'. It's nice having the place to myself, but it's also great having someone else to break up the silence.

I knock on the bathroom door. "Hey bud, I'm home... so keep your towel on, yeah?" I chuckle. If I know Mick, he'll come out starker's just to prove he doesn't care. *Don't I know it!* We've lived together so long now that I don't even blink anymore. Knowing I was shy only made him more determined to break me.

In the kitchen, Patch barrels through the dog door once she hears me. *She mustn't have heard the car over the Cold Chisel murder in the bathroom.* "Hey, girl! Come on, let's get you some dinner and fix up this water bowl, hey?" She follows my every move, tail whacking everything she passes.

Mick emerges, fully clothed in old cargo shorts and a tee with several holes exposing tanned skin beneath. His hair sticks up at uneven angles, obviously not brushed after a rough towel dry.

"Hi. How was camping? Catch anything?" I ask.

"Nah. Nothin' worth mentioning. Was fun though, you shoulda come. You remember Old-Man-Johnny that used to live up there? The one with those two snobby little girls who used to rat on us when we were up to no good?"

The faint memory of a fair-haired girl poking her tongue out at me, claiming she was 'dobbing' comes into focus.

"Yeah, vaguely. Little blondies, weren't they? Always in either pigtails or plaits?"

"Yep, that's them. Well, let me tell you… no pigtails there anymore. We went into town for a counter meal and I ran into one of them. Hoo-ey, has she grown up or what! Legs for forever and honestly, I don't know if they were real or fake, but her tits—" Mick makes hand gestures to display two generous mounds against his chest. He isn't a total douche but god, it's a wonder he hasn't had his teeth knocked in more often. "They felt real. Certainly seemed too soft to me for plastic. She made the frosty night easier to bear; I'll tell you that much."

I grit my teeth. I don't want to hear anymore.

"Mick, do me a favour. I've never mentioned it before, but Dani's been through some pretty traumatic shit! So, when you get around to meeting her, don't talk about women like that, okay?! And I hope for all the women out there who cross your path, that you're not as big of an ass-hole as you sound right now." Picking up my glass of water, I leave him standing beside the fridge and head for the lounge.

"Hey, what the hell, Kev?" He saunters out and stands between the TV and me, blocking my view. "I was only mucking around. Well, not about the sleeping together part. We did that, but it was nice. She was nice. What's got you all tangled up? Has something happened to Dani?"

Dani's words come quickly to my mind *Why do NTs call it that? Sex has nothing to do with sleeping.'* Hearing her voice in my head brings a smile to my lips. *How can I miss her already? I just came from there.* "If you're re-ferring to the trauma, it was a few months back… And a few years ago." I hunch for-ward. To think of the animal who claimed her virginity by force. *What I wouldn't give to punch him in the mouth. As for her old boss, well, it's a bloody good thing I don't know what he looks like, now that she's told me he's walking free!*

"Geez, man, I'm sorry. You just find out?" Mick sits on the edge of the coffee ta-ble, looking like he just saw a ghost.

"Nah, she told me pretty early on. Wanted to be up front about it, given her parents' protectiveness when I started hang-ing around. Completely understandable."

"Oh, for sure. So, I got your text about going around there for dinner tonight. How'd that go? Meeting the parents… I'd be shit-ting myself." Mick ploughs his thick fin-gers through his almost-dry hair as if he's stressed just thinking about the idea.

"Yep, I was pretty shitting. Few hairy moments when things got real." The fresh memory of Dani virtually yelling at her par-ents over the dinner table that 'Yes, we'd had sex' hits me hard and I can feel the heat ris-ing up from my neck and into my face. I make a dash for the bathroom to escape Mick and his intuitive eyes.

"Oh wow! You guys did it, didn't ya?"

"Leave it alone, Mick." I warn. *Damn him for knowing me so well!*

"Leaving!" He raises his hands in surender. "But for what it's worth… you're a good guy, Kev. I'm here if ya ever need a sounding board." At the threat of anything resembling emotions, Mick ends the moment, returning to the lounge room.

Without turning around, I hear the couch springs squeak and the television switch over to sports. I grab my gear and head in for a quick shower.

Lying in bed, Dani and I finish the evening with our usual text messages back and forth. Dani is always far less guarded through text messages. Blunter, but open.

We can talk about topics this way, that I know she would clam up over if I asked her in person. Every time we text like this, I learn a few new pieces of her. I love that she's willing to share them with me. Tonight, we finally agree that it is time she met Mick. *I need to go through so much with him before this happens. Maybe I could ask Michelle and Luke to come along too? That'd give her a couple of familiar faces. I'll ask them tomorrow. Shit… I need to get some sleep!*

36

Danielle

I've been staring at the ceiling for what feels like hours, but it's still too dark outside to be anywhere near a reasonable hour of morning. Instead of checking my phone and waking Rebel, I lay quietly, contemplating the day ahead.

Today is the day. Kevin has arranged for a group of us to go on a picnic together so I can meet his cousin Mick. Michelle and Luke are also coming and apparently Mick is bringing a friend along—a boy, I think—and since it's a dog-friendly place, we're also taking Patch. We're all leaving from Kevin and Mick's house right after breakfast.

Just getting ready is almost too much for me. The pretty babydoll style shirt I wanted to wear seems determined to unravel me. I have worn it dozens of times before without issue. Today, however, it has morphed into an itchy hessian sack, stitched together with barbed wire! Of course, it hasn't really, but that is what it feels like against my skin. *God damn, I hate you!* I sit on the edge of my bed, contemplating cancelling.

The top lies in a crumpled mess on the floor. *It's just because you're meeting Mick and you don't know what to expect. Once you get past this, things will settle down. Get dressed. Go with 'every-dayers.' You don't want another 'itchy attack' while you're out.* So, with my usual—and very boring—doubled-up singlets on and knee length denim shorts, I climb into my car and make my way to his house.

Kevin and Mick are loading a large esky into the boot of Mick's X-trail when I pull up out front. Patch waddles around the front yard. Fear dominates me and I am frozen behind the wheel. My white-knuckle grip threatens to split the skin. *Don't be such a fraidy-cat! Just go, be polite, keep it brief. Kevin's right there. Oh shit, he's coming over!* I remind myself to keep breathing.

His smile is instantaneous, and he opens my door for me. *Do I look like a completely crazy person? Probably. Shit!* Kevin is calm and natural. Normal. Nothing at all like myself.

"Hiya. How did you sleep?" He asks, a schoolboy grin on his face. I'm glued. Nothing is working. I try to nod in subtle agreement, but even that feels jerky and forced.

"You okay, babe? You're nervous, I get that. Just remember… you like me and you like Luke. Mick's pretty similar. We all grew up together. The others aren't here yet. Do you want to stay here? Maybe listen to some music for a bit or do you want to come in? I don't mind. Whatever makes you comfortable. Plenty of time later for introductions." He kisses me on the forehead. I close my eyes. His touch is very calming to me. He is like my very own anti-anxiety drug.

"Maybe… music," I say. It's all I can get free.

"No worries. I'm just going to help Mick finish loading, but I'll come back shortly, okay?" he asks. I nod, a tight smile reflecting back at me from the rear-view mirror.

Meditation music comes through the car speakers from my iPod. It's the type of piece I should be listening to, but my nerves have me looking for something faster-paced. I skip through several songs until I find one to match my mind's chaos. It is too early in the morning to crank it up. Even in my sealed car, I know people outside would hear it, so I listen at a respectable volume. Leaning against the headrest with eyes closed, I absorb the music and try to forget everything beyond my car.

A tap on the window interrupts me and I squint through a partially open lid to inspect the noise source; Michelle. Reaching out for the button, I put my window down halfway.

"Watcha doing?" Is all she says. I return to my previous pose, eyes closed.

"Listening to music. Freaking out. Kevin knows I'm here."

"Mmm… Is this really all over Mick? What's got you so worried? You've met plenty of new people. Especially since our wedding. What's so scary about meeting one more?"

"He's younger than the others. He'll think I'm stupid—"

~ Oh, I think he'll KNOW that! ~

Oh god, not now, She-Devil! "He lives with Kevin. What if I freak out or something when I'm here? What if he hears us—" I look around before whispering, "having sex? I'll die. How do people do this?" I smack my forehead with the heal of my palm, eyes still shut. The logistics of carrying out a relationship, too confusing and scary.

"Whoa, hold up a sec. Firstly… one step at a time. We're talking about *meeting* him, not moving in. Secondly… do you honestly think Kev's going to sit back and let Mick make fun of you if you have a *moment*? Of course he isn't! He is going to wrap you in his arms and protect you. He's already proven that at the wedding and the night of the restaurant. And thirdly… Have you thought about the noises *you* might hear coming out of Mick's bedroom? Trust me, he's got enough girls on the go that I'd be way more concerned by what you might see and hear! So what do you say? Should we get this over with and enjoy a great day in the mountains? I already know you're going to love where we're going. It's so pretty up there."

"Okay," I agree. I lock the car up and—because I'm thorough—I click the lock button two more times to make sure it is definitely locked. *Always stalling!* The boys are all leaning against and sitting on the tailgate of Kevin's dual-cab, laughing at each other. Their laughter fades as we approach.

~ *Yep, they were laughing at you sitting in your car like a loser, freakazoid!* ~

She-Devil does her best to sabotage me before I've even started. *She's so mean!*

"Whatever disgusting boy jokes you guys are swapping, put them away. We're here now and we don't want to know. Grubs!" Michelle rolls her eyes when they all share another secret smirk.

Kevin leaves his spot to come stand by my side. Using his body as a shield to separate me from the others, he claims my hands and ducks his gaze to meet mine. "You okay?" His words are soft and his hands feel warm. Calming. With a deep breath, I nod. He releases one of my hands and turns us towards everyone. "Guys... this is my gorgeous Dani. Dani, this is my cousin, Mick, and is his good friend, Joe."

"Hi, Dani. Nice to meet you." Mick raises his hand in a friendly wave from beside the ute. Joe does the same.

"Hello," I say. It's all I can offer in my nervous state. *At least I got that out!*

"Alright. Shall we get moving?" Mick breaks up the awkwardness. "Shell, Luke... Joe and I thought you guys could ride with us, save on fuel. Kev and Dani are gonna have Patchy-Pooh snoring on their back seat so… might be a little cramped there." He chuckles to no one in particular, and everyone agrees. Kevin hooks Patch's harness in and she flops down immediately, clearly familiar with the car routine.

Window to window, Mick and Kevin decide that Mick will lead, and we will follow. It isn't long before we're on the highway and leaving the suburbs behind us. I can breathe again. Kevin smiles from his side of the cab. It is so easy and natural. Pure, amongst an ocean full of fake and misleading attempts. I rest my hand on his thigh. His body heat seeps through his thin board shorts quickly. It feels too intimate. Before I can pull away, he places his over the top. Instantly relaxing me. I smile and enjoy our connection.

"So, where are we going?" I ask.

"Surprise. It's a bit of a drive, but it's worth it, I promise."

It doesn't take long for the scenery to shift. Gum trees and pine forests line both sides of the highway. I am content. The only background noise is the faint snore coming from Patch as she snoozes.

My phone blips with a message…

Michelle: Apparently Mick was under instruction to 'not crowd you' this morning. He was just telling us so thought I'd

let you know in case you thought he was
stand-offish.

Was he standoffish? I didn't notice that.

"Everything okay?" Kevin squeezes my hand affectionately.

"Huh? Oh, yeah. Just Michelle. Did you tell Mick not to crowd me? Apparently, he is saying that. Michelle just wanted to let me know in case I thought he was stand-of-fish."

"I just told him to give you a little space because you were a bit nervous about meeting him. Are you mad?" he looks my way. I have to process what he's asked for a minute before I can reply. "You're mad." He sighs, shaking his head.

"Give me a sec." I say before falling silent again. I sift through my thoughts. "No, I'm not mad. I *do* need space and I am nervous to meet him. So... no, not mad. It's kind of sweet, actually." I meet his gaze. The more time I spend with him, the more I'm learning that his need for eye contact is a re-assurance thing. He seeks it when he thinks I'm hiding from him. Although I often find the action uncomfortable—when I'm stressed—I am content at the moment, so am able to soothe his concerns. *Our role reversal makes for a nice change.*

Weaving our way inland, the land-scape changes again. The heavy vegetation gives way to fenced paddocks with only a few metres of scrub separating them from the tarmac. Huge ghost gums and ironbarks tower up from the road's edge. Their long, twisting limbs reach out over the bitumen with Old Man's Beard and Australian Mistletoe, clinging to its host in an intricate knot of plant life. At ground level, tiny flowers and wild cotton plants grow among the weeds. The change outside brings fresh smells into the cab. The earthy aroma of eucalyptus mingles with the crisp and peppery scent of lantana shrubs.

Patch wakes and sits up in her seat. She shuffles and pants. Kevin turns off the air conditioning and rolls all the windows down. My hair whips in my face as gusts of wind enter the cab from all different directions. Patch lets out a loud bark, making me jump with fright. She goes from one window to the other. Her sudden excitement tells me we must be getting close to our destination. The excitement is infectious, and I too feel jittery. A strange balance between nerves and excitement. I squirm in my seat and start flicking against my denim clad pant leg with a finger. Kevin notices.

"You okay?" He drops his gaze to my fingers, his thoughts obvious.

"Yeah, just restless. Are we nearly there? Patch seems to think so."

"Maybe she can sense it in me. She hasn't been here in a very long time. I doubt she'd remember. I think she reads me better than I do most days."

"That's nice though, don't you think? I swear Rebel does the same. It's like he knows when I need him the most. He'll stay close and yet, when I'm okay, he goes off by himself. Animals are so much more intuitive than humans."

"Definitely. What're you thinking so far? About today, I mean." I haven't realised I am flicking the denim with intensity now as Kevin points it out. Glancing that way again.

"Oh, sorry. Guess I'm a bit nervous. Oh, but I'm excited too!" I try to correct, too late.

"It's okay. Still nervous about Mick or something else worrying you?"

"Um… mostly Mick. I'm not great at surprises though either, so that's probably playing a part too. Knowing what I should expect and what is expected of me helps things. I'm a planner. And a worrier… god, I sound like such a bore, even to me!"

"Dani, you're fascinating. Not in a 'science experiment' kind of way. You're unique. You're so… real. More than any other girl I've ever met. Not all shoes, hair, makeup and money."

"Agh, I hate pretty much *all* of those things. Give me animals, nature and my books any day. And you and Patch, of course." I smile at Kevin before patting Patch, who is still excitedly wearing down the back seat with her to-ing and fro-ing.

Mick's X-trail pulls off and we make the turn behind them. *Is it a driveway? I don't even know.* The bright pink flowers of a bougainvillea vine creep up and over the top of what I have to assume is a ranch-style archway. Though I can't see any of the structure, I know that the ornamental climber needs something to cling to.

Despite its undeniable beauty, I am reminded of poison dart frogs with their aposematic colouring. The bright fuchsia flowers acting as a similar warning to any who dare enter her gates. Long, sharp thorns protruding from her tentacle-like arms backup her threat.

"Where are we? Are we allowed here? It seems... Guarded," I state.

"It's a place we all used to come as kids. Our parents brought us camping here. Sometimes together, sometimes separately." He shrugs. "That vine is full of thorns though, so we need to put the windows up, until we're through... I don't want it flicking in and scratching any of us."

"Yeah, it's a bougainvillea. It's very healthy, by the looks of all those flowers."

"What's it called?"

"It's a Boug- AARRHH!" A big, creepy looking insect crawls in my—still partially open—window, catching me by surprise and throwing me completely off our original conversation. I continue to scream and wriggle, tethered by the seatbelt but without the brain capacity to undo it. Kevin leans across me with very little effort or fear and scoops up the critter against the hood lining. In a seamless motion, he opens my door, chucks the insect a short distance away before closing it again. Still stretched across me, he pulls on the button for my window, closing it the rest of the way. My breathing is heavy and I'm fidgeting madly. He remains across me. Close. Concern and something else I don't recognise etched on his face.

"Breathe, babe. It was just a cricket, but it's okay, he's gone now." Kevin's voice is soft. Comforting. My body is rigid against the seat. I'm having a kind of out-of-body experience, like I can see myself from his angle. *You look ridiculous! Having a breakdown over a defenceless little cricket. Get yourself together! Why is he looking at me like that? He looks weird... cute, but weird.*

"Why're you looking at me like that? You have a strange expression and I don't know what it means?" I drop my gaze. I hate admitting that I'm confused.

When no response comes, I'm forced to peek up at him again. He looks from my eyes to my lips and back again. Add this to his close proximity and something stirs inside me.

He remains unmoving and saying nothing. Flutters spark in my gut. I'm not sure what's happening, but I'm curious to find out. I mimic his eye movements, letting them drop to his lips before searching his beautiful eyes again. A smile tips up one side of his mouth. *He is so beautiful.* Tentatively, I lean forward experimenting, with this new non-verbal language I think we're sharing. I kiss him. He returns it with vigour, confirming my understanding of his body language. Fireworks go crazy inside my head. *I did it! I finally got it right!*

The celebration within is grand and the energy it brings is too much for sitting still. My body and brain need an outlet for it all. A chuckle sneaks out before I run my fingers up through his hair and tug gently. My necessity for movement and sensation has me craving more of him. More touch, more pressure. I hold him firm when he starts to pull back from me, my greed not nearly satisfied. He tries again and this time, the sound of a car horn penetrates my oasis.

"I think we're being summoned." Only inches from my face, Kevin winks at me. His lack of embarrassment or apprehension over the intrusion buoys my own mood, and I giggle. He watches me from his close vantage point, grinning like the Cheshire Cat.

"How embarrassing! I didn't realise they were waiting for us." I whisper.

"Well, they probably heard your scream and stayed close by, just in case we needed help. You were pretty loud." He has his cheeky smile back. The one that brings out his dimple that I love so much.

"I know. I don't usually mind bugs, but all bets are off when they surprise the shit outta me!"

Kevin bursts into laughter, startling me. He moves back across to his own seat and I watch his retreat with curiosity. *What's so funny about that?* I wonder to myself.

"I've never heard you swear before," he says. I try to recall if I have but can't remember. "Come on, the others have gone. Let's catch up before Patch pees in my car."

On the other side of the cattle grid and thorny vines, we open the windows again. The remnants of an old dirt track winds down and around a small valley. I can make out the road, but it hasn't been used in a while and has tall grass growing up the middle of the tread marks.

At the bottom of the valley, we reach a creek crossing that has shallow water running over it. Patch stands up on the armrest for a better look, and whimpers and pants with excitement. I too am drawn to the scenery.

The soft sound of water trickling down the far side of the crossing into the next section is heavenly. Cicadas pick up a high-pitched tune as we disturb the quiet with our sloshing of tyres through the water.

It is the type of place I let my imagination wander to, in search of calm. Seeing it in real life... I am the bearer of magic. It is wonderful. Kevin takes my hand, lacing his fingers through mine.

The track follows the creek's edge. The creek itself shifts from a fine trickle in some parts with barely enough force to keep it flowing into large pools of water that have rope swings hanging from side-lining trees.

Next to one such pool—equipped with its own thick rope and log swing—I see the X-trail parked under a magnificent fig tree. The others are getting out. Kevin pulls up alongside them with a car's length between the two vehicles. Picnic tables are dotted all over the vastness.

The fig tree has an enormous girth. Large roots protrude from the ground beneath in a stubborn effort to keep the monster from toppling over. Its dense foliage offers us protection against the hot mid-morning sun.

Kevin opens the rear door for Patch, who bounds out and gives an all-over shake before charging off to explore.

From the X-trail comes a football and it doesn't take long for the boys to give up unloading in favour of footy.

"Go, Luke!" Michelle cheers as he sets the ball down across the invisible line of success. She goes to join in their game.

Patch runs amongst them, barking with excitement as the players around her dart and weave away from each other. I chuckle at her crazy antics. From the ute, I pull out a large rubber-backed picnic rug.

Next to our designated picnic table, I spread out the rug and spot a random tap coming up out of the ground. Knowing that Kevin keeps an old stainless steel dog bowl in the ute, I go grab it. *She'll need a drink after all that running around.*

As if they've heard my thoughts, the game ends. Everyone is laughing and puffing. They're walking back while Patch trots ahead, her tongue hanging out the side of her mouth.

"How does it look?" I ask him. "Here, Patch. This is for you, sweetheart." She is quick to find the cool water.

"Looks great!" He smiles broadly. "Thank you. You didn't have to do it all, though. We were coming back." He leans in—for a kiss, I think—I pull back, repelled by the sweat glistening on his top lip and brow.

"What's wrong?" Kevin goes from smiling to frowning in a second. His sudden shift in moods puzzles me. *What's wrong with ME?... What's wrong with HIM?*

"Nothing's wrong with me. Why are you frowning at me?" I ask.

"You pulled away. Why? If nothing's wrong..." His frown deepens. A thick crease between his eyes. *Is he mad at me? What's happening here?*

"You're all sweaty. Surely you know this, can't you feel it? It's running down your forehead." I state the obvious. Well, obvious to me, at least.

A few snickers from those around us raise the hairs on the back of my neck. *Am I the only person that sees this? Why are they laughing?* I clench my fists into two tight balls by my sides. It takes all my concentration to keep from stamping my foot. I turn sharply, walking away without a word.

"Dani, wait up!" Kevin calls after me. I hear Michelle tell him to 'let her go' I think, before I can't hear them anymore.

37

Kevin

Watching Dani storm off, my first reaction is to chase after her and find out what's going on.

"Let her go," Michelle says, staring off towards her sister's back. Her words don't feel right to me. *She was clearly distressed!* Michelle calculates my next move and counteracts it, stepping in front of me, blocking my view of my—now disappearing—girlfriend's back.

"She will come back. You going after her now isn't going to help. She's so mad that I'd guess she can't voice her issues, anyway. Just leave her." Michelle tries to pat me on the shoulder. More so, to turn me back towards the group, away from where I still want to run after Dani.

Mick, Joe and Luke jump into some stupid footy conversation, feigning disinterest in everything that's just unfolded.

Someone gets the esky out, and soft drinks are passed around. I'm here in body only. My mind races back and forth, trying to understand the exact moment I stuffed it. A swig from the can in my hand tells me I've got orange. *I hate orange.* Thirsty from the game but too preoccupied with my thoughts, I take another slug of the vile fizzy drink. *Bugger this. I gotta talk to her.*

38

Danielle

People are so frustrating! If we were here by our-selves, none of this would've happened! Not only be-cause we wouldn't be playing football, but because his silly friends wouldn't have been here to laugh at me. And the stupid part is… it wasn't even funny! Nothing about sweat is funny! I wrinkle my nose in disgust.

Away from the group, I find a picnic table and listen to the noises of nature. A cicada plays its high-pitched song. Adding to the tune is the sound of leaves rustling in the breeze. The wind stirs my hair and blows softly against my face.

The creek here is narrow, no more than a metre across. Water trickles over river rocks and into the next section, to carry on its mysterious journey. Its gentle melody re-leases the tension in me and I travel back down the escalator from rage to contentment.

Calmer now, I'm absorbed by the scenery surrounding me. Plants, both native and introduced, have taken up residence here, with no apparent order to their placement. Most likely spread by birds. The constant flow of the creek providing them with the nutrients they need to thrive. *If only human life were so simple.* I sigh.

Cabbage moths and fairy wrens dart through the long grass, silencing cicadas and crickets in their hiding spots. I sit still and watch the proceedings quietly.

Remaining quiet, the place comes to life. Following the delicate trill of a wren, I spot the brightly coloured Red-Backed Fairy Wren. The black plumage against his scarlet red collar, easy to see among the thin wisps of grass. His females echo his call. Their dusty brown appearance making them harder to spot.

The creatures disappear into the shadows and denser shrubs. Their pretty songs fall silent. Something has scared them. I catch the sight of a person in my peripheral vision and twist to get a better look. It's Kevin. He's wearing a different shirt, but I can tell that it's him. His steps slow when our eyes meet.

"Can I sit?" He asks. I nod in tentative agreement.

We sit side by side for the longest time saying nothing, just staring out at the grass, bending with the breeze.

"Dani—"

I cut him off with a finger over his lips. I move the finger to my lips before slowly pointing it towards the shrubbery where I last saw the birds flying. Kevin scans the area beyond my fingertip, obviously not seeing yet. Another twenty seconds pass before the wary little male flutters again. This time, further out, making his way towards the creek. I can tell the instant Kevin spies him, because his eyes dart quickly with the wren's erratic flight plan. Together, we watch him return to the safety of his shrub before I turn to Kevin.

"Isn't he pretty?" I whisper.

"Sure is. Cute little guy too," he replies. "Dani, can we please talk about what happened back there? One minute we were laughing, the next minute you ran off."

"I wasn't laughing. Everyone else was!" I state firmly, picking at some loose paint flakes on the table.

"Okay… is that what the problem was? Because the way I remember it… I tried to kiss you. You pulled away. Then all hell broke loose and you left. I want to understand, but you've got to help me. I've got no idea." He twists to face me, straddling the bench seat.

"You were all sweaty. You all came back from your game wet and sweaty! Why would I want a kiss when you're sweating?" *Why do I need to explain this? Isn't it obvious?*

"Right, so… making a mental note that my girl doesn't like *sweaty Kevin*." His lip twists up in a devilish schoolboy grin. It is the cutest smile I've seen on him yet. He is trying to soften me, I think, but I'm not giving in so quickly today.

"Does anyone?" I throw him the rhetorical question, shuddering at the thought.

"Well… it might surprise you to learn that some women actually *do* like their men a little… messed up and steamy."

"Eeeew! Which women? That's disgusting!" I shake my head back and forth, trying to ignore the image now vivid in my mind. Kevin arches backward with a roar of laughter. His cheeks are pink. I think he is remembering another time with another girl.

"Was it 'Angry Lady' at the restaurant?" I blurt out, needing to know.

Kevin's laughter dies off and his eyes return to mine, a faint smile still present on his pink face. He shakes his head, no, but he must see I don't believe him. He raises his hands in surrender and chuckles.

"Honest! I haven't personally come across any that I can think of. But, ah… well… I'm led to believe that a certain sister of yours likes a messed up Lukey every now and then. Or so I've heard." His cheeks blaze brighter.

"I shouldn't be surprised. That's so gross. Why are you blushing? Your cheeks are bright red." I reach out to touch one with the back of my fingers. It is hot, like I expect. "I like it when you blush. It's something your body does without your consent or control and yet, visible to everyone. That's how it is for me when I meltdown. It makes me feel like we are the same, if only in this one small way." My fingers slide away.

"We're the same in so many ways. I know you feel lost sometimes and like you're the only one 'not getting the joke,' but I have been stumbling through my life since the day I lost my best friend! Thing is… I didn't even realise it until I met you. Then everything started making sense." I want to tell him it isn't the same, but I keep quiet instead.

"And now I find out that Mick and Luke figured all this out years ago, but they never said anything because they thought I needed more time. You're so much more in tune with who you are and what you like or need. You kinda scare me a bit." He dips his head in the familiar way, chasing eye contact. I pick at a non-existent piece of fluff on my shorts for something to do. He continues, "but you know what scares me most?"

I shake my head no.

"That one day you'll figure out how boring I am and leave me. I have no clue what I'll do when that day comes."

"You think you're boring? You have friends. The only friends I have are fictional or have four legs!" I frown. Kevin chuckles at my words.

"I guess that's that, then. We'll have to stay together forever, so we always have each other." Kevin pauses thoughtfully. "So... am I allowed to kiss you now that I'm all cooled down and dry again, or do I need to wait until after we get home and I've had a proper shower? I *did* get a partial wash when the guys thought it'd be funny to push me into the freezing cold creek while I was busy worrying about you, if that counts?"

"I guess so. Just so we're clear… if they ever do that to me, I will be *extremely* unimpressed! I don't find that kind of thing funny, *especially* if it's happening to me!"

"Duly noted," he says, leaning in. His lips are so soft and warm. The tip of his hot tongue dances across my lip, inviting me to deepen the kiss. I melt against him. His strong arms encircle me. The kiss grows awkward as we try for physical closeness but are hindered by bumping knees.

With seemingly little effort, Kevin hoists me up. Shifting my legs to wrap around him, I'm higher now that I'm straddling his legs but not by enough to break our kiss. Our positioning means I have his hard flesh pressed against my most intimate parts. A spark ignites in the pit of my stomach.

As always, it's Kevin who breaks contact first. I am wired now. Ready to go. His withdrawal leaves me exasperated. "Please don't stop. I love the feel of you against me." I demand another wet kiss before he frees his lips again.

"Babe, we're in the middle of the day area. You know what you were saying about my blushing giving me away? Well, that's not the only thing that *everyone* can see... you know? Anyone could drive—or worse— walk past and see us." He looks around as if to emphasise his point.

"Okay... but when?" I ask impatiently.

"You can stay at my place tonight if you want?"

"Really?"

"Yeah, 'course. If your parents are fine with it."

"They will be. Oh, do you need to ask Mick, though?" I chew on my lip nervously as thoughts of Kevin's cousin return.

"Shit, no! I'll tell him we're doing it and he'll go to the pub." My mouth falls wide with embarrassment and Kevin laughs. "Relax! It was a joke. I'm not going to tell him that. God, you should've seen your face." He chuckles again.

"Thank god, I'd die!"

"He'll probably guess, but that's only because he's always thinking about sex. Speaking of them though... do you think we should go back and have some lunch and see what they're all up to? I'm starved, but I couldn't eat knowing you were upset with me."

"Do we have to? I'm much happier here. Just us two and the peace and quiet."

"Don't forget mister 'scarlet-letter' over there." Kevin points towards the shrub. It's my turn to laugh. The name he's given the little wren seems quite fitting with his brightly coloured feathers. After another long kiss, we rise from the bench and head back towards the others.

As our group comes into sight, I spot Patch's tail twitching above the knee high grass as she wanders around searching for something. She sees us in the same moment and barrels across the field towards us. Someone laying on the rug lifts a head to see after her but drops it again when they realise we are the reason. At our feet, Patch thrashes against us with her tail.

"I know, I found her," Kevin says affectionately.

Remnants of lunch are scattered along the tabletop. Crumbs on the ground are being devoured by small armies of ants.

"So glad you waited for us," Kevin says flatly to no one in particular.

"We were hungry! You guys were gone a while. Michelle said to start," Mick replies. Winning himself a scowl from Kevin, Mick retreats. "Who's up for a swim?

You can meet us over there once you're done."

"Yep, sounds good," someone says.

"Great idea," another agrees.

Mick and Joe race each other, stripping off their T-shirts as they run. Luke and Michelle are on their tail, shoulder to shoulder. Mick is the first one to enter. He jumps, knees to chest. Water erupts, splashing the others. Michelle squeals in protest as the icy droplets hit her.

Encouraged by her discomfort, Joe does the same. Watching them, I feel both jealous of their camaraderie yet disinclined to join them.

"We can swim up the other end if you like? When we're done," Kevin says, as if reading my mind.

"Oh, thanks, but I'm not swimming. I don't like it when I can't see the bottom," I reply, a little sheepishly. *Or when my scar is still an angry pink line. The doctor better be right about it fading!*

"Oh really? I was hoping we would have some fun together."

"Hm, thanks, but I might just take the rug and lay down at the edge. That's as close as I'd like to get."

"Well, if we take it up where I was thinking, it's lovely and quiet. Not sure if there'd be anymore wrens, but maybe," he offers.

"Sounds perfect."

We scoff down our bread rolls. Kevin scoops up the rug and we make our way around a large outcropping of dense vegetation and trees. Once on the far side, we are sealed off from the others visually. Their laughter, reduced to a distant muffle.

Together, we spread the rug out over the semi-long grass and stamp it down with our feet.

"Aren't *you* swimming?" I ask when Kevin lies down beside me, stretching out.

"Trying to get rid of me?" He smiles.

"No, it's not that. Just thought... I was going to get a perve session." I chuckle under my breath.

"Oh, it's like that, is it?" He grins. "Why should you get to perve if I don't?"

"You don't want to perve on me," I say, full of doubt and embarrassment. Flashes of my fluoro-tube legs and 'never-seen-sun' belly come to mind, cementing my decision. *No one wants to see that!*

"The hell I don't! Why wouldn't I want to? You're gorgeous." He pivots forward, leaning closer to kiss me. It's gentle and turns my insides to mush. *I can see how some girls could lose their heads over a guy.* When I open my eyes, he's still there. His breath warms my cheek as he exhales. His beautiful eyes penetrate right through to the very depths of my being. *I will never get tired of this...*

"What are you doing?" I blurt out when he shuffles.

"Taking my shirt off. Isn't that what you wanted?" *Yes. But now I'm shy and I don't know what to do or where to look!* I roll to my back, searching the clouds in a fluster. "Would you rather I left it on?"

"Yes. No." I throw my arm over my eyes to hide. I feel the heat in my cheeks, but I don't know if it is just from the dappled sunlight and lack of breeze making me hot. *Please don't let him see.*

"Dani?" he asks. I remain in hiding. He comes closer, I hear him move on the rug.

"Babe?" he whispers in my ear and does something strange to it. *Is he eating my earlobe?* Goosebumps travel along my skin. The tingling hairs rise along my arm as I keep it rammed across my eyes. I concentrate on breathing.

Kevin nuzzles and plucks kisses along my neckline, nudging at my stubbornly locked arm. Lying across me, his weight feels so inviting. I feel his fingertips against my stomach as the stretchy fabric of my t-shirts rides up, exposing my bare skin. Self-consciously, I tug the shirts back in to place, which ends up trapping his hand awkwardly inside. *SHIT!*

"What're you thinking right now?" he asks.

"Um… breathing," I say truthfully.

"You look worried. Why?"

I am! "Um… I don't want to say." *What was he doing to my ear again? Maybe if I could do it back, he'll forget.* I duck into the crevice of his neck.

Kissing his ear feels really weird, so I opt for his neck instead. He leans away, but since we're tangled together now, the balance shifts and I'm pulled over on top of him. Steading us both, Kevin's hands land on my hips. He keeps them there. I panic he will feel or see the raised scar that sits dangerously close beneath his hand. *It is ugly. I don't want him to see it.* My anxiety prickles and the two most beautiful hands in the world suddenly become two hot irons, burning my skin.

Should I sit up? Slide off? Agh! My shirt rides too high, and that's now really annoying me as well!

I am busy deciding when he lifts me to sit squarely on top of him. Straddling his body free's my hands, and I use the opportunity to tug the singlets back down quickly before he can see.

"Please don't hide from me. If I'm making you uncomfortable, I need to know that you can tell me. That you will. It's important."

Is this that whole protective thing again? Just tell him or he'll never believe you. "It's got nothing to do with that! Well, it does, in a technical sense, I guess. But not from my perspective, it doesn't." I sigh. "It's a lot brighter out here than it was in your bedroom last weekend."

"And?" He looks around at the trees for answers, it seems.

"And… I have an ugly purple scar across my hip that hasn't faded yet! But… the doc promises me that it should mostly fade to nothing." I tack on the end, dropping my gaze to pick at fibres of the rug.

"Is that what this's about? Your scar?" Kevin surprises me, sitting up effortlessly, despite me straddling him. His eyes are only fractionally lower than my own. He looks purposefully at me. "Babe, is that what this is about?" he repeats slowly. I nod, yes. It's all I can do. My tongue, suddenly glued to the roof of my mouth.

"Don't *ever* be ashamed of your scars. This is something I know. For so long after the car crash, I hated my scars. They were reminders of my best friend who died... who died because of me, yet I lived. I wouldn't look at myself when I showered, and I covered up the mirror in my room, so I never had to see them. You know?" he asks.

I lace my fingers through his, wishing I could erase his pain. *He's too beautiful to have suffered this.* I stay quiet. "Our scars are not our fault. We didn't choose them. They're our body's reminder of how hard we've fought and how far we've come. You're strong, Dani. That scar tells the world that. It should tell *you* that, too."

I lunge at him, bumping foreheads but unperturbed. Clutching his face to my own with a fierce need, I skip straight past the delicate kissing and race ahead to a deeper, wetter connection. We crash down on the rug together, but it doesn't slow my progress. Kevin makes a noise; half moan, half mutter. He's probably trying to speak. I don't care right now, I'm too in love with his beautiful soul. I need connection. Physical connection. *How did I come to be with this incredible human? He is so perfect and knows how to reach me. Like no one ever has before. He is like an angel. My very own earth angel. How did I get so lucky? Dear god, don't let me ever mess this up!*

I scurry backwards, kissing first one nipple, then its twin. Making my way lower, I place a ring of kisses around his belly button. My inexperienced hands fumble with his board shorts strings.

"Babe, whoa. What're you—" he never finishes his sentence. I finally reach my target and thrive on the sounds of his pleasure. Listening carefully to his unintelligible groans, I learn what he likes and how fast. My body awakens, tingling all over. Kevin's breathing speeds up. I take his cue and do the same, speeding up my pace. He taps my shoulder, startling me out of my euphoria.

"What's wrong?" I look to him, confused. His head is arched backwards so I can't see his face. He groans and grabs my hand. Placing it over his hard length, he guides me a time or two. Understanding dawns, and I take control once again. I'm rewarded with the unguarded view of his climax. *He is so beautiful.*

Feeling accomplished and inwardly thrilled by my newfound power. I lay down beside him, watching him return from bliss. His head flops sideways, facing me. He smiles crookedly.

"Hi," I say.

"Hi, yourself. Well, that was… unexpected."

"I know! For me too."

"Mmm, remind me to talk about our scars more often! Least, I think that's where we got… Hey, wow… look at that!" Kevin points to something behind me. I twist to see.

"Oh wow! I've never seen that species before. It's so big! And colourful!" On a plant I don't recognise, about two metres away, is an enormous butterfly. Fluttering and floating around. Its wings are a blue-green colour blended with areas of yellow and outlined in black. "I wonder what type of butterfly he is?"

"I'm not sure. Something for us to look up when we get home."

We sit a minute longer, silent. Watching it cruise through the secluded area in a dip and climb pattern of flight. Finally, he disappears.

"Incredible!" says Kevin.

"I'll say! I can't wait to research him!"

With the insect gone and no risk of scaring the creature, Kevin pulls his pants up and cleans himself up with his beach towel.

"I think we should start making tracks if we're to beat some of the traffic. Let's go round up the others." Kevin leaps up, offering an outstretched hand to pull me up. Together, we pack up the rug and leave our secret hideaway. *I'm glad the trees can't talk.*

39

———

Danielle

Everything's organised. We stopped in to collect some clothes and toiletries for me to stay over. Mum wasn't home—perfect timing—so I just told Dad what was happening and that I wouldn't need dinner. Michelle advised me to *tell* them, not ask. Dad made it easy and only asked if I had my phone and charger for safety. Of course I did, so that was painless.

"You alright? Seem quiet?" Kevin says, breaking as we come to an amber traffic light.

"Am I? I feel okay. Think it's just been a big day. Looking forward to a shower and a cup o—" *Oh no! I didn't bring my teacup! I can't have milk without my teacup! I can't sleep without my milk!*

"Dani? What's wrong?"

"My teacup!" My brain is on a loop. No other words form to explain what I'm talking about, I'm stuck on repeat, I can't remember if I've told him about my bedtime rituals before or not. The cab is silent as we drive away from the lights.

"Should I go back?" he looks over to me. "I'll turn around."

"No. It'll be fine… It'll be fine. I can drink it out of a glass. Yeah, I can do that for one night. Can't I?" I look to Kevin for encouragement, trying to convince myself. *I don't want to be a pain. Just drink it out of a glass. It's only one night.* "Yeah, I can." I say, but I'm not sure if it's for his benefit or my own.

"You sure? I can go back. If that's easier or if you want it."

"No, I'm sure. It'll be fine." *Please let it be fine!*

Arriving at his house, Patch wakes in the backseat. Mick's four-wheel-drive is parked beside Kevin's work van, but there's no sign of anyone. The others must have left already. The esky has been cleaned out and is leaning up against the garage to dry. That's when the front screen door opens.

"You guys need a hand?" Mick calls.

"Nah, we got it; thanks, bud. Come on, girl. Outcha' get," Kevin taps his thigh.

Here again. Just the two boys and me. I'm back to weird again. *Just breathe.* I remind myself, toying with the strap on my backpack.

Sport plays on the television. Condensation runs down the outside of a half-filled glass sitting on the coffee table. The house smells of male cologne, but it isn't Kevin's. It is overpowering and tickles my nose. Mick has obviously showered already.

"I'm gonna wash my stuff from today. If you guys wanna chuck yours in too, I'll turn it on shortly." Mick says to Kevin. "Shell said to give her a call if you need her or wanna talk," he says to me.

"Thanks."

"Too easy, bud. Dani's staying the night, so we might jump in the shower before we start up the washing machine." Kevin turns to me. "How do you want to do this? You want to shower together or separate? You can go first if you want?"

Shower together? Do people shower together? I guess so. Do I want to share the hot water though? An image of Kevin's naked body covered in suds and water turns my legs to custard. *I want to wash him! Oh, but Mick… that's a bit weird, he'd know we're both naked in there…* "I might go first, if that's okay?" I ask. The hot water will be good after a day of roller-coaster emotions, anyway.

"Okay. I'll get you a towel. You can put your stuff in my room if you want or take it into the bathroom with you, whatever suits."

I put my bag on his bed, taking out my PJs. *Wait… am I supposed to wear my PJs in front of Mick? But what else would I wear? Michelle would know. I need to call her. Damn it.* Kevin appears in the doorway, towel and washer in hand.

"Actually, do you mind going first? I need to give Michelle a quick call," I say.

"Oh, sure. Well, I'll get in then. If you change your mind about joining me, come right in. The lock doesn't work and I don't mind." He winks at me, his cheeky smile in place. As tempting as it sounds, Mick sitting right there in the lounge room is enough to keep my feet rooted to the floor. Water hisses through the old pipes. I grab my phone and head outside.

"I'm just going out the back for a minute. I need to call Michelle," I say to Mick, trying to be polite.

"Too easy," he replies, looking over the back of the couch.

Outside, I get straight on the phone.

"Hi," Michelle answers.

"Hi. I'm… um, having a problem. We're about to have showers and… well, is it a bit weird to be in my PJs between now and bedtime? With Mick here too, I mean?"

"Oh, I thought we were going somewhere else with this. Um, I don't think it matters. Wear whatever makes you feel most comfortable. If you want to wear PJs, then just put your bra on underneath them until you go to bed is what I'd do or put some clean clothes on and just change into your jammies when you go to bed"

"But… I only bought clothes to put on for tomorrow and my PJs?" I ask, stressed.

"Yeah, you can just wear your clothes for tomorrow, tonight. You're only going to be in them for a few hours and you're fresh clean outta the shower, so they're perfectly acceptable to wear again in the morning. Just don't spill your dinner on them. You'll be fine." I hear Michelle laugh softly at the other end. "It's totally acceptable to wear your jammies if you prefer, though. It really is your choice. Mick's not going to care, he's had girlfriends before… if you can call them that, anyway."

"Okay. Well, I better go. Is it normal for people to shower together?" I ask last minute.

"Um, yeah... it can be. Depends on the couple. But you don't have to! You never do anything that doesn't feel right. Okay? Anyone who tells you 'you should,' is no good. So only do what you're comfortable with!"

"Yes, I will. Well, I better go. Hey, Michelle... Thanks."

"Any time! Now, go have fun."

Hanging up, I tap my thigh. "Coming inside Patchy?" She comes without any further prompting.

Kevin is just opening the bathroom door. His hair looks brushed, but I can't tell for sure. A pale blue towel sits low on his hips, tied snuggly. The contrast of it against his tanned skin is striking and incredibly inviting. I struggle to pull my eyes away. This afternoon replays in my mind. My heart thumps inside my chest. *Shower. PJs... get your PJs!* I make my feet move. He is right behind me when I enter his bedroom. I tuck my clean underwear inside my PJs to hide them and escape past him without looking at him or his half naked body again.

"Dani?" I pause and turn back to him. "You forgot your towel."

"Oh." I try to chuckle, but it just sounds like I'm choking.

"Hey, babe... Just breathe," he says. He leans in, kisses my forehead gently, and then closes his bedroom door between us. *Right, shower.*

After stressing about the bathroom door that doesn't lock in a house of boys for a solid five minutes... I convince myself that Kevin wouldn't let Mick come in and Kevin's already seen me nude, anyway. I get in, my eyes remain glued to the bathroom door. The water is heavenly. It soothes my nerves. Scenarios of the evening ahead roll through my head like cars on the highway. I try to plan for everything that might come up so that I'm well-rehearsed and not taken by surprise. *You just need to get through the next few hours. Once it's just you and Kevin, in bed, you'll feel comfortable and happy again. It's just sitting on the couch between now and then.* Mick on one side, Kevin on the other. *That's going to be weird.*

Clean, dry and dressed in PJs with bra and undies on, there is nothing left to do in here. I hang my towel over the shower screen and turn out the light, leaving the steamy bathroom behind. The house is quiet. The only thing to be heard is the TV. When I enter the lounge room, though, it's empty. Kevin comes around the corner from the kitchen at the same moment.

"Feel better?" he asks.

"Yes, much. Thank you. Where's Mick?"

"Oh, he got a better offer. Something about beer and pizza at Joe's place. I think he's giving us privacy." Kevin shrugs.

"I see. So…" the suggestion of privacy is very welcome.

"So… are you hungry? You wanna get something to eat? Or… we could…" he takes a single step towards me from across the other side of the room.

"Yeah, I'm thinking… we could, too" I walk towards him slowly. When I get there, Kevin puts his arms to my shoulders, halting my progress.

"Babe, I'm sorry I keep harping on this but… I just need to say something first. I know we're moving fast. We suddenly do-ing this a lot. Please assure me that you know you don't have to. I *need* you to under-stand this! It's okay to not want to some-times. I'm afraid that you're doing it for me. To please me. I only want to do it, if you do too. You're so damn good at it that I'm having trouble being the responsible one, but it isn't expected... just because you're staying the night or for any other reason at all."

Don't say it. You're not supposed to say that. Don't say it! "Yes, we do!" *He's frowning... told you not to say it!* "I've been jittery all afternoon. Since we were together at the creek. I want to be close to you. I *need* to. To feel your skin., Run my hands over your gorgeous arms and chest. I want to touch you, and I *really* want you to touch me, too. So, yes, we *do* have to. And if it's alright with you, I'd like to soon... now even."

~ You're such an idiot! Do you have any idea how creepy you sound? He's gonna think you're a stalker. ~

In a hurry to silence the horrible witch in my head, I go up on tiptoes, take his face in my hands, and kiss him. Softly at first— proving to She-Devil that I'm not aggressive—then letting both our desires build naturally and steadily together.

40

Danielle

Waking up next to Kevin isn't nearly as strange as I'd thought it would be. Returning to consciousness after a night of sensual bliss, I feel him wrapped around me like a koala hugs a tree. His body is burning, pressed against mine. *Is that his hand on my boob? Inside my top?* I lay stoically still. Tense. I'm not even sure I'm breathing. My muscles tire quickly. *I need to roll over.*

His arm is a dead weight in his sleepy state. I wriggle gently so as not to disturb him, but the instant I start, he stirs. His eyes flutter open, but his brain is still catching up. I watch him with fascination. He blinks and scans the room before his gaze lands on me. His boyish smile turns up one side of his face, the other hidden against his pillow.

His chest is bare and on display with the sheet hung low across his hips. Several scars of different shapes and sizes are visible on his torso, the largest of which is a thick line running along his hip bone. I reach out to touch him, tracing it and the others with my fingertip. I study them as my finger glides from one to the next. Making me jump, he swats my hand away and rubs his chest roughly. I search his face, confused. He's smiling. *Not angry? Why did he smack me then?* Understanding dawns on me.

"You're ticklish!" I blurt out in realisation.

"Maybe." His smile widens and he chuckles once. He draws his arm closer to his belly, defensively.

"How did I not know this before?" I ask, more to myself. He clears his throat, trying to hide a laugh, I think. The sound of it draws me back to the current moment. Mischief in mind.

"Don't look at me like that! Dani… I'm warning you!" Even I can see that there is no concern or fear in his words. His megawatt smile, still firmly in place.

I lunge at him, and we fall back together. Unsure of the exact spot he's ticklish, I straddle his bulk, trapping him. He laughs nervously, but his eyes radiate playfulness. I wiggle two fingers in the air, letting anticipation build.

"You know I'm going to find it, right?" I challenge. He says nothing but shakes his head, no. A huge grin on his face.

My fingers lash out, aiming for the soft flesh of his waist, but he anticipates my move and blocks it.

"Oh, it's in there, is it?" I laugh.

"I'll never tell! You want it, you find it," he chuckles nervously, again.

I rush to worm a finger into his side. He wriggles and bucks. We shove and wrestle against each other. I explore each new opening that emerges. He does his best to block me, but his hands fail to catch and confine me. We are laughing hard and lose our breath quickly. A truce only lasts long enough for me to get mine back and we spar again.

The bed and pillows are in ruins by the time we're through. Lying in each other's arms, we're quiet. Content. *What brought that on? He makes me so playful. Less serious... It's wonderful!*

"Thanks for staying over last night. I've loved having you here," Kevin says out of nowhere.

"You're welcome. I loved it too. You're very easy to sleep with. I thought it would be hard… weird… but it really wasn't. I like who I am when I'm with you." *Did that sound dumb? Probably. Well, it's the truth.* I shake off the internal chatter.

"I'm glad. I feel the same way."

"Is it always like this?" I ask, curious. Kevin stares at me, no answer.

Confused by his silence, I rephrase my question. "How many girlfriends have you had?" Kevin rolls his eyes. "How many?" I probe.

"Actual girlfriends? Two, I think. One in third grade and another in ninth." He smirks. It's my turn to roll my eyes.

"I'm serious. How many women have you had sex with?"

"Dani, come on. I don't wanna talk about this." He plumps his pillow higher under his head. "People don't talk about their ex's, it's taboo."

"Why? How's anyone supposed to know if they need to be safe or not?"

Kevin frowns, but his posture softens, confusing me. "You're supposed to be safe regardless. Until you know if they're a jerk or not."

"Oh. Does that mean we can stop now? Because I know you're not a jerk," I ask. Kevin laughs.

"No, babe... we can't. You're not on the pill, so we need to be safe for other reasons, too. Not just STIs." He winks at me.

"Oh, right. Course. So... How many women have you been with?"

"Agh, you're not gonna let this go?" he asks. I shake my head no. "I haven't had many girlfriends, but I've had my share of girls." He looks at me and I just stare back at him, unmoving. Waiting.

"Six! I've been with six women. Now... can we please stop talking about this?"

"No way. What were they like?"

"Agh, nothing like you! They were fake and high maintenance. Cantankerous mostly, and not what I wanted in a partner," he finishes, rolling over and getting out of bed.

"And I'm not those things? I think I'm high maintenance, too."

"You have higher needs. That doesn't make you high maintenance. You aren't doing it on purpose. The girls I've known were nasty. Wasps that leave a sting and piss off! Now, can we *please* get up and talk about something else while I make us breakfast?" Dressed only in shorts, he kneels one knee on the bed and kisses my forehead.

"Hm… for now. But don't think this is over. I'm fascinated to know more."

Kevin grimaces.

By the time we've finished breakfast and done the dishes side by side, dark clouds have rolled in and the first spits of rain hit the landing with a plip-plip.

"Crap, the washing." Kevin races out the back door and I follow to help him. Reaching the clothesline, the rain comes heavier. Kevin rips at clothes pegs and towels, chucking them all into the basket together. Water beads on his skin and runs down his shirtless body. We both tug faster at the items, spinning the line around as we go. "Go inside, babe. You're getting drenched. I'll get 'em," he yells across the loud rain. We're soaked. I see rain running down his face and I can feel the same happening to my own.

"I'll get the door." I run towards the back of the house, waiting on the soggy little landing for him to catch up with the heavy basket. He takes the two steps in one leap and crashes through the now open doorway, dumping the basket down on the dining room floor. We both remain where we are, lost as to what we should do now, soaking wet and torn between letting the water pool here or traipsing it through the house to get fresh towels.

My hair clings to my neck. I hate how it sticks to me, like it's trying to strangle me. I scoop it up in my hand, pulling it high, away from my skin. As I move, my clothes are stuck similarly, making me shudder. The rain outside pours down.

"You're cold. Come on."

"No. Maybe a bit. My hair and clothes are clinging to me. That's all. I hate that." I look at the puddle on the floor, trying not to move anything but my eyes.

"Oh. Do you want to have a warm shower or just get dried off with a towel?"

"Um, a shower might be nice." I pull my shirt front away from my skin.

"Okay. You go get in, then I'll have one after you."

"That's silly, you'll get cold then... come in with me."

"Nah, you don't have to do that. I'll just hang here. It'll be fine." Kevin grabs the tea towel off the bench to pat himself down with.

"Please. I feel bad."

Kevin just stares at me. An odd expression on his face. One I've seen a few times before but still can't identify. "What are you thinking?" He hesitates, I think.

"I'm trying to decide. A massive part of me wants to and a smaller part of me thinks you don't want me to. I'm deciding if I'm honourable or not." Kevin's gaze is fixed on me. I have to look away, their gravity too strong. *Am I allowed to want this? Am I allowed to share the shower? Michelle said I could. Do I want him there? Yeah, I really do.*

"Is the decision easier if I tell you I genuinely want you to come in with me?" I ask the floor.

"I wonder if you're just saying that because you know it's what I want?" his voice is quiet. Soft. It comforts me and I search out his eyes again.

"It's what I want too. But... Since I don't exactly know what it's all about. Do we have to have sex in there? I thought maybe we could just cuddle? Or not? I don't know the rules. Another first for me." *Stop talking!*

"I would like that. There aren't any 'rules,' babe. We go as far or as little as we feel okay with. We don't need to decide now. We can see how we feel in the moment. We can always stop if we go too far and we aren't happy with it anymore. Always. Both of us. Relationships are mutual. Either person can stop things *at any time*. You need to know; you can ALWAYS tell someone to stop if they're doing anything you don't want them to.

"Please tell me you understand this. It's really important that we can always talk about things, okay? I'm sorry if I keep saying this and you get it, but I need to know that you understand. Real people don't just take without asking. Not like those other bastards did. That's not the norm, and it's not okay!" He swallows, and I see his jaw muscles bulge as he clenches them. I get a glimpse of a different side to him. A side that *could* be threatening or scary and I fear for any person that wrongs him. A shiver runs over my wet skin. *Okay… Now I'm cold.*

"I know. And I do understand. I promise, I'd never make you do anything you didn't want to do. Now… I'm really getting cold, so I need to get in that warm water. I'd love it if you joined me, but there is absolutely no pressure. I'll let you decide, while I go jump in." As I tip-toe through the kitchen, trying not to drip water on the floor along the way, I am giggling to myself. Having used Kevin's own words from last night back at him just now, I crack myself up! Stripping down to my underwear, I'm still chuckling when I hear Kevin's wet footsteps coming. I smile in anticipation of his humorous comeback.

"Dani, I'm... Why the hell are you smiling?"

Uh-oh... why isn't he laughing? He looks mad. Why's he so upset?

"I wasn't talking about me back there! Your past scares the hell outta me! Do you know that? Your experiences with men have been tainted in the worst possible way, and yet your perspective of it all seems dangerously detached. I'm terrified that at some point you're going to snap and reality will take hold and it will be my fault. Something I accidentally do that will cause or trigger it." Clutching his head in his hands, he rubs at his forehead savagely. He looks worried. My heart hurts for him. I wish he didn't worry about me like this. *Why doesn't anyone understand my view? If I could just make him see. How do I explain it right so that he can get past this?* I think a minute longer.

"Sit." I grab his hand and pull him towards the edge of the bath, tugging him down beside me. A take a steady breath. "Firstly... if I go mute here, give me a minute." He nods in understanding, keeping his eyes on the tiled floor. I take in his pose and posture. *He looks so much like me right now.*

"My view is often simpler than most… black and white, some say. I can't tell you if it's my autism or if it's just a 'me thing'. It's all interlinked and perception is never clear cut, as I'm sure you realise. I'm going to try to break it down so you can understand. The first time… with Jack. Well, he felt he was 'owed' for his effort. I believed then that he had a point—" Kevin opens his mouth and shakes his head violently. I raise my hand to silence him, knowing all too well what he will say.

"I learned later that what he did was wrong. But how I felt *at the time* can't be discounted in my mind. The other side of it was that I just kind of… switched off. Yes, he used my body, but he didn't get near my sacred place. My mind, soul, heart… I don't know what to call it. I was kind of dead or sealed off or something. It was only time that I lost. Nothing more. Almost like… like when you're sleeping.

"The second was easier… and harder. I got hurt, so I had to tell people, which I didn't like. But it was easier for me personally because he didn't actually do anything…

you know? He didn't get *that* far before Tom arrived and stopped him. I know I'm not technically a virgin, but I felt like I was for our first time. I wanted it. It was my choice this time. And I've loved it every time since. It's been beyond amazing. My happy place and reality all merged into one beautiful experience." My cheeks burn and I'm certain they're bright red, but I push through.

"I always thought girls weren't supposed to like sex. No... That's not right. They're... supposed to be modest. Prudent. That's what I've always seen and read in books. It makes me a little shy to ask for what I want but, on the inside, in my sacred hideout... I'm loving every minute of being with you. I want all of you, so much. So yes, I know you want me to tell you when I don't feel comfortable, but I don't think that's going to happen. I'm curious and excited to explore all of you. I feel safe with you. Powerful, in a way. Like I'm finally in control and not my usual aspie-self. You make me feel worthy of more, and that is something new to me. So, from my side... you're stuck with me." Kevin strokes my cheek, sending heat through me like cinders igniting. In the back of my mind, though, a deeply rooted fear trickles through, threatening to destroy my happiness.

"Why're you crying?" He whispers, sounding choked himself.

"One tear doesn't constitute crying." I swipe away the culprit.

"Hey. What is it?" He caresses my cheek, and I lean into his tender touch.

"I just hope you never get tired of me." Another stubborn tear plops off my lashes, hitting my cheek. Kevin wipes it away and leans in to kiss me slowly. I shiver and goosebumps rise along my skin. My desire and the cold temperature both fighting for domination over my senses.

"Let's get in and warm up." Kevin says. Helping me up from the edge of the tub, he grips my waist. "Just to be clear... there is nothing sexier in a man's eyes than a confident woman who knows what she wants and isn't afraid to ask for it." Lacing our fingers together, he tugs me towards the shower.

41

Kevin

God, she's beautiful! I don't know what I did to deserve her, but I'm sure glad I went looking for her outside that night at the wedding.

Driving to work, I can barely keep my smile contained. You know... the shit-eating, he's got it bad kind of grin your mates tease you about, but secretly wish they had what you have. I follow Dad's handwritten directions to the newest part of the estate and snag a car park in front of his van. We scored the contract for most of the houses in this complex. It's nice to have a set workplace for a few months.

Grabbing the small esky from my passenger seat, I head inside.

"Hey, Dad. Where we up to?" I ask.

"Hey, bud. Pretty self-explanatory, Plans are laid out in the kitchen. Final hook-up. Kitchen, bathroom, laundry, ensuite, two toilets and a separate sink in the butler's pantry. Waters turned off but that's as far as I got. Thought I'd start in the bathroom if you wanna start here?" Dad points to the kitchen around us.

"Too easy. I'll grab my gear and get straight into it."

"Yep, I'll come too... I wanted to get the layout before I brought my gear in."

The two van doors roll back along their tracks in unison. "So... your mum hasn't shut up about this Danielle bird you brought over the other week."

"Oh, yeah... that a good or a bad thing?"

"Think she was pretty impressed. I heard all about how she picked up Prickles. Girl's got spunk; I'll give her that. I wouldn't pick up an echidna... and I've been around 'em longer than most. Think the pair of them are conspiring about something, but to be honest, I got no idea what."

Realising he has switched gears back to Mum and Danielle, I ask. "Really? What makes you think that? She *did* pick up Prickles, though I saw her. But she loves animals. You should've seen her face the night I told her about mum and the wildlife. She wanted to go straight over there." I chuckle to my-self, remembering her excitement that night.

"Mm, just a feeling. Your mum's been harassing the crew at the shelter quite a bit. Seems keen to get young Dani on the books down there."

"Yeah? I know Dani would love that. Here's hoping. You need a hand carrying any of that?"

"Nah, I'm balanced. Let's go."

Cramped in the small butler's pantry, I reach blindly under the sink to connect the taps. My phone rings loudly in my pocket. I let it go to message bank while I fight with the stubborn hunk of metal. "Come on, ya bastard!" *Maybe a few months of this won't be as great as I first thought!* Shifting positions, I try for a better angle. My phone rings again. Grateful for a distraction, I retrieve it and smile pleasantly when I see Dani's name across the screen.

"Hi," I answer.

"You won't believe what's just hap-pened!" Dani screams into the phone. I sit bolt upright, smacking my head on the cup-board front. *Ouch!* Fear makes my muscles tense.

"What? What's wrong?"

"The refuge just rang! They want to see me! They want me to go down there tomorrow for a meeting! Can you believe that?" I hear Dani giggle on the other end of the line. She sounds short of breath.

"That's great, babe. Are you alright, you sound puffed?" I ask. Now that I can breathe again, I probe along my hairline to inspect for blood. Finding none, I give it a rub.

"Oh, yeah... I'm just bouncing with excitement. I can't believe they actually rang. I was sure they wouldn't!"

"That's fantastic news. I'm so happy for you. And you'd be perfect for a job with them. Hey, can I call you a little later? I've gotta keep going here."

"Oh... of course. Sorry, I just had to tell you. I'll let you go. Talk to you tonight."

Hearing her voice and good news resets my mood and I return to my work with renewed patience.

"Same time and place tomorrow, then?" I ask Dad as we leave. The sun has begun its descent, out to the west, but we still have a couple of hours of daylight left.

"Yep. We're in that one there tomorrow for memory, but I'll check that tonight and let you know. See you in the morning."

"Yeah, you too, Dad. Tell Mum I say hi."

Depositing my esky back to the passenger's seat, I switch on the van and pull out my phone while the air conditioning kicks in.

Dani: Mum and Dad (and me) want to know if you'd like to come over for tea tonight to celebrate my getting a meeting with the wildlife shelter tomorrow. You could stay over too, if you want?
Kevin: Dinner sounds great. Probably shouldn't stay, though. I have an early start tomorrow. What time?

I shoot off a text to Mick while I remember letting him know I won't be home for dinner. Chucking the phone into the cup holder, I pull out and head home for a shower.

42

Danielle

Dinner last night was a complete success. Mum and Dad were both genuinely thrilled with my news of a potential job interest. Kevin arrived with a beautiful bunch of flowers especially for me, making me feel very special. Mum made my favourite—spaghetti Bolognese—and even though I'm a terrible judge of moody undercurrents, I'm almost certain everyone was happy. Happy for me!

Word has made it to Michelle and consequently Luke because I've received text messages from both of them wishing me good luck. *I probably should've thought to message them myself. Ah well… I was so excited and have been so busy preparing that I forgot.* With little remorse for my actions—or lack thereof—I start putting together my folder of illustrations, research print outs, notes and pencil case. My whole body feels bubbly with anticipation. I've never felt so ready in all my life. *I just hope they listen. Hope they like my ideas.*

~ Why would they? No one gets you! Never have! What makes you think this time will be any different? ~

My hands pause on my zip. My lips are pursed tight in annoyance.

"Because… these people care about animals and nature, *just like me!* They said they wanted to hear my ideas and discuss possible new opportunities for their government funding and a new grant application which involves *me*, that's why. Now, you've had your time, She-Devil, but you aren't welcome here anymore. You are horrible and unkind and I'm choosing *not* to listen anymore! Yep, I'm gonna have self-doubt. Yep, I'm gonna have anxiety… probably over stupid stuff! But you know what… *everyone* does sometimes. So, you can just shove off! because today… I'm finally ready!" I say with conviction to the emptiness of my bedroom. Silence.

A strange tranquillity settles around me. It feels almost tangible, yet unreachable at once. A lightness creeps in, filling my soul or my body. I can't tell which. I feel airy; a helium balloon, tethered only by a thin string compared to someone bound by the monumental pull of gravity to the earth. *What's happening? Did I just...*

Understanding and joy come together, images form in my mind's eye. All the peaceful worlds of my inner brain come together in one divine collage of happiness. Animals roam through fields, eating grass. Flowers litter the outskirts, perfuming the air with their scent. Butterflies cover the skies. I'm drawn to a leaf. A shiny chrysalis dances in the sunlight. When I reach to turn the leaf over gently. I gasp. It is open. Beside it, is the most beautiful butterfly I've ever seen. It is brightly coloured in speckles of the rainbow.

It's ME! The butterfly has morphed, and it is me! Tears of jubilation spill from my eyes and I rush to the bathroom for a tissue before they wreck my modest application of make-up. Dabbing at them delicately in the mirror, all I can focus on is the smile staring back at me. With a slow, steady breath, I blot my eyes one last time and go to get my bag. *Time to go.*

Pulling up in the unsurfaced carpark of the refuge, I grab my bag and climb out of the car. *Please don't let me freeze up and go mute*, I plead silently. The main reception building is a dated apricot colour. It could use some maintenance, but its weathered look only tells me that the workers here choose animal care over building appearances. And that is fine by me!

Inside, a counter divides the room. The public waiting area, on one side and the staff office, on the other. Metal bars prevent anyone from scaling the counter to gain access to the office.

On my side, pamphlets sit in neat piles. There is everything from 'Is your pet hurting our wildlife' to 'what to do if you find an injured native?' Amongst them is a doorbell buzzer with 'Please Ring for Assistance' handwritten on paper and stuck down with sticky tape. The office behind the counter is messy. Papers, cages, and medical paraphernalia litter every horizontal surface. The place is empty—of people, at least. I press the button and hear it ring loudly through a speaker somewhere beyond the small building.

From deep in the back of the office, I hear the squeak of a screen door opening. A woman rounds the corner into my view. Only one side of her button-up shirt is tucked in. The other hangs freely. The woman's sandy-blonde hair has all but fallen free from the ponytail she put it into this morning. A pen shoved through it threatens to fall out without the tight up-do to hold it in place.

"Hi. Can I help you?"

"Yes, I'm Danielle. I'm here for a meeting with Lauren."

"Oh, wow... Is it eleven o'clock already? Come on through and I'll take you 'round to her office." The woman opens an adjoining door between the two areas of the reception building. She leads me out the back door—the squeaky one I heard a moment ago. I follow her along a paved walkway towards a small demountable building, set off the ground and not much bigger than an oversized garden shed. The woman leading me takes the stairs two at a time, leaping quickly despite her knee-high, skull-ridden gumboots. I, however, am careful of my footing and take them one at a time. At the top, she knocks once, but opens the door before receiving a response.

"Danielle's here to see you," she tells someone inside the structure. "She's ready. Go on in," she tells me before heading back the way we came.

"Hi, Danielle. I'm Lauren. It's lovely to meet you. We spoke on the phone yesterday. Please come in and take a seat. Can I get you anything? Tea, coffee?"

Lauren Whittleman is a strange combination of a woman in power, yet dressed like she's one of the hired labourers of this place. Dressed in King Gee shorts and a tan coloured button-up shirt; their Wildlife logo embroidered on the breast panel. Lauren's hair, however, is in a neat bun and her hair is a much darker brown. She wears lace-up work boots and her thick socks are scrunched down above the boot top.

"Maybe a water, please?" I squeak. My nerves build, unravelling my confidence. I sit up straighter in my chair. *You got this, remember!*

"Sure. My good friend, John, will join us soon, I hope. He works for the council and is helping us navigate the hoops we must jump through to successfully obtain this added conservation grant. While we're waiting, tell me a bit about yourself."

Walking out of the meeting an hour and a half later, I struggle to grasp everything that we've achieved. Feeling like I'm perched on a fluffy cloud, I all but float out the refuge. Climbing into my car, I close the door and my excitement erupts. With a massive smile making my cheeks hurt, I do a few punches in the air and break into a boppy dance groove. A squeal of elation escapes me and I realise the enormity of my happiness. *I need to go thank Kevin's mum. She'll be waiting to hear how it went! I'll go straight there.*

On the way to Kevin's parents' house, my buoyant mood cannot be muted. 'Jessie's Girl' comes on the radio. A song I would normally change station's on... today, however, I crank it up loud and sing along at the top of my lungs. The next three they play are melancholy and I switch from station to station until I find something upbeat.

I drive up to the house, through the over-grown scrub of their driveway, and bounce out to find her. I pound on the front screen door with more force than necessary.

"We did it! Can you believe we did it? I shout through the mesh." Kevin's mum comes into view, carrying a pair of knitting needles attached to a blue-threaded creation.

"Well, whaddya know! That's wonderful news! Come in, come in! You got time for a cuppa?"

"Not for me, thanks. I don't think I could sit still long enough to drink it! I'm on such a high. You should've seen them. Lauren was so lovely and listened to everything I had to say. Really listened!"

"I told you she would. Your idea is fantastic and you should be so proud of all the work you've done to prepare for it. I'm so happy for you. I can't wait to see it in action, it's going to be wonderful! And what did Lauren say about in the meantime? Does she have anywhere for you while it's being finalised?"

"Oh, yeah… I almost forgot. So… she wants me to fill the reception roll at the refuge for now so that I can get a feel for how things operate and how the systems work so that I'll be ready to jump right in when the new zone is complete! Can you believe it? I can't! I'm shaking, I'm so excited! She wants me to start as soon as we can get the paperwork completed." On impulse, I reach forward and give the older woman a boisterous hug before leaping back out of her arms.

I'm 'Tigger' from Winnie the Pooh… bouncing my way through the afternoon. "Did you tell Kevin about our little study session yesterday?" I ask.

"Nope, just like you asked. Though hubby was pestering me for answers when he saw you leaving here yesterday. Told him to mind his own business and not to tell Kev you were here."

I smile, drawn to this earthly woman whose values feel so parallel to my own. It's easy to see how Kevin is so amazing and kind.

"Thank you! It doesn't feel like enough, but it's all I have. Thank you! I'm going to go, so you can get back to your knitting. There is so much to tell Kevin. I need to go home and run off my energy, I think." I laugh at myself.

"Any time, lovely. Any time. You go now. I'll see you soon at the refuge, no doubt. Say hi to that son of mine when you see him. Oh, I trust I can let the cat out of the bag now when hubby gets home, yes?"

"Oh… Yes, of course. Thank you again… for everything. I'll see you soon. Say hello to Prickles for me," I shout, walking backwards towards my car again. *I can't wait to tell Kevin! Maybe I could meet him at his house after work?*

43

Danielle

A text message to Kevin has established that he needs to get home and have a shower before I come over. Because I am insanely excited to tell him all about my day and meeting with Lauren, I've sat at home chewing my nails down to the skin, waiting for his message for me to come over. When it finally does, I almost trip over Rebel in my haste and skid out of the driveway—accidentally, I promise. Something I'm sure Mum will lecture me about when I get home.

Today, I don't care. All the pieces of my best self are slotting into place. I have purpose and someone special to share it with. Today is a magical day!

At Kevin's house, I pull up sharply along the curb directly in front of his letterbox. In one motion, I'm out of the car and skipping hurriedly up his driveway. Patch barks once from behind the front door and then stops to wag her tail when she sees who it is.

Too forcefully, I pound on the front door in excitement. *I'm going to be exhausted tomorrow!*

"It's open!" I hear Kevin's voice from the kitchen and let myself in. He rounds the corner, drying his hands on a tea towel. He is devilishly handsome in only a pair of denim shorts. A sight I'm quickly becoming accustomed to. My eyes roam over his chest and follow the thin scattering of golden hair down to his navel. When our eyes meet, I realise he has just caught me ogling him. His cheeks turn a faint shade of pink. It is so sexy on him. The corner of my mouth tips up. Guilty but not sorry. *I could launch myself straight into those arms! Perhaps we could make love and then I could tell him about the interview after-wards? Stop getting side-tracked!*

"Hi," I say.

"Hi," he replies, coming towards me with open arms. "Good day, huh?"

His naked chest, the firmness of his skin. It's all so inviting; I struggle to remember what I came here for. "Hello? You with me, or did I lose you to the charm of my irresistible body?" His laughter rumbles through his chest.

"Well… you *do* make it hard for a girl to concentrate when you're parading around in your sexy denim shorts!" I giggle.

"Sexy shorts? These are as old as ever! I'd hardly call them sexy."

"They're denim… I'm a denim girl. They're sexy." I shrug.

"Ah, note to self… The pretty lady's attracted to jeans and jean shorts. One to remember. Now… we're getting off topic. How'd it go today?"

Kevin's words pull me back to the real reason I'm here. I drag him towards the couch so we can sit down while I retell the whole story.

"I have so much to tell you! Where to start? Well… I didn't tell you before because I didn't want to jinx myself, but yesterday when Lauren rang me, I started talking about butterflies. She quickly realised my obsession with them. Our phone call quickly took a different turn, and she mentioned a separate project they've been trying to establish for ages. She asked to see my notes and information on some research I've done. To bring them to our meeting."

"What kind of project?"

"That's just it. They couldn't come up with a specific cause for the conservation grant, so they've been deliberating for months, but everything was essentially ready to go!"

"And this affects you, how?" He frowns.

"Okay… Part two. You might not know *how* obsessed I am with butterflies. See… I've always kind of admired the caterpillar. You know… they're dealt a simple life, then curl up somewhere safe and transform into a beautiful creature of symmetry and grace. Their best self. They morph and fly free. Unlike myself, who'll always be 'awkward me'. Forever the one with a 'different brain'… flawed. But… Because I'm so in love with them, the bigger part of my obsession is researching them. Their different types, where they live, what plants they're attracted to and so on." I use my hands to list off all the different topics. I notice his eyes following my movements as I ramble excitedly.

"Do you remember that butterfly we saw at the picnic? Well, when I got home… I discovered that they're nearly extinct! Can you imagine this world without that amazing creature in it? I can't! So together, with Lauren's friend's help from the council. We're going to build a research and conservation facility, especially dedicated to some of the smaller wonders of our world. It will also focus on specific plant and sub-species that have altered over time, forcing the numbers of certain insects to drop. A major part of the project is promoting the importance of these little guys in our environment and day-to-day lives. That is a job that will be decided later but until then, Lauren wants me to be heavily involved in the ideas and fact-finding side of it all. Can you believe it?"

"Dani, that's incredible! I'm so proud of you!"

"Thanks! Until the location's decided and the building is built, she wants me to work at the refuge, learning the computer systems and stuff so that I can step straight across to the new role smoothly once it's running."

Telling him about it all reignites the excitement in me, and I bounce my leg rapidly to expel some of the energy.

"There was something else that happened today, too." I pick at my fingers shyly while I consider if I should reveal my secret inner world to him. *If he's scared off now, I'll be*

devastated. Tell him! Let him be there for you.
"So… this is weird to tell you… Anyone, actually! But here goes…"

I take a steadying breath. "From as far back as I can remember, I've had a negative voice in my head. She's mean and loud, like an actual person lurking inside my brain. She always arrives at the most inconvenient times, often making me more nervous than necessary and knocking me down when I'm already in my low moments. My psych years ago told me to name her. So I did… I called her She-Devil, because that's what she is to me." I look up to see if Kevin is still listening. His eyes are right there, staring back at me. He waits, allowing me to tell my story.

"So… today when she came to sink her fangs into me before the meeting, I wasn't surprised BUT… Her words didn't hurt me. I stood in my room like a complete nutter, telling her to shove off because she'd over-stayed her visit! The second I did that, I had deathly silence on the other end. I saw myself… I morphed into the most colourful butterfly I've ever seen. Not really, of course. In my mind or my imagination or something. It was incredible!

"Do you understand? I'm not stuck anymore! Everything is turning out for once, and I swear… it's all because you came into my life. I love you so much, Kevin!" I launch into his arms and lap. Annoying tears of overwhelming emotion leak from my eyes and I swipe at them, embarrassed.

"Oh, babe." His muscular arms tighten around me. My safe house. "I'm so proud of you. Gosh, what a big day, hey? What'd your parents say? They must be proud, too." He keeps me close.

"They weren't home yet when I left. I sent them a message saying I got the job, though."

"Got the job? Babe… you smashed it! You *made* the job! I'm so happy for you."

"You don't think I'm crazy for thinking I'm a butterfly?"

"Maybe a little," he chuckles. "Nuh, I think it's sorta neat, actually. It's a great metaphor. What animal do you think I'd be?" He puffs his chest out playfully, or maybe it's proudly…

I think about his question seriously. "Umm… maybe like… a bee."

"Oh geez, thanks!" He scowls.

"What? You're very much a communal creature. You need your loved ones around you. You're a hard worker, which bees definitely are. To those who know you best, you're kind of soft and fuzzy around the edges. And you seem to like flowers because you've bought some for my mum and now, for me too."

"Yeah, And I've got a sting in my tail!" He pouts dramatically.

"But you'd only use that in a threatening atmosphere, which you steer away from because you don't want to hurt people. Bees are incredibly important to the survival of so many things! Without them, there'd be no plants or flowers. No crops mean no food for us or other animals to eat. They're very special and needed for our survival! You're needed. You're very important for my survival." I smile affectionately at him. He softens, I think.

"Well… I guess when you put it like that."

A four-wheel-drive pulls into the driveway out front. It's Mick. I wriggle to untangle myself from Kevin's lap. We hear the car door close as he heads in from work.

"Where are you going? Stay put." He holds me firmly in place on his lap. "He'll go straight for the shower, anyway." The front screen door bangs against the metal railing outside as Mick swings it wide. His arms, laden with groceries. "Hey, bud. Oh… hey,

Dani. You staying for dinner? I'm making a wicked Thai Green Curry." He disappears around the corner, to the kitchen. The rustling of plastic bags and fridge shelves getting stocked filters through to us in the lounge room.

"You wanna stay?" Kevin asks.

"Mm, as tempting as that is... I don't do spicy, remember? And... I should probably get home, anyway. Mum and Dad will want to know how I went." Unable to help myself, I gently stroke his cheek, drawing him closer for a lingering kiss. *Agh, I could totally stay! After today... that would be the icing on the cake! Thank god, Mick's cooking in the kitchen, I could do this for sooo—*

"I'm just gonna... eww, guys! Can't you do that in your room? Some of us wanna keep our lunch down." He laughs loudly. I feel Kevin's arm move from behind me. I don't look up to catch it, but I'm pretty sure he's giving Mick the finger. *Well, that's not half embarrassing.* "Sorry," I whisper.

"I'm not! I love kissing you. And trust me... I've had to endure a lot of his make out sessions, in our time living together. We've got so many more to pay him back." Kevin tips his lop-sided smile into place. He is ridiculously handsome when he uses his cheeky-boy smile on me like this. I cave and we're kissing deeply again. He nips my upper lip, sending tingles straight to my privates. An ache. Nerve endings I didn't know I have come alive like electricity running through live wires. I run the tip of my tongue slowly along his upper lip in return. A moan escapes him, and I feel his excitement springing to life beneath me. *God, he turns me on! I really need to go.*

"God, you're turning me own. Please say you'll stay?" Kevin pleads, as if plucking the thought right out of my head and twisting it around.

"Agh, I wish I could, but I got to go." I try to sound convincing, every cell of my body questioning my sanity and making it impossible to leave. *One last kiss!* I keep it short, or risk weakening. He doesn't let me break off the kiss easily. Another moan, deeper this time. When I finally rise from his lap, the true magnitude of his hunger becomes clear. Now it is my turn to grin cheekily. It is fun, knowing I have the power to unravel his self-control like he does mine.

"I'm going down to the refuge to sign paperwork tomorrow afternoon. Perhaps I could swing by on my way home to say hello?" *And maybe we could pick this up again then?*

"I'd love that. Sounds perfect. Send me a message though from the refuge so you know if I'm home yet. Come on, I'll walk you out."

"Not with that you won't... anyone could walk past and see it!" I point to his bulging shorts, a smile on my face. *I really* do *love this power!*

"Well, I can walk you to the door at least." After another delicious kiss against the front door, I make my exit and leave for home.

44

Kevin

Seeing Dani drive off, I can't get the idea out of my head. An idea that sounds absurd to my own ears, yet here I am, tossing it around with serious consideration.

The bathroom door opens and a thick haze of steam clouds the hallway. Mick emerges in a fresh pair of shorts and shirt. More dressed because of Dani's presence.

"Where'd she go?" he looks around the room on his way to the kitchen.

"She had to get home. She got a job at the wildlife refuge today, so headed home to tell her folks."

"Hey, that's great news! Tell her I said congrats." Mick pulls a cutting board from under the sink. A knife from the drawer. "Isn't it?" he questions.

"Huh? Oh, sorry. Yeah, nuh… it's awesome news. She's gonna rock at it!" I reply.

"You don't sound convinced," Mick probes.

"Nuh. It's not that. It's… well. This is crazy! Would you think I was completely mad if I invited her to live with us?"

"Whoa! Shit, Kev, that's epic!" He slices through a fistful of greens before looking up.

"I know, right? Is it too crazy? We're closer to the refuge here than her place is." I try to justify. "Would you mind? Totally no pressure to say yes here. This has got to be alright by you too."

"Shit no, man! I haven't seen ya this happy in… forever! So long as she does her bit to keep the place running, I'm happy. Oh… but no sex on the couch, remember? That rule still stands. I can't be worried about where you pair have sprogged while I'm watching telly, ka-peesh?"

I laugh at his colourful depiction. "Completely agree! No sex in the main living areas. Deal. Hey, you mind if I go after her now? I gotta ask her. Put some in the microwave for me? I won't be late and I'll have mine when I get home."

Already three quarters of the way down the hall, I snatch up a semi-decent t-shirt from my wardrobe and slam my feet into my black Vans, forgoing socks in my haste. A quick go over with the body spray and I'm grabbing up my car keys. "Wish me luck. Back soon."

Out the door before he has time to re-ply, I pull out and the tyres chirp before gaining traction and propelling my ute for-ward. *I must be crazy. She's gonna think I am!* I can't bring myself to believe the words roll-ing around in my head. The longer I think about it though, nothing about this idea feels wrong. I'm excited beyond words at the prospect of falling asleep beside her beauti-ful face every night and laughing with her until the early hours. The limited time we've spent together weighs no more than a feather against the idea. There is no one else like Dani. Not for me.

In her driveway, I jump out and leap up the two front steps. With my hand raised to knock, Michelle opens it, surprising me and throwing me off for a second. "Michelle? Hi."

"Hi. Come on in." She steps back in greeting.

"Oh, thanks, but I can't stay long." I see Dani's head pop sideways from behind the kitchen wall. She skips up to the door, a puzzled frown on her face. *Maybe I should've messaged her first.*

"Hi," I say.

"Hi."

"Can we talk for a sec?"

"Sure." She wanders out the door, aiming for the swing chair on the verandah. Michelle frowns at me before returning inside to give us some privacy. "What's up?"

"I was thinking as you left this arvo… I know it sounds a little crazy… and it's okay if you don't want to…"

"Babe, what? Just say it already, whatever you're trying to say."

Here goes nothing… "I thought maybe you could move in with me? Well… with *Mick and I* realistically." Without warning, Dani lets out a squeal and launches herself at me. Her feet leave the ground and she's wrapped around me. Her surprise attack threatens to overbalance me and send us toppling, but luckily, I'm able to keep us upright. Gripping me around the neck as she is, her face is buried against me. I can't see her. I don't know what she's thinking.

Michelle, who I'd thought had gone back to the kitchen, appears in the doorway. "You alright, Dani?" she calls, still frowning.

I turn towards her, Dani clutched to my front like a koala. Finally, Dani releases her suffocating grip and looks at Michelle, a huge smile on her beautiful face. Seeing it, I can breathe again. *Phew, she's not panicked. She's happy.*

She looks into my eyes. A rare moment when I get to see hers so closely and clearly. She blinks and the contact is broken, but she leans down to kiss me instead. A warm, soft kiss. Nothing like the intense and hearty ones we shared back at my place. This one is gentle. Mutual love.

As the kiss ends, a frown creeps across her forehead and she lowers her legs back down to the verandah floor. "What about Rebel?" she asks. Obviously now thinking about the logistics of such a move. *Shit, I hadn't thought of him.*

"Well... he and Patch will have to meet. If they get on okay, maybe he can come too? We can try it at least and see how it goes." *I hope Mick is okay with that? Ah well... I guess we'll find out soon enough.*

Michelle has stopped frowning, but I can see she's still guarded about what's going on. She is being the protective big sister. *I need to explain…*

"I'm going to move in with Kevin and Mick!" Dani beats me to it. I wait to see Michelle's reaction to the news. She smiles, relief floods her face as she lets out a massive sigh.

"God, I thought you were breaking up with her, thought I was going to have to kick your arse!" she says. I chuckle, imagining Michelle coming after me.

"Hell no! You're out of your mind if you think I'm letting her get away!" I squeeze Dani affectionately, still in my arms but supporting her own weight now. I turn to face her and find her staring back at me, her smile beaming. Her beauty radiating from the very deepest part of her being. *She's the purest soul I've ever met. The brightest star in my sky. Please don't ever let her change.*

My beautiful butterfly.

EPILOGUE

Kevin

Ten months later

Seeing Dani's car parked in our driveway every afternoon still gives me jitters. She finishes earlier than Mick and I, so she's usually showered and out of the bathroom by the time we arrive home.

She and Mick share an enthusiasm for cooking that I will never understand, but hey, I'm not complaining! They have regular bake-off's, making me swear to be an unbiased judge. *Thank god they invited Michelle and Luke over last time to share the judging duties.*

Michelle has been super supportive of the move and pops in often for a cuppa and catch up. She is helping us convince Dani's mum that this is the real thing.

"Hi, babe. I'm home. How'd it go?" Dropping my keys in the bowl by the front door, I close the screen behind me. I can't see or hear her, but the house is open and her car's out front, so she's got to be here.

Patch pads out from our bedroom, more subdued than her usual gushy greeting. *Hmm… that's odd.* I look to the couch for Rebel. He claimed its high side soon after the move, realising it was out of 'dog slobber' reach.

I kick off my boots and head for our bedroom. Patch rarely leaves Dani's side when she's home. *There she is.* Asleep on our bed from the look of it. She is curled up on top of the doona. She's still in her work uniform. Another oddity for my little routine-reveller.

Stepping closer, I hear her let out a sob and realise she isn't sleeping. She is crying.

"Babe? What's the matter?" I sit on the bed and try to tug her gently to face me, but she resists. "Hey, what's going on?" I encourage softly. *Today was her first day at the new office. I thought she'd be bouncing with excitement after being with the butterflies all day.*

"Talk to me, baby." Such an automatic response. *She probably can't, you idiot! Seriously*

wish I could erase that sentence from my vocabulary!
"Sorry, dumb choice of words. Want a hug?
I'm good at hugs."

Like a loaded spring letting go, she un-ravels. She crushes me to her. My heart aches seeing her like this. I wait to see if she will say something. Anything. I grip her tightly, understanding that a firm squeeze is what she needs most right now.

"I… I'm sorry." She sobs.

"For what? What's got you so upset, beautiful? Whatever it is, we'll work it out."

"I'm sorry for… everything. I haven't had a shower. I'm on our bed in my work clothes. I just… I needed to lie down. Today was… today was terrible." She breaks into a fresh round of tears and muffled crying against my chest.

"Hey, shhh. It's okay. Have a cry, let it all out. Then we can talk about it, and I'll tell you all about my first day as a plumber? All I know is… first day's suck! They're sup-posed to be exciting, but I don't know a sin-gle person who had a good first day yet. But it's going to get better, you'll see." I stroke her hair softly while her tears fade, her breaths becoming more even. I keep going.

Sitting up together on the edge of the bed, Dani rubs my hand with her fingers. It's just one of her things. *I love that I can be what she needs.*

"So, anyway… this Belinda woman slams the empty coffee jar down on my desk and starts screaming at me. I felt so stupid and embarrassed! How was I supposed to know it was my job to order it? No one wrote it on the list, and I don't even drink the stuff. That's when I ran away and locked myself in the storeroom." Dani's chin quivers, tears threatening again. "I'm sorry I dirtied your doona cover with my shoes." She chokes out.

"Oh, babe… I don't even care about the doona. I have four more in the cupboard! That's so easy fixed, it's not even on my radar. All I'm worried about is you. What about a nice hot shower? You always feel calmer after a shower. Or a bath? You've still got some of your bath salts there if you'd rather do that?" She shakes her head, no.

"Will you come with me?"

My sweet girl… for as long as you will let me comfort you, I will always be here. I smile, thinking of her favourite expression. "Do butterflies have wings?"

Her smile is radiant, despite her tear-streaked face. She snuggles into me awkwardly. Lifting her spirits, watching her fly… it's the best feeling in the world.

We go through this every time she has a meltdown. I know she thinks I'll get tired and leave her to be with someone 'normal', but she doesn't see what I see.

She doesn't see the quirky enchantress, always fighting the good fight.

How could I ever be content with normal when I've flown with my beautiful butterfly?

ACKNOWLEDGEMENTS

This book has been a long time in the making, a labour of love. Between life, family and work… my writing has taken a back seat. However, recently learning that a friend's cancer is devastatingly back for the fourth time. I've decided that life is far too short. Because I'm scared, I don't think I'm ready yet, I can't focus on marketing it properly right now. No more excuses. I'm hitting go!

Surrounded by neurodiverse family and friends, I drew upon my experiences as a neurodivergent woman to discover Dani's characteristics, challenges, and superpowers. She does not and positively could not represent every person on the autism spectrum. She is simply a young woman trying to find her way in the world and how she fits into it.

There are several people who I must thank for being there through it all. These people have pushed me when I needed it, supported me through the gruelling editing process, and guided me through the labyrinth of the publishing industry.

To my husband and two little people... thank you for putting up with me when I am hyper focussed and nudging me along when I am low on spoons and motivation. Your ongoing support and love means everything to me.

To my family for always supporting me on this crazy journey. I know I wasn't an easy child and as a mother myself, I now fully understand the strength, dedication and energy it takes to keep getting up, picking up the pieces and trying again tomorrow. Thank you for always loving and encouraging me to be the best I can be.

To Jodie, Dee and Fi... I can't believe it's finally here!

Jodie... I could never have guessed that one blind lunch date (is that what we should call it?!) could have changed my life so profoundly. I thank my angels for your love and friendship every day; my wise, brave, fiercely passionate about all things close to her heart, friend. Thank you for always being there for me.

Dee... You have and continue to be an absolute pillar of strength. You are an inspiration and someone I admire deeply. You have taught me so much and I am a better human and writer for it (even if I *do* hate "killing off my darlings")! Thank you for everything.

Fi... My beautiful romance-loving soul sister. Always longing for, needing, and wanting to find that romantic element that drives us towards any good book, story or plot line as we all sit around that restaurant table. Together, we discuss everything from writing struggles to life, parenting, and more worldly issues. Thank you for indulging with me on all things hunky and spunky to keep life fun.

To my friend, Renae... I believe the universe puts us where we need to be, when we need to be there. I can't put our friendship down to anything short of fate. To meet the way we did is too much of a coincidence. Thank you for coming into my life when I needed your beautiful positive influence, encouraging motivation and 'go getter' attitude to keep pushing me forward.

To my beautiful friends and ongoing cheer squad, thank you for always believing in me and supporting me throughout this journey. You all know who you are.

To all my beautiful readers, thank you for sticking with me. To know that you are out there, enjoying my work and sending me your encouraging words of support, means more than I can say. Never in my wildest dreams did I think I would get this far with my writing adventure.

THANK YOU!

Liked this story?

Stay up-to-date with her other stories and new releases on her Facebook page, J.H Nelson.

Or you can send her an email at:

jhnelson.author@gmail.com